BILL BRIDGES

MY TIME AMONG THE STARS

Tales of the Fading Suns

My Time Among the Stars
Tales from the Fading Suns
(The Collected Alustro's Journals)
by Bill Bridges

Additional writing: Christopher Howard ("The Letter")
Cover art & design, interior illustrations: John Bridges

The chapters in this book originally appeared in the following Fading Suns books: "Prologue" (from *Fading Suns* rulebook, first edition); "The Letter" (from *Byzantium Secundus*); "Sins of the Past" (from *Forbidden Lore: Technology*); "On Meeting a Noble" (from *Lords of the Known Worlds*); "Tall Tales" (from *Weird Places*); "Visions" (from *Priests of the Celestial Sun*); "Melting Pot" (from *Fading Suns Players Companion*); "The Rampart Plea" (from *The Dark Between the Stars*); "Blink" (from *Merchants of the Jumpweb*); "An Open Mind" (from *Children of the Gods: Obun & Ukar*); "Fragments" (from *The Sinful Stars: Tales of the Fading Suns*); "Tangled Web" (from *War in the Heavens: Lifeweb*); "My Quest" (from *Fading Suns* rulebook, second edition); "Loyal Service" (from *Legions of the Empire*); "Margins of the Wild" (from *Star Crusade*); "Obligations" (from *Passion Play, Fading Suns Live Action Role Playing*); "Strange Communion" (from *Lost Worlds: Star Crusade 2*); "Approbations" (from *War in the Heavens: Hegemony*); "All For One" (from *Vorox*); "Ghost Story" (from *Into the Dark*); "Witness" (from *Spies & Revolutionaries*); "Aeolus Solaris" (from *Fading Suns d20*); "On Wings of Prophecy" (from *Character Codex*); "Hidden Faith" (from *Heretics & Outsiders*); "Lost Time" (from *Arcane Tech*)

For more information on Fading Suns, visit fadingsuns.com.

Visit Bill at bill-bridges.com. Sign up to be notified by email of Bill's new releases.

Pilgrims:

Though long days may pass between our meetings, our mirrors still receive each other's light, even across the incomprehensible gulfs and even in defiance of the laws of light. For the spark of the Pancreator within us accepts no limits, evades all barriers, and obeys no laws except Love.

— The Prophet's parting words to his Disciples, from *The Omega Gospels* (apocryphal)

Table of Contents

Introduction

My Time Among the Stars is set in the far-future Fading Suns universe, which has appeared in roleplaying games and computer games. Those new to Fading Suns might wish to first read the Appendix, to familiarize themselves with the worlds in which our narrator, Guissepe Alustro, writes and travels. These journal entries first appeared in various Fading Suns roleplaying game sourcebooks.

Guissepe Alustro is a young member of the Eskatonic Order, a fringe sect of the Universal Church with interests in occult study. In joining this near-heretical order, Guissepe earned the disapproval of his powerful Uncle Palamon, Archishop of Byzantium Secundus. But he gained an influential ally — Lady Erian Li Halan chose him to be her personal confessor. He has spent the last five years traveling the Known Worlds with his liege and the rest of her entourage: Cardanzo, Erian's bodyguard; Julia Abrams, a caustic but able Charioteer star-pilot; Onganggarak, a Vorox warrior; and Sanjuk oj Kaval, an Ukari "reclamations" specialist (she joined the group in "An Open Mind").

Erian Li Halan eventually swore allegiance to Emperor Alexius Hawkwood and was admitted to his order of Questing Knights. Alustro, along with Erian's other companions, joined the Emperor's cause as an Imperial Cohort, sworn to aid Erian in her quests (see "My Quest," in Volume Two: Provost).

Alustro keeps a journal of his travels, both as a historical record and a forum for his musings on Known Worlds life. He has published some of these journals in small press editions, often including some of his sketches. While his journals are not widely known, they are popular among a small readership. Apparently, these journals are even read by the Vau (see "Approbations," in Volume Two: Provost).

After a time of rest and meditation on Byzantium Secundus (see Volume Two: Provost — "Approbations," "All For One," "Ghost Story," and "Witness"), Alustro has collected all of his previous journal entries (except for the most private or those dealing with Erian's secret missions) and published them in two new editions, entitled "My Time Among the Stars, Volumes One and Two." He later added Volume Three, which included more journal entries ("Aeolus Solaris," "On Wings of Prophecy," "Hidden Faith" and "Lost Time"). This book

Volume One: Novitiate

Prologue

Thrülday 3, Shenri moon, 4996 (Leminkainen calendar); Tuesday, June 6th, 4996 (Holy Terra calendar)

Greetings Uncle Palamon,

Forgive the years of silence between this and my last letter to you. It is only now that I can again write you, for the years have opened my eyes and greatly changed my soul. I am not the youth you once knew, your dutiful nephew, son to your dear sister, my beloved mother. I realize that you harshly disapprove of the course my life has taken, and your reaction to this letter may cause you to burn it before it is fully read. I ask in my mother's name that you read further. If not for me, then for her, to whom you were indebted for tutelage and upbringing after the tragic death of both your parents. If you still bear her any love — and I know that you do — then read the words of her only son, your nephew who once looked to you as a dog does its master, with both love and fear in its eyes.

Two years have passed since I left Midian to follow Erian Li Halan, my liege, to the stars. Four years since I left the fold of the Orthodoxy to join the Eskatonic Order. You could not then understand my choice; you took it as an insult. But that was never intended. I hope this letter will lead you now to better know the fire that burns in my soul and demands the choices that I have made. Can an archbishop not understand the yearning of the soul for the Pancreator? The yearning for answers to the deepest questions of life, and the thread of meaning that is woven between its inception and departure? I have so many questions, and I have chosen the path that will allow me to answer them, among the stars.

Can you not understand why my life could not be the same as yours? The noble quietude of cathedral, although nourishing as a sanctuary from the world's pain, is to me only a retreat. The career you had outlined for me in the Orthodoxy would have led to my slow pining and suffocation. I mean no insult. You did as you thought best, with the kindest intentions. It must chaff to read a surly youth's attack on your beloved institutions. I know what the cathedral, the Orb and the rites mean to you. They mean much to me, too. I have grown, yes, but that boy to whom you taught the chants will always be a part of me.

I made vows to another order not because I was rebellious or discontented, but because it promised escape. Unlike the Orthodoxy, the Eskatonic Order requires that its priests quest, and questing was the first virtue extolled by the Prophet after his vision of the Holy Flame. Of course, you know that. But why act otherwise? I have met priests of the Orthodoxy who chaff under the strict rules laid down by the archbishops. Do you not know their need? Do you deny it? I tell you, it is not the illusions of demons that cause them to rebel, but the call of creation. Call it heresy if you will. This is a charge my order suffers under all too often. The truth is that your fellow priests refuse to see, to ask, to really discover the wisdom nurtured by the Eskatonics.

But I spend too much time arguing theological knots. This is not what I intended when I picked up pen to write. I mean this as an explanation, not a reconciliation. If you choose to forgive me after reading this, you must do so without my repentance. I am what the Pancreator has made me, and can be no more or less.

I mean to tell you why I changed, what seed was planted in my breast that sprouted roots and branches. Do not feel guilty when I tell you it was your fault. You could not know how the Emperor's coronation would light in me a flame which only grows hotter with each year. When you invited mother and I to Byzantium Secundus to witness the crowning of the new Emperor, I am sure you only thought to introduce me to the grandeur of your great cathedral. Grand it was,

11

I do not deny that. Indeed, had it been but a trip to see the holy sight where Vladimir was crowned, I might then and there have given up all other ambitions but the Orthodoxy. But the cathedral was not the nexus of that visit. The new Emperor was.

You cannot imagine what it is like to know only war in one's lifetime. You are old enough to remember a time before the Emperor Wars, when the houses were not constantly at each others' throats. Of course, they always have been, I suppose. But in the times of your youth, they at least were discreet and kept their quarrels among themselves. But once Darius Hawkwood made his bid for the throne, the hatreds of the houses, guilds and, yes, even the sects of the Universal Church were naked before all. Since my birth and until Alexius was crowned, I knew only war. A war that killed my mother not long after the coronation, as the last malcontents made their final, failed bid.

But you know this. My point is only that, after Alexius took the throne, peace was finally a possibility. It is now, as I write this, a reality. How long will it last? I do not dare guess. But I pray every morning and night that it does last, that it is eternal.

The other factor in my current development was also your doing. It was you who pulled the strings that placed me in the service of House Li Halan. I was still new to my vows, and stumbled over the chants often, and was imperfect in the eyes of the traditional and stern Li Halan royals. It was the mild ostracism I received there that drew Erian Li Halan's interest. She was coming of age and struggled against the preconceptions her family held her to. We became compatriots against the stodgy elders around us. She chose me as her confessor, to the annoyance of her father, who wished her to be kept under closer scrutiny by one of his own choosing. The fact that I soon after forsook the Orthodoxy to join the Eskatonics became a minor scandal in the house. But Erian supported my choice, although I suppose it was merely a rebellion for her, a means to snub her father again.

She doubts too much. She has many questions of faith, and I am hard put to give her sufficient answers. How can I, when I still have so many questions myself? But I do not doubt. My faith is strong. Regardless of the conundrums and paradoxes of existence, I see One hand behind all actions, that of the Pancreator. It is my duty to ensure that Erian comes to see this also. I must endeavor at all times to bolster her faith.

When her father passed away and left her disenfranchised, having given all his lands to her brother, she had little choice but to leave Midian. I had to follow, not just because she asked it of me, but because I had yearned for the stars for so long. I had secretly contemplated leaving, of begging Erian to let me go. But the time to cut the final bonds that held me to the Orthodoxy and Midian had finally come of its own.

The jumproads became my new home. I have always been fascinated with the jumpgates and all the relics of the Anunnaki, that race also called the Ur. Who were they? Where are they now? Did they know the Pancreator as we do? What names did they use to address the Mystery? I was consumed with curiosity concerning the Great Ones and their ways. Now, I could pursue this obsession freely.

I presume you know more of them than even I have discovered. You are, after all, Archbishop of Byzantium Secundus. One does not rise so high without learning some secrets. I am certain the Church fathers know more than they reveal, especially concerning history and the mysterious, inhuman race that left us our star-faring legacy. Like most outside of the Patriarch's favor, there are many things I will never know. All the more reason to seek answers elsewhere.

I have enclosed some sketches from my travels. I include for you the one I made of the Gargoyle of Nowhere, the great monument of the wastes known to give omens and visions to certain pilgrims. I remember when I was very little that you talked about the Gargoyle. Is it surprising that I remember this? How could I forget it? As you spoke, there was excitement in your eyes and your gaze looked off into spaces immaterial. You had been to the wastes on a great pilgrimage with many nobles, sent to guide their penance in return for Church forgiveness. But it affected you more than it did them. You received no vision, but its presence alone was enough for you. It thrummed with Mystery. Imagine now what you felt then and you will begin to understand my whole life. My quest.

In my travels, I have discovered that the Known Worlds are not what we are told they are. You know this already. I suspect your hand in much of the Church's creed. Why? I know the political reasons for the lies, but why do you participate in this scheme of ignorance? I ask knowing that I will never get an answer. You will say you are protecting their souls, but I know you cannot believe that. Not really believe it.

The places I have seen! The people are so different… yet so much the same. The Pancreator's creation is a wondrous tapestry. I could not begin to detail for you the incredible people of the worlds I have walked upon. How the peasants of Madoc, living on their great, sprawling boats, know generosity without measure, sharing all they have with those in need — and they are canny distinguishers of want and need. Their fishers, those most revered among them, know where the largest herds of fish are without any outward clue. They simply know, with an instinct of sorts, the way the old men of Midian know when the weather is growing bad well before the Engineers' terraforming towers tell them anything. How is this?

How is it that the downtrodden, brutally punished rebels of Cadavus still dream and yearn for more when everything the nobles tell them denies the value of hope? I have seen hope, uncle. It is no fleeting thing, but a tenacious, living thing in the heart, in the eyes of those who have it. Those who lack it are empty vessels waiting and desperate to be filled. All too often, they drink first of hate and violence.

The people of the Known Worlds group themselves together in cliques and gangs, guilds and sects, houses and whatever else they want to call themselves. For protection, for companionship, for some sense that they are not alone in the growing darkness. I know from experience that you cannot go alone, through life or the universe. That is death for the asking. All too many prey upon the lone traveler, he with no one to vouch for him or pay his ransom.

I am no fool; I have many friends on the road. We are brought up believing that we cannot trust those who are not sworn to the same allegiances as we, whether it be another house, guild or sect. But it is a myth, a lie like many others made to serve the political needs of the war. Besides my liege, I have friends among the Charioteers and the Vorox. They are boon companions, and we have shared wonders and dangers together. I would gladly give my life for any of them, and they would do the same for me. This is not what I was taught as a child. There were many lies in my youth.

A friend of Erian's, Sanjuk oj Kaval, has a saying she heard among the youth gangs on her homeworld of Ukar: "The older you get, the more lies you wear on your skin."

This, of course, refers to the Ukar custom of writing an Ukari's deeds in scars on her skin, and the fact that adults come to conclusions about how things really are and rarely deviate from those convictions thereafter. But youth is questioning. Why not maturity as well? It is clear that our immediate predecessors did not have the answers to all questions, and our distant ancestors, while mighty in thought and deed, failed in humility. We pay the price for their hubris.

Strange that many of the things our ancestors of the Second Republic achieved and were proud of are now considered vain or evil. Their technology was remarkable, but we spurn it as if it were the tools of demons. So we say, yet without it we could not travel the stars or maintain life on barren worlds such as Nowhere. Though we curse the fruits of our ancestor's labor, it does not prevent us from using that labor and its yield. All recognize the necessity for tech, but the Church teaches that tech taints those who use it, that their egos will grow too mighty, and self-importance will surpass their love for the Pancreator. This, it is said, was the sin of the Second Republic citizens.

They are said to have been a godless people, spurning belief in a deity and exalting themselves in the Pancreator's place. But I find this hard to believe. How can anyone not recognize the works of the Pancreator and his hand behind them? I find this to be the greatest lie we are told about our sinful ancestors, that they knew not the Pancreator. Was not the Church in existence then? Did not the Prophet preach before the Second Republic was formed? I have seen ignorance and willful denial of the truth, but rarely on such a scale as is claimed here. No, I refuse to believe that anyone who could mold the very substance of a planet to make it pleasing to the body, mind and spirit is one who is without knowledge or love of the Pancreator. The ego alone cannot work such feats, although some will attempt to argue otherwise.

On blessed worlds such as Holy Terra, the maintenance of elder tech is unnecessary. The Pancreator molded that world for humans, and little is needed to maintain it. But on other planets, such as the tragic Pandemonium, upkeep of tech is vital to life. I know that monks now build a cathedral there in denial of the cataclysms caused by terraforming engine failure, expecting the Pancreator to save them from any harm. We are gifted with intelligence and insight; to so foolishly ignore these gifts in the face of disaster is an insult to the Pancreator. Is not the wisdom of science but the perception of the Pancreator's laws? Certainly, we need to beware our own greed and pride when utilizing tech, but this does not mean we must forsake it entirely.

Outside the cloister, people live life as they must; they use what they can to survive. While the Church chants about the sins of tech in its hallowed halls, those living outside the walls scrape as they must. It was eye-opening, I tell you, when I first realized just how many people ignore the laws of the Church. Not just mendicant monks, but peasants, yeoman and nobles — even bishops! They say one thing but mean another, especially when it concerns their comfort and power.

Since the end of the war, the jumproads have opened again. As people travel to neighboring planets long sundered by their ruler's rivalries, they meet strange people, once so much like them but now changed through years of isolation. Some greet old family or friends from other worlds. But others remember old hatreds and simmering feuds. New conflicts have broken out on these worlds, so long united by their lords against rival houses or guilds. But with no direction, they fall back to their old conflicts as if they were instinctual.

Such is the case with Malignatius. Long under the rule of the Li Halan, the morally lax Decados now own the world. People are returning to the ancient sects of their ancestors, denying the Orthodoxy that was imposed on them for so long. Wars have erupted over religious issues; pain and misery is the result. How can those who claim to worship one creator fight so much over the details of his grace?

Yet still I think the best of the Pancreator's creatures, whether human or alien. For while I have seen violence and greed, lust and all the other sins paraded unashamedly, I have also seen the virtues. I have seen peasants suffer the lash of their lords to rescue a fallen comrade. I have seen mercy and forgiveness from nobles when severity was surely the wiser course. Tenderness from a mercenary who had seen the darkest of shadows on Stigmata and survived.

I have grown in ways the cloister would never have allowed. I am convinced that holiness resides not only in the monastery, but among the people, the worlds and the stars. I am not naive, however. I know that evil abounds. I have seen not only the good but the foul. Traveling affords a vision of an evil tapestry as wide and varied as that of good. As the Prophet said, demons lurk in the dark between the stars, waiting for a fallen person whose flesh to take.

I was witness to one such possessed soul, whose poor family pleaded with me to exorcise him of the taint. But I had to refuse, for I cannot perform such a feat. Only those who have mastered the theurgic rites of the Orthodoxy can dream of attempting it. The possessed one was finally lynched by the townsfolk, who had tired of his tricks and black ways.

Have you ever lost one of your flock? Of course you must have, for you are far older than I. This man was not even one of mine, for I am itinerant and have a flock of one to preach to. But I knew then what it must be like to feel responsible for a soul and then to lose it.

How much more such loss must pain you, for your flock includes all the Known Worlds. Even were there no individual sin and misery, there are the dying suns to doom us all. How do you cope? Penitents must flood your cathedral daily, begging for salvation from the dimming light. What comfort do you give them? Surely you do not tell them the standard canon, that their sins are the cause of the darkening skies? If that were so, then would not the collective penance from all the years since the Fall of the Second Republic have made up for all sins committed or contemplated since the beginning of time?

What be the cause? It is truly the end of history, it seems. Judgment is near. Yet, I cannot accept that we are to be rewarded for sitting still and waiting for death. If that were so, why did the Prophet say: "A sun must burn to birth light. When your passion burns, you give off light." Perhaps the suns die because we lack passion. Passion for life. For the struggle necessary to unlock the Mystery. We are bored with everything, having accomplished all. History has returned to the point at which it began.

Or perhaps the answer still waits for us. Perhaps the dying suns are our spur to greatness, a necessary quest on which we will finally understand ourselves and our place in the universe.

This is a quest I gladly undertake. Erian Li Halan has also taken it, although she knows it not. Indeed, anyone who seeks outward for new horizons seeks to renew the light, wittingly or no.

Farewell, uncle. My liege calls and I must go. To what planet we next travel I do not know. Perhaps I will write again once we've arrived. This letter will probably not reach you until I have left for yet another world, so if you choose to answer this letter, you must send it care of Erian's mother on Midian. There is no guarantee I will receive it, but I will look for it with hope nonetheless.

Your nephew,

Guissepe Alustro

The Letter

August 15th, 4996 (Holy Terra calendar)

Brother Guissepe Alustro,

A month has passed since I received your letter. I read it, though I debated burning it as you suggested. Still, if nothing else, I believe you deserve the dignity of a reply.

I send this missive through the hands of the most worthy Lady Tira Li Halan, as you suggested. She is a gracious woman, and I heard from her a somewhat different accounting of your stay on Midian. Her family saw your conversion away from the Orthodox Church and to the Eskatonic Order as more than the "minor scandal" you described to me. Her son, the baron, told me that he suspected you in the theft of Saint Urda's bones, a sacred relic of the Li Halan. I assured him, truthfully, that you were in no way responsible for the outrage. I told him that you were young and naive, yes, but that you were in no way a thief. You may wish to carefully scrutinize your choice of friends in the future, however. One of them was a well-known thief from the planet's Ipswich region. (And yes, in answer to your unspoken question, I have been keeping watch over you. I owe this much, at least, to my sister.) I suggested that the baroness have him arrested; they recovered the relics and you are, at least partially, returned to the good woman's graces.

I relate this story for two reasons. The first is to make you aware of your choice of companions. While your liege, Erian Li Halan, is no doubt a worthy, though overly-spirited, young lady, you must watch her retinue. The worst ruffians follow even the best noble trains. Your eyes are so fixed on the stars that you do not watch where you set your feet.

19

Still, that is the way of your order, is it not? If nothing else, consider your lady's safety in all this and exercise greater diligence in the future. I do not believe I need to further belabor your responsibilities as her spiritual counselor. The second reason for this parable is to illustrate what consequences your order's lack of respectability may have on your future career, if any, in the Church.

Petty miscreants, such as the one you met on Midian, are the least of your concerns. Although you know my disapproval of your newfound sect, at least they, in the end, are mostly loyal clergy of the Universal Church. If you hearken to the Eskatonic Order's more responsible injunctions then you are, perhaps, not consigned to the icy shades of perdition after all. You see? I am not as humorless as you had supposed. You must, however, beware the siren song of alien and heretical philosophies. Ideas have a seductive quality. A heresy of deed almost inevitably follows a heresy of thought. Some priests of your order are freethinkers, anarchists or secret Republicans.

I say nothing here that I have not said more forcefully before the bishopric council. The Eskatonic Order is overly concerned with ephemeral matters. They teach that ideas in and of themselves are not dangerous. "A heresy restricted to one's private meditations is not a true heresy." Some in your order even preach the odious doctrine of moral relativism. Still, it is not your sect, per se, that is my concern. I once knew a curate of your order who spent a year among the Ur-Obun on an "anthropological grant." The Church paid for this expedition, yet when he returned the unfortunate sinner was parroting the Ur-Obun's dubious, animistic philosophies. That a primitive race such as they would have anything to offer the Universal Church beyond their admittedly technically proficient art is a notion more foolish than heretical. (And, yes, I detect something of their style in the sketches you sent me.) Their work is currently en vogue among certain Byzantine nobles. But enough; I trust I have made my point. I believe I need not fear you becoming a tree-worshipping pagan.

Still, one of your acquaintances is Ur-Ukar, is she not? In your letter you quoted to me some of her no doubt endless homespun wisdom. If the Ur-Obun are dangerous only in thought, the Ur-Ukar are dangerous in thought and deed. Despite our ministrations among them, many remain malcontents, saboteurs and murderers. They live in the sewers and feed on filth. I have known a respectable Ur-Ukar or two in my time, but few have found the light of the Pancreator, despite the words they so readily mouth. If nothing else, I suggest you hide your relationship to me while you are among them. There are many of their number who would ransom or kill you just to strike a blow against the Holy Church and me.

There are many such pitfalls throughout the Empire for one such as you. Alien fallacies and human perversions are rampant. All this despite the benign efforts of the Church, of which (I will again remind you), you are still a member. As a youth I too met with many such temptations. Cleverly wrought sophistry and salacious lies conjured by honeyed tongues can divert even the most devout believers from the true faith. You were always an intelligent youth; you excelled in all but a few of the Church's disciplines, and I admit that your accomplishments filled me with a sense of pride. It is because of this that your recent sea-change in attitude proves so vexing to me. Intelligence, however, is no defense against the many false paths of knowledge. Indeed, promises of false wisdom bait some of the surest traps. Others are baited with more fleshly, worldly desires. Your order's overemphasis on the Prophet's sermons on questing make you particularly vulnerable to such snares. You were ever an obstinate heretic in your quest for knowledge; I read little in your letter to allay my fears in this regard.

It is not easy to watch the child one cared for as a son defy all that one has taught him. Unthankful child. So I saw you then; so I see you now. I will further note that your conversion has caused me some small political discomfort in my administration of the Holy See. Still, I will give you what you so guardedly asked for — my forgiveness. In answer to your conditions on my forgiveness, however, I must add one of my own. As I must extend you my forgiveness without your contrition, so must you accept my forgiveness without my approval. I ask not for your repentance; for I see that you are not yet ready to do so. There are places on the roads between the stars where I fear this lack of penitence and humility will serve you ill. I say this, not as some sinister veiled threat, but as a simple observance of spiritual truth.

I look at you and I see myself at your age. I was young, brash and so sure that I was on the threshold of all the secrets of the universe. They called it hubris, and so it was. The old father at Saint Horace's shook that out of me soon enough. I went to the Cloud Caves against temple law. The old father caught and rightly punished me, for the caves were filled with carnivorous rats the size of Bannockburn hounds. He put a penance on me, greater than any I have ever laid at your door. Still, I learned a great lesson that day: The hand that chastises also protects.

And so I come, at last, to your question of what I say to my flock. Do I give them the "standard canon," that their sins are in some way responsible for the darkening skies? That we humans, as a race, are not in some way responsible is inconceivable to me. Can it be that you doubt this truth? During the Second Republic we spat our contempt to the heavens. "See?" we said. "We have conquered all the powers of nature. We have controlled the force of earthquakes and storms with our terraforming engines and weather control satellites. Behold! We are no longer merely beasts imbued with a divine spark; we are ourselves divine!" The Pancreator justly punished us for this blasphemy, just as the Prophet foretold. The Pancreator notices the fall of the smallest dust mote on the most dead and distant world. Think you that he does not see the wickedness in the human heart? A heretic may hide his sins from his community, his family and even himself, but not from the all-seeing eye of Creation.

You are knowledgeable in the arts of rhetoric and debate. The Prophet said "quest," and so you do. The Prophet said: "A sun must burn to birth light. When your passion burns, you give off light." You take this as an admonition against what you see as the burdensome responsibilities of order and tradition. You, like many who follow this new Emperor, misinterpret the Prophet's teachings on the Quest. The Prophet spoke not of an outward seeking passion, nor was he a proponent of a dubious quest for "self-enlightenment." The Prophet spoke of a passion for building the one true Church, so that all throughout the Known Worlds may know the divine touch of the Pancreator. Humans are creatures of two instincts, one base and profane, the other divine. If the Church must discipline its flock to save their souls, so be it. If, as you said, many ignore the "petty" laws of the Church — what of it? Dereliction of duty by the weak should in no way dictate the actions of a man of conscience. At the end of all things, our souls must be in right order, before the final judgment of the Pancreator.

But again, enough. I will not rebut your letter point for point. You no doubt view it as your "Manifesto of Freedom" against the stifling old ways. I wrote many such documents in my own youth; they molder even now in the great cathedral vaults beneath my feet. No, the impetuousness of youth will in no way admit to the wisdom of age in its quest for "truth." I understand, perhaps even envy, the unbridled freedom that you believe your travels afford you. You must, in the final analysis, make your own mistakes (although many Inquisitors may be less lenient in their judgment). As long as you remain true to the ideals of the Universal Church, I will strive to protect you as best I can. I do this out of a love for my dearly departed sister, and because of a lingering belief that you may yet become a productive member of the Church. I have spoken with Bishop Vestrus. He assures me that his parish is still open to you, despite the unfortunate events surrounding your final parting with him.

If not, you are set on an altogether more dangerous path than any I ever attempted. You have traveled much, from Midian to Leminkainen. If you in any way still heed my word, then take heed off this: Midian is a relatively stable world, Leminkainen less so. Yet, still you have not walked the dark paths. There are planets, and you know of which ones I speak, that are far more treacherous than any you have yet encountered. As you and the Prophet said: "Darkness walks among the stars." I have had visions of hidden hands at work throughout the Known Worlds. I fear that a time of great tribulation is upon us. There are nightmare paths, some unknown to the Charioteers or the lower castes of your order. Questing does not mean the reckless courting of needless dangers. If you walk these cursed paths, you pass beyond the borders of all help and I will not be able to aid you.

You are, no doubt, tested by my old man's warnings. So I will end by allaying at least one of the fears addressed in your letter. I bear you no animosity for the choices you have made… thus far. I may still feel the brunt of your rejection of Orthodoxy, but if you repent it must be to yourself and to the Pancreator. If your path should bring you to the seat of the Empire, you will find my door open to you.

Your Uncle,
Marcus Aurelius Palamon
Archbishop, Byzantium Secundus

Sins of the Past

October 31st, 4996 (Holy Terra calendar)

Since it always calms my nerves to compose in my journal, I undertake to do so now, for rarely has my need for calm been so great or my nerves so aflame. For so long have I heard the priests who tutored me condemn crime and the criminal, painting with words a picture of terror for he who commits such an error. Never did I think while a youth in the rectory that such a litany would be turned against me.

I am now faced with the moral quandary Julia Abrams mockingly warned me of when first we joined company in the entourage of Lady Erian Li Halan. "Wipe the mother's milk from your lip, priest," she had said, "If you travel with us, you're going to break all the rules."

I smiled then, used to such airs of superiority from working class freemen, who seemed convinced that only they knew the ways of the worlds and that only their feet were not weary from walking them. "Let not thy vows to Mother Church be forsaken, and all resistance will yield to thee," I quoted, so confident, even though the Avestites were then on our heels. But I knew that their hunt was only political. At least, it was then. I fear our actions have made it otherwise. I have broken my vows to Mother Church and touched the sleek and cold brilliance of technology, risking my soul in the act, and the souls of others in my care.

My sojourn into sin began when Earl Sebastian Hazat de Aragon made loan to Lady Erian of a starship in his family's care. He did so in return for my liege's later favor in an as yet undisclosed matter. The vexing charity of the nobility is best left unaccepted, but we were in dire need of transport to Kurga, for on that embattled world was rumored to be a long-buried secret vital to House Li Halan. Possession of this secret could very well restore land to Lady Erian.

We took possession of the craft with Julia Abrams as pilot. Even though we had traveled far already in her company and had become fast friends, sharing life and death struggles together, she proved her guild ties once we were in the craft. A loud argument ensued when she raised the matter of compensation for her piloting the craft. She dared to ask her boon companions — nay, the Lady who succored her — for money. The guilds bathe in such filth, preferring the clink of coin to life-giving water. The matter was finally resolved when all of us threatened in return to charge her for our once-freely given aid in future matters. She relented and consented to pilot the craft in return for a share of any profit our group's endeavors might one day yield.

I shall perhaps later add an entry concerning our journey though the vast spaces between Aragon and her jumpgate, and the void that awaited us on the other side of that gate. But I am eager to address the matter of which I now write — of technology and its misuse in the eyes of the Church, and the rabid hate invoked in those whose mission it is to guard the faithful from such sin. My sin.

We landed on Kurga undetected, for the Hazat and the Kurgan rebels were fully engaged in bitter warfare at the gates of the capitol, a battle which, as with many others in that location before, would come to naught but death for many soldiers with victory for none. The capitol stood firm.

Far from it, in the deep forests to the north, we landed our craft near the spot to which our data had led us. From a long-slumbering think machine on Aylon I had retrieved a map of this very place, detailing from a millennia ago the city which once thrived here, but was now swallowed by root and loam, canopied by leaf and vine.

Such wilderness expeditions were not unknown to us, and our Vorox companion, Onganggorak, led us through the winding paths to the remains of a structure wherein rested our secret find. After digging a while to gain egress, we traveled by fusion torch light through corridors untouched for generations. After nearly a day of such travel, with many false turns and dead-end alleys, we finally came to the vast vault.

I gasped in astonishment at what lay before us. I had seen weapons of war before, but rarely so grand as these. They stood in perfect ranks, unblemished by the centuries, perfect metal cannons of destruction such as have never been seen by the faithful souls of our modern-day Empire. Such Second Republic monsters could have been crafted only by godless men, who knew not compunction or remorse for the horrors their metal children would wreak.

It was our mission to retrieve one of these beasts, of the same design and type clearly once used by the Li Halan long ago when they had secured their fiefs from the sinful Republicans. But as I looked upon them now, I shuddered, and remembered the legends of the early Li Halan, how they had made pacts with demons and slaughtered their enemies with such ferocity as to make the Pancreator weep. I knew doubt then. Could I aid even my sworn liege in this task? To return to the Known Worlds with such weaponry? Surely, to hand over this technology would return Erian to the graces of her family — but to what use would it then be put? These things could only deliver horror and soul-death. Oh, the Emperor Wars had been one long night of terror for too many, with similar rediscovered weaponry shifting the balance of power for each house who discovered them. What if these weapons convinced the Li Halan that they could defy the power of the new Emperor?

I pleaded with Erian to realize what we had done, and to leave these things untouched, to destroy the data which had brought us here. But she was flush with the power of these things, and heeded me not.

Even with the burns that now pain my arm, I thank the Pancreator for the delivery of his punishment then.

We were fools to think that the Avestites had not followed us here. Ong had said too much in public under the influence of drink, and

27

word had spread of our goal. They burst into the room brandishing flameguns and screaming their litany of seizure.

Of course, we all resisted. We hid behind the monstrous carcasses of the cannons and fired our weapons while they fired theirs. But it was a short fight, for Erian was struck when her shield burned out. We pleaded surrender, knowing that because Erian was noble, they would have to return her for trial rather than let her die here. There was always the hope of escape then.

While I ministered to her wound under their watchful gaze, they demanded that Julia show them the workings of the cannons. She refused at first, but their brands convinced her flesh, and her resolve soon followed.

Let what bad words I said of the guildsmembers earlier be mitigated by my thankful admiration for their cleverness — as dangerous as it is. They are all trained in the art of talking, used to befuddle their customers so that they might sell faulty merchandise for good price before the dupe is aware of what he has bought. Such a gift served Julia here, as she maneuvered the Avestites to inspect the mouth of the cannon as she pressed the remote control unit she had pocketed during the firefight.

The ensuing chaos allowed us to escape down a side tunnel, which Ong collapsed behind us to stifle pursuit. I followed in a daze, ashamed at my extreme relief. Like a child who had avoided punishment, I was elated — but great Pancreator, others suffered in my stead.

I can never forget the sight of the Avestites blown apart by the fires belched forth from the metal beast, asleep for so many years, awakened now at an instant to destroy all in its path — including its own brethren, standing in ranks before it. The fellow cannons' screams pained the ears. They did not go gentle to their doom, for the fires in their innards erupted outward, released from their long captivity by ruptured steel.

It was only the fire-retardant robes of the Avestite who stood before me that prevented my burning in the blight. He burned for me.

My clothes were alit and my skin hot, but I was alive. Ong's fur was singed terribly, as was Erian's clothing, but our fear helped us ignore the pain as we bolted from that fiery chamber.

We suffered two days without food or water in the winding caverns before finding escape from that tomb. Our craft was still where we had left it, although the Avestites had tried to search it. Of them, there was no sign. Did any survive the conflagration? I pray for their sakes and ours that the answer is no.

I have received a harsh lesson, and one that I will endeavor to heed. But not so my companions. Erian has resolved to not give up her search for similar engines of her family's past. Julia is positively ecstatic about the power she wielded with but the movement of her thumb on a switch. Cardanzo, Erian's bodyguard, has sworn to be more cautious around such technology, but has developed no fear of it. Only Onganggorak has realized the full import of what we have seen. Bred among little technology, on a world where only one's own strength can prevail over others, he rightly fears what destruction can be wielded with such machines.

I have thought deeply on this but have no easy answers. It was such technology that aided Alexius in his ascent, and I am not one to deny the greater good he now delivers to us. Indeed, I write this from inside a cocoon of metal speeding through the void towards a machine greater than any yet conceived, the jumpgate of the Annunaki. The Prophet admired such space quests, yet abjured the cannons we have seen. He knew the terrible, seductive temptation to use them.

I am only a young priest, but I know that technology is a greater force than I, awakening desires within me and others to remake the worlds in images not of our choosing.

On Meeting a Noble

Nobles are most perplexing. My time in Lady Erian Li Halan's service has taught me that, but offered little insight otherwise. I have not the upbringing to fathom their thoughts, and thus their deeds remain largely unpredictable to me. I live by the guidelines of the Prophet, with compassion before all. They have other... priorities. I say this not to diminish them. How can one such as I, a novitiate in a small and ill-famed order, through word or deed ever tarnish those of noble blood? If, as some say, they were born to their high peak by the Pancreator's will, then the words of those below them can mean little, even those words blessed to reach them past the furious winds which blow at such heights.

No, I in no way infer a political statement behind my musings. I simply wonder at times. If but a few nobles could put aside their obsessive duties and place the well being of their charges first in their hearts, then perhaps the darkness which devours the suns would not seem so cold to those who suffer in its dimming light.

Perhaps I had best give example before my confusing thoughts yield heresy.

I had returned with Erian and her entourage to Vera Cruz after our harrowing expedition to the barbarian world of Kurga, of which I will say no more here. We were forced to abandon our starship for fear that it would lead the Inquisitors to us. We set out on beastback to hide ourselves in the remote mountains for a time, hoping the Inquisitors would turn their hunt to another world, figuring we had moved on. With minimal supplies, we left the last settlement listed on our maps and went to the wilderness.

We soon found that the maps were wrong. Drawn up and made

available by noble decree, they omitted what the nobility hid in shame.

Two days into our journey, with no sign of any village or even a manor house, we came upon a field of peasant workers. I know they saw us, but they nonetheless pretended they had not. We could hear a commotion up the road, concealed around a bend. By the furtive glances the peasants gave this area, I knew it was the source of their fear.

We rounded the corner and saw a cruel scene. A man was on the ground, writhing in the mud and grunting in pain, suffering the terrible lashes of a whip, which was thrashed wildly by a stripling in noble garb.

I acted without thinking and only later realized how foolish it was. My compassion got the better of me, but I endangered my Lady with it. Without even considering that the victim of such torture might be a criminal who deserved this treatment, I jumped off my horse and ran to him. I grasped the long tail of the whip as it was drawn back before it could strike again, and yelled in anger at the startled boy who held it.

His eyes widened in shock but he quickly recovered, snarled at me, and sent me reeling with a backhand. I flopped into the mud alongside the whipping victim, and immediately felt the lash myself. Oh, I will never understand how the man beside me withstood 10 lashings let alone one without crying like a babe from the sheer pain of it. I could not withstand the one lash, and did cry out.

There did not come another. When I opened my teary eyes, the noble boy was lying in the mud before me, unhorsed himself. Beyond him stood Erian, sword drawn.

"Get up, boy," she said. "If you would dare to strike a member of my entourage — a priest, for Prophet's sake — then you would surely be bold enough to settle the matter properly. Draw your blade!"

The boy scowled at her with a most ugly expression. Indeed, he looked the most ill-bred of any noble I have yet seen. But he certainly had reflexes, for he was up with sword drawn in a second, with his steel aimed straight for Erian's throat.

She casually tapped the thrust aside and flicked her blade at his wrist, drawing a thin line of blood. His scowled deepened, if it can be imagined, and he began a hail of blows, all easily parried by my Lady.

I looked to Cardanzo, Erian's bodyguard, who had not even dismounted. He sat on his horse smirking. I knew Erian was in no danger. Few men can size up an opponent as quickly as Cardanzo, and if he saw no danger for our Lady, then there was none.

I picked myself up and bent down to attend to the poor wretch I had attempted to save from misery. The clang of swords continued behind me as I examined the man. The lashes had cut deep in some areas, now splattered with mud. He would need washing and a bed to properly heal.

I turned to watch the duel in time to see it end. Erian, finally tired of toying with the boy, disarmed him and sent his blade flying into the field. A few peasants ran from the spot at which it landed, afraid to be near it. The boy was panting and exhausted, but his anger seethed from him, hot enough to warm a small hut on a cold winter's night.

"Admit your defeat, boy," Erian said. "Or fetch your blade for more."

The boy growled and ran to his sword. He was soon back, hacking furiously at Erian, who was actually surprised and somewhat angry now herself.

Anger is the great undoer. He pushes us to precipices we would rather not fall from.

Erian struck out and sliced the boy's forearm, not enough to cripple, but enough to end his days as a duelist for a long time. As he fell to the ground screaming and clutching his wounded arm, horse's hooves sounded loudly on the road ahead. In moments, a horse rounded the bend and stopped short, kicking mud up into the air.

A wild, blacktressed demoness leapt from the mount and marched toward the boy. Never have I seen such an impressive lady or such a seething anger. But I could not tell at whom it was directed — the boy or us?

She said nothing but I could tell by the way the boy's eyes beseeched her that she was his mother. She looked at the wound in contempt and then turned her attention to Erian.

"You have wounded my son, lady," she said. "Are you prepared to stand trial for restitution?"

"I'll do no such thing," Erian cried. "I had just right to challenge your boy. You'd know that for sure, but then, you're the one who raised him to strike priests!"

"I raised him no such way!" the lady yelled. "Defend your actions then!" She drew sword and waited for Erian.

I could not believe this. I had thought the matter swiftly ended, but here was yet another noble seeking yet another duel. And Erian, without a moment's hesitation, gave it to her.

Their swords flashed in the light of the coming sunset as they paced about each other, each seeking the other's measure. I looked to Cardanzo to see that he had left his mount and now watched the battle intently. By the way his eyes never wavered from the blades, I knew that Erian had perhaps met her match. All because I had foolishly acted, creating a chain of events which inevitably led to this, vendetta upon vendetta.

Fear gripped my heart, for I knew that my Lady's energy shield was inoperative, for our fusion batteries had long since run out. I could not allow this! I cried out: "Hold your sword! My lady is at a disadvantage — I can see that you have an energy shield while she does not!"

"Still your tongue, Alustro!" Erian yelled.

But her opponent stepped back and dropped her blade. "Good priest, I thank you. I would not have it be said that my accouterments won a battle rather than my hand. I remove my shield." She unhooked an elaborate brooch which she wore on her cloak, and placed it in her saddlebags. "Now, have at you!" she yelled and engaged Erian.

I prayed for my Lady, using no theurgy or rite which was unseemly to a duel, but with the simple means of faith instead. If she was in the right, surely the Pancreator would grant her victory. I winced as the first full strike hit steel, sending a clang echoing across the field. The peasants had all stopped their work and were staring gape-jawed at the fight.

Swords moved so swiftly I could not mark the battle. Parry became riposte, becoming feint and then slash, punctuated by moments of supernal stillness, then broken once again by flashing blades. Both combatants were nicked and bloody, but with no major wounds on either side.

But as the sun moved closer to the horizon and the sky grew red, the mysterious lady's face grew softer, and her grim expression slowly became a smile, which rose to her eyes. Then, she drew back and raised her sword for truce.

"You fight well, lady," she said. "We are both tired and have not yet got the full measure of the other. What say we call a truce and end this duel?"

"I accept your terms," Erian, panting, replied. "You fight most well indeed. It would seem we are both the match for the other. I doubt that even another hour of dueling would decide the outcome."

The swordswoman laughed. "True. True, indeed. It is rare to meet such an accomplished and honorable noble in these parts. Would you return with me to my manor and be my guest? I am most curious about you now, and would be offended were you to refuse."

How odd! She had wanted to soundly thrash my lady moments before. Now, her rage was turned to... affection? The offer seemed to be most genuine, with no hint of guile behind it, and I am glad my Lady accepted it, for we had as yet no place to stay for the night.

But our host's boy was not happy about the offer. He scowled at his mother, climbed on his mount, and rode off down the road. I was surprised to see that she cared little about his actions, even rolling her eyes as if to suggest to us that the boy was overly dramatic in his actions. Most perplexing, indeed.

The manor was but a mile up the road. Not the richest lodging we had seen, but it was most comfortable. The lady had even graciously helped me to place the wounded peasant on my mount and offered her chuirgeon to aid him. Thus, I joined our entourage at supper a bit late, as I took it upon myself to ensure that the wounded man was put to bed well. As I entered the dining room, I was greeted with laughter and joy. Our hostess was listening to some of Erian's tales of our lighter adventures, and she seemed fully caught up in the humor of them. A most remarkable change from earlier.

"Ah, Alustro," Erian said as I sat down, "Is all well with your charge?"

"Yes, my Lady," I replied. "He will do fine. His wounds will heal aright." Our host's face darkened somewhat as I said this, not out of anger, but shame.

"Our gracious host, Baroness Shariza Hazat de Laguna, has explained the incident to us," Erian said.

"But I owe an explanation to the priest, also," the baroness said. "My son learned only the ways of cruelty from my husband. He knows not how to treat the serfs in a manner befitting the Pancreator's creations. Had you not already intervened, and had it not been a matter of family honor to defend him before strangers, I would have lashed him with his own whip. Of all the misery my dishonored husband left me, he is the worst."

"I... I am sorry, baroness," I stammered.

"Why? It is not your doing. No, my husband chose to betray his liege during the wars, and in return his widow is given only the least of his manors on the least — and now last — of his lands, a prisoner far from society where she can no longer harm his reputation."

It seemed to me that her exile perhaps had less to do with her husband than with her own outspoken manner. She seemed a great lady, but in the fashion of many nobles, greatness leads to great enemies. Indeed, as the night went on, we talked long about our exploits and listened intently to hers. She and Erian had built a bond of sorts on the field which only grew tighter as time passed. They had so much in common, both wronged by their royal connections.

We stayed at the Baroness Shariza Hazat de Laguna's manor for a week. During that time, Erian cemented a friendship it seems will last a lifetime. Rarely were those two apart, talking always about noble affairs and how to overturn their bad fortunes. By the end of our stay, we knew we had an ally for whenever we needed it. I don't think Erian wanted to leave when we did, for the baroness was the first compatriot she had meet since her exile. But the vision afforded by the Gargoyle of Nowhere drove us on.

The whole affair was most perplexing, even if it did have good outcome. How can the shattering sounds of steel upon steel lead to such a true friendship? Most people make their friends in more civil ways, but it seems that nobles must first ascertain the power of another before they can be unguarded before them. Is this any basis for true human companionship?

Perhaps it's the truest and most enduring basis. I hope not. It would be a crueler world than I imagine if all human interaction was reduced to hierarchies of power. But then again, there is surely evil out to thwart all good people. Perhaps only in the heat of such passion, tested where there is little chance for guile, can we truly come to know another.

Tall Tales

"Hell, I've got the scar to prove it!"

"I understand the trophy value of these wounds," I said, "but they are not healthy. At least, not in such numbers. Surely so much scar tissue must lead to health complications later on in life. If you anticipated such dangers, why did you not travel with a trained physick, or at least learn something of the arts of healing yourself, so that you could properly bind your own wounds?"

"I did pretty damn good by myself, son," Foote said, holding his head high. "But for this one — the jagged tear in my bicep opened up by that grackle fox — I didn't have any thread. I had to use the sinews of the grackle itself. Almost fainted from blood loss by the time I'd skinned him enough to get at the tough cords. If I didn't have my Martech Gold with me, never would've cut through it at all. That's stuff's tough! A knife'll go dull before slicing a grackle fox's guts up!"

I looked at my companions. Cardanzo nodded knowingly, as if Foote had stated some eternal verity. Even Ong nodded eagerly. Grackle foxes were native to his world; he surely had some experience in such matters. If he agreed, perhaps it was so. But I felt it more likely that the beast served the same purpose for Vorox hunters that it did now for Gabriel — a prey whose capture is greater in the telling than in the deed.

It was Julia who introduced us to Gabriel. She knew him from her apprentice days among the Charioteers. Actually, we had all heard of him. Who in the Known Worlds has not? The famed Captain Foote and his exploits for the guilds are well-told tales throughout the Known Worlds, providing proof of the virtues of heroism and duty. Of course, the occasional parish priest sermonizes against Foote, fearful that his exploits will provide example for fools to venture forth to the stars, and thus meet useless deaths on distant worlds. But his reputation was enshrined in most houses.

But now that I had met the legend, I thought him a blowhard. Most of his stories were sheer illusion, tall tales that — amazingly — everyone seemed to believe. Even my Lady, Erian Li Halan, was genuinely excited at meeting a man who, in most circumstances, would be her social inferior to an extreme degree. But she treated him with the deference due a count. For such he was, in her mind and the minds of others. A hero, regardless of actual worldly rank and station, is often considered a de facto lord.

And here this lord sat, on his well-worn bench in the Rampant Gurdvulf, the throne on which he gave audience to his visitors. The requirement for admission to such an audience? As much alcohol as the lord requested. And should the well run dry, the audience would end, the supplicants sent on their way to make room for the next batch. Such is the life of retirement for Captain Gabriel Foote, former pilot and explorer.

We had already been overlong on Criticorum when Julia heard word of Foote and his night roost. Now, we had spent another three nights here, plying Foote with liquor in return for tales of his exploits. The longer we stayed in one place, the closer the Inquisition would come. But Foote assured us that no Inquisitor would dare step foot in this district of Nueva Janeiro. So far, he was correct. But could we risk an exception to his rule?

My Lady believed the risk worth the prize, for she had grown up hearing of Foote's legendary adventurers, told among the noble youth of Midian when their instructors were not listening. Such exciting stories, especially ones about a guildsman, were not considered proper for Li Halan lords and ladies, but they heard them nonetheless, spread by the children of householders, whose connection to the bustling world outside the palace was greater. For my Lady, Foote was a childhood hero, and she was proud to meet him. His slovenly ways and colorful language seemed only to reinforce his legend.

And so we listened to Foote. How many exploits can one man possible have? His seemed innumerable.

"Julia," Foote said, "Didn't you say you'd been to Nowhere?"

"Yeah," Julia replied. "We saw that Gargoyle thing in the desert. Erian and Alustro got some weird dreams after seeing it."

"Visions," I said. "We both had the same true vision."

"Okay, right," Julia said. "But we've been there. Why?"

"I've been there, too," Foote said. "Saw the Gargoyle also. I didn't get a vision, but my passenger did."

We all waited as he took a swig of ale. He certainly knew the art of suspense, purposefully pausing at just the right point in his narrative.

"Whatever it was he saw lit a fire under his butt," Foote continued. "We were off again the next day, hurrying to Shaprut. Over the journey, he wouldn't tell anyone about it or why we were going to Shaprut. When we landed a week later —"

"A week?!" Julia said. "From Nowhere to Shaprut? That's at least half a month's journey, what with the time it takes to get to the gates—"

"Well, we had a fast ship."

"Fast is one thing, but that's not even counting the shakedown you get from the Stigmata Garrison before they let you take the jump out of the Stigmata system. How'd you avoid that?"

Foote shrugged. "The regent could go where he wanted, when he wanted."

"Regent! You mean Alexius was your passenger! No way!"

Foote smiled. "Ask anybody in the guild, Julia. I served as the regent's pilot for three years. Luckily, I went freelance before he crowned himself Emperor. Things would have gotten a bit hot even for my taste."

I rolled my eyes, but Julia saw me.

"All right, Alustro," she said. "I'm sick of your attitude. Gabriel's been an excellent host to us, yet you seem bored. Or disgusted. I can't tell which. What the hell's the problem?"

I gave her a glare. How dare she say this in front of Foote! I did not wish to openly insult the man, but I could not lie about my feelings once asked directly. "I am most grateful for your time and entertainment, Captain Foote."

"Gabriel, please," Foote said, "I'm retired now, and my first name's good enough for friends." He flashed a smile that charmed them all. Friends of the great Gabriel Foote. What a high honor.

"Gabriel. Thank you," I said. "But… Well… It just seems so… elaborate."

Foote raised a single eyebrow.

"I mean… You seem to have done an awful lot of things. So many things…"

Everyone was looking at me now, staring me down, telling me with intent alone not to say what I was about to say.

"They cannot all be true. These are tall tales."

"Alustro!" Erian said. "How dare you!"

Foote chuckled. "Can't fool a confessor, I guess. Of course some of it's overblown, priest. Tales grow in the telling even if you don't mean them to. Do you think your friends here don't know that? Only a fool would take it all at face value. But I tell you this: the important things happened. I did fly for Alexius, for a time. Were we friends? No. I doubt he'd even remember me. Hell, boy! Ask me anything about any place you know and I'll bet I've been there. Go ahead, ask."

I frowned, but thought for a moment. "Pentateuch. Have you been there?"

"Ha! Of course."

"Then surely you visited Heliopolis. In which quarter is the Basilica?"

"Son, anybody could answer that question even if they'd never been there. Let me ask you: Have you been in the Sirocco from atop Mount Tabor?"

"No. And you have?"

"Aye, I have. An old friend of mine led me there — we went through flight school together here on Criticorum when we were as wet behind the ears as you were. He's a Marabout now. Saw the World Fire and it changed his life. Out of remembrance for our youth, he took me there when I asked him to. I waited for three nights and nothing happened. I gave up and left.

"But on the way down, the storm came. Next I knew, I was in the desert, miles from where I'd been standing, my friend and pack beast no where to be seen. I had to walk without water or food for three more days before I came across the Ur-Obun pilgrims train. But I did it without complaint. I'd seen something in that storm. Something I've never talked about to anyone. But I'll tell you. As naive as you are in the ways of people and the worlds, I think you'd understand this best of all — begging the Lady's forgiveness, of course, but she's not a priest and you are."

He leaned forward, staring intently at me. All the bluster had left him, and he seemed instantly sober, as if his drunken cheer was all just in jest. Despite my earlier feelings, I had a slight chill. He seemed to be in the grip of some deep passion as he spoke about his holy experience. I could not help but respect it.

"I saw myself in the cockpit of my ship, flying through an atmospheric storm. My instruments were out and it was too dark to steer by sight. I was freaking out, flying wild. Then my navigator told me to fly by instinct, that faith in myself would get me through this. And he was right. I calmed down and just flew like there was nothing I couldn't fly through. Next thing I knew, the storm cleared, and the sun broke through, so bright I had to squint. It felt like victory. And only then did I remember that I don't have a navigator — I fly alone.

"I looked at the seat next to me and there was this pilot, smiling at me. I knew he was a pilot, 'cause he had on flight gear, except it was old, like they used to wear a long, long time ago. He said that only when everybody could trust themselves enough to weather any storm would the light of the sun shine bright enough to blind us. I knew then

41

who it was. I can tell by the look on your face that you also know."

"Yes," I said in awe. "Saint Paulus. Those were the words the Prophet spoke to him after he had safely flown through the terrible storms of Manitou, before the Prophet made his final journey. But this is not in the Omega Gospels! It appears only in the apocryphal scripture of Darius, apprentice to Paulus after the Prophet's death. Only the Eskatonic Order keeps this scripture and they do not reveal it to the unordained. How did you know this?"

"I certainly didn't read it in your books. It was what the World Fire gave me. And it changed by life. You think I'd travel to all those worlds and get into all the trouble I told you about because I like it? What kind of idiot prefers getting shot at, stabbed, chased, locked in dungeons or possessed by demons just for the fun of it? I was questing, son, because the Prophet demanded it. Only out there, among the stars, was the answer to my fate.

"Only on worlds unseen by other men, in places damned by priests and peasants, did the answer to my destiny lie. And I wasn't alone. It was my going to such places that led me to Alexius's service. My time with him saw some of the strangest things I've yet seen. Weird things that I'm under vow not to tell of — a vow which I'll keep. You don't break an oath to the Emperor. Hell, if he hadn't gone questing, he wouldn't be Emperor now and we'd probably have some Decados or Hazat pig ruling us all.

"And my travels weren't all heroic, either. There was a lot of misery, too. And heartbreak. Times of such despair that I'd liked to have killed myself — and I almost did, taking risks no sane man would. But I survived it all, lived to tell of it. And the telling's just as important as the doing. When someone hears about such quests, it's sort of like they're participating in them, even when they're just sitting on a barstool farting. What's the difference between questing in the body and questing in the mind? It's questing either way. 'As long as our hearts are ever expanding to distant orbits.'"

"Paulus 23:5," I said.

"I'm not just telling stories, I'm telling sermons. Parables of sorts about the places I've been and what they mean to me. What they could mean to others. If it gets even one person up off his butt to find out what's what — what his purpose is — then it's not a lie."

I nodded, beginning to understand. Gabriel Foote was no priest and no lord. He sought to change the world the only way he knew how: through example.

"It is true that our own experiences would not be believed even were I tell them with no art whatsoever," I said.

"But the secret of storytelling," Foote said, "is to weave the truth with a little art — even with a lie. If the art's good enough, they'll want to believe it with all their hearts. The Prophet knew that. When you tell folks about your own adventures — and you will, come time — remember that." He sat back and winked at Julia. "Sorry I never told you any of this. I hope you understand."

Julia nodded. "Oh, I understand."

And I too finally understood Julia's fondness for the man. His deeds light the way for us. Without the possibility of great deeds, what use are our travails? Is our suffering and hardship simply for naught? Or can we forge from them something worthy of the telling?

Visions

For too long have I delayed writing of the two most significant events in my life. I feared to put them into words lest their power disappear like a dream upon the morning. But over the years and months since, they remain with me, as powerful as when I first experienced them. The vision from my youth and the dream of the Gargoyle of Nowhere have changed me, and I cannot yet say where they shall take me.

I am aware that these things are uncomfortable to many, who would rather not read such intimate portraits of another's inner life when they are often too confused to read their own. Faith — even quiet, enduring faith — unnerves many, for they either equate it with foolery or with the fires of the punishing Inquisition. Most would prefer to leave spiritual matters to experts. If this is so for you, reader, then read no further. For I will write of naked experience and the raw power of the Pancreator. If such beliefs make you nervous, turn the pages and return to matters more mundane.

When I was little, I was fed on the bread and milk of the Church. Raised in pious fashion on Midian, I knew no other ambition than that of the vestry. My dear, sweet mother wished only ordination for me, as did my well-placed uncle, none other than the Archbishop of Byzantium Secundus. But the Pancreator often has his own goals for our futures, and reveals them in his own time.

I was 14 years old when I took vows and received my novitiates' robes. My family connections ushered me in early to such duties, for my friends were still altar boys and cantors. This neither bothered me, nor was I overjoyed. My career in the Church was a given, not something to which I looked with any excitement nor misgiving. This changed in the gardens of Lady Tara Li Halan.

Walking there alone one afternoon on a gray day, I came upon a dying wuwei bird. The mokuto neko that had mauled it slipped away as I came down the path, leaving the bird to weakly flutter in fear and pain. I bent down to watch its last moments, more from curiosity than compassion. Dying animals are no rare occurrence. But as I watched its weak struggles, I realized that my presence caused it only more pain. Foolishly, I reached down to stroke it, hoping to allay its fears. Birds, of course, do not like being petted. I do not know what I was thinking. Stupid boy.

Then, a remarkable thing occurred. The bird stilled, not yet dead, but calm, as if it accepted my weak gesture of peace. Its eyes looked into mine and I saw in them an inner light. Indeed, I now saw a light limned about its entire tiny body, a warm glow that spread outward. As I watched, my vision became clearer, as if fogs rolled aside so that I could truly see, for the first time, another being in its full glory. The light radiated out and met another brilliance, a deeper, brighter light descending from above. When the lights met, the entire area was suffused with the glow, spreading all around, engulfing me within it.

I gasped. Light now escaped from me, as if a furnace burned in my breast and my flesh could not contain the glow. I looked again at the dying bird and saw its light burst from its heart and shoot into the sky. As it disappeared into the heavy clouds, the radiance around me dimmed and returned to gray. My own light retreated within once more.

I was exhausted. The world returned to its previous state. The fog rolled in again, concealing the secret luminosity of the world. The bird's body lay unmoving, a dead husk.

I believe that I was gifted with a vision of the Pancreator's Descent of Grace, and the Luminous Return to the Empyrean of one of its divine creatures. But the experience was different from what I was taught by my Orthodox tutors. For the bird had revealed a flame within itself — and its display had in turn revealed to me my own light, drawn outward by the Pancreator's presence.

This holy vision changed my entire outlook on my career, my very life. Yet I could not tell my teachers, for it departed too far from their doctrines. I knew even then, as a young boy, that my vision was truer than the theology carried in books for over a millennia. I knew then and there that I would eventually leave my order to join the Eskatonics, whose own doctrines spoke of the very thing I had experienced.

I have since spoken with many priests, my age and older, and discovered that such a vision as was afforded me is rare. Most travel through life with no such experience, relying only on faith as proof of the Pancreator. I understood why the Church was important to them; it was their only experience of the divine, mediated through the accounts of those who had touched Creation. I knew how truly blessed I was, that I had received what so many others have not. I did not need books and debates; the truth of the Pancreator resided in my memory, in my soul.

But I also knew that to count my self above them for such a gift was wrong, and would lead only to hubris. To the contrary, I believed myself humbled. Why was such vision afforded me? Surely it meant that I must perform a duty for the Pancreator, to give my life in service to him. I began to envy those who were blind to visions, for they could choose their courses as they saw fit, with no divine prodding to sway them. I began to question all my actions in the light of my vision. I was paralyzed with indecision, lest I choose wrongly.

Only time has allayed such fears in me. Only the rhythms of the mundane over the months and years have brought me to a sense of peace with my self. I must trust my heart, my own light. Why else was my burning heart shown to me if not for this meaning, that the truth lies within?

But I could not forget the heavens, to which the dying soul of the bird had fled. My yearning for the stars and for questing began there. It is still strong in me. It is this yearning and the memory of that early vision which prepared me for the quest given by the Gargoyle.

My Lady Erian Li Halan led me to Nowhere to seek the famed oracle. With the rest of her entourage, we bought access past Stigmata to Nowhere, realizing that we might not be allowed to return should the garrison fear Symbiot taint among us. But to Erian, it was worth the risk. Her lands were stolen from her and she was rootless.

An old matron of her pious house had told her of the Gargoyle, which had delivered to her grandfather a vision long ago, one which revealed to him the secret needed to rise to power within the family. Returning from that oracle, her grandfather had, within a number of years, deftly rid himself of all his rivals and uncannily predicted which of his allies would betray him. Emboldened by this tale, Erian swore to seek the oracle herself.

Once on Nowhere, we had to purchase transportation and a guide to take us to the wastes, where the Gargoyle had sat for more years than recorded history. Few ships can risk landing in the wastes, lest the winds of the upper atmosphere scour the vessel's hull and breach it. Yet the winds on the lower plain are eerily still and dead. The atmosphere of the wasted planet required that we wear breathing masks, although atmosphere suits were not needed. After a journey of a week, we finally saw the thing across the vast plain.

After setting up camp, we approached and examined it. Its architecture was impressive, its sculpting so lifelike, that it seemed a creature frozen rather than carved. But it did not move, and thus could not be alive as we know it.

I then performed a rite so that I might view its occult properties. When I opened my eyes with the Second Sight, I saw that it was staring at me. Its eyes had moved, rolling in their massive sockets to peer down at me. I shuddered, for its gaze was inhuman. No emotion could be read from it, except perhaps that of fear.

I looked to Erian and saw that she was the only one of my companions who remained. The others were gone. Even the wastes were gone, replaced by lush grass over a purplish-green plain dotted with groves of oddly shaped trees. We stood in the Garden of Nowhere, the legendary state of the planet long ago, before it was turned to waste by mysterious forces.

Erian looked up at the Gargoyle and beseeched it. "Show me," she said, with a pride and bearing which I hoped would not insult the artifact. But it was, as ever, unmoved. Its eyes had rolled to gaze upon her, but its silence was supernal.

"Blessed be the works of the Pancreator," I said in prayer. "Let wisdom come to those who are open to it, whose cups are empty and whose minds are as guileless as those of small children. Show us thy will so that we may complete it."

I do not remember exactly what happened next, but I know that I dreamed. I saw more than I can recall, but what I saw was strange enough. I was back aboard the pilgrim ship we had arrived in, but it was empty of pilgrims and my companions. I found my way to the bridge and discovered that it, too, was empty. Looking out the port, I saw that the ship approached a jumpgate. Although no pilot had willed it so, the gate began to open, space and light warping within its hoop to open a strange portal to another star system. As the ship entered, I realized with a shock of fear (in that form of dream logic where one knows things which have not been told) that the Sathra Damper was disabled and that my soul was at risk.

Instead of the fabled euphoria, however, I saw a mist outside the ship. The pilot (yes, for there was now a pilot there, as if he had always been there) turned to me and asked me why it had taken me so long to get here. I replied that I had been on the bridge since before the jump, but he said that that was not what he meant.

The ship then exited another gate and we were back in normal space. A ship awaited us, but it did not belong to any noble house, guild or sect. It was Vau. The pilot was gone again and the ship flew randomly. The Vau ship shot forth a beam and caught my ship in a cocoon of light. I went to the hatch to greet the visitors (which I knew would be coming).

I was then in a sumptuous dining room, eating with a Vau

mandarin. Soldiers stood by the doors and half-naked servants brought us plates of oddly colored plants and meats, but they all tasted good. The mandarin turned to me and said, "Now that you have truly traveled space, you must become a priest."

I got up from the table and left the room, returning (instantly in the way of dreams) to the bridge of my ship (although it was now a different ship — the very one we would later acquire from one of Erian's Hazat allies). Julia Abrams flew the ship and asked me where I had found the strange clothes I wore. I realized that I was wearing Vau priestly robes, and replied, "I earned them."

She told me to strap in, because we were going to have to fight the Symbiots to get out of there. "There" was a different place than I had been before. We were now back in the Stigmata system, apparently pursued by a Symbiot spacefighter. It was faster than us, and shot forth a spiderweb from its guns. The web wrapped about our ship and I could see tiny spiders crawling across our hull, strengthening the web with their own silk. Our ship slowed to a crawl as the web dragged us back.

The spiders were now in the ship, crawling underfoot. I shooed them away, but Julia was frantic. I told her to calm down, for we would all one day be food for the spiders. I said that we must climb the web to get home. I led her to the hatch and we crawled out onto the hull (without spacesuits!) and grasped the sticky webbing around it. Using it as a ladder, we climbed out into space, toward the sun. Julia complained about the cold, but I said that the sun was hot and we'd be warm when we would arrive there.

But as we got closer, it only got colder. The sun seemed less bright. I knew that we had to connect the web to the sun, but I did not know why. I then realized that my own inner light would keep us warm. A small sun seemed to be inside my breast, and it radiated heat into space. I then remembered a Vau word to shape the light, and began to weave it into an extension of the web, building a ladder from our ship to the sun.

I woke on the wastelands of Nowhere at the foot of the Gargoyle. I had been unconscious for nearly a day. Our guide had instructed Cardanzo and Julia to shade my body, but told them that this coma was the way of visions.

Erian had dreamed also, but not the same dream as I. Her dream was populated by famous figures of her family's past, many from before the Conversion, when her relatives were demons among men. She has yet to tell all that she saw, but one of the elements of her dream was the discovery of a family relic on some unnamed world. Whether this world is one of those we know or a Lost World is unclear, as is the nature of the relic. Erian seems to remember less of her dream than I, but traces of it return to her in dreams.

As to the meaning of my dream, I cannot say for sure. I am still trying to unravel it. Perhaps I must bring the word of the Pancreator and the Holy Flame to the Vau and Symbiots? But this seems too simple an explanation for such a profound seeming vision — and profound for me it was, even if such emotion is lost in dry writing.

Whomever reads this account in my journals, temper any charge of heresy that you may have with the knowledge that even the Prophet revered the Gargoyles, and believed that they represented a purpose as yet to be revealed to Creation.

Melting Pot

August 8th, 4997, 9:00 am (Holy Terra calendar)

I am in awe at the immensity of this spacestation.

Its engineers are powerful indeed to keep it operating so many years after the Fall and under extreme pressure from the Church to abandon it. Cumulus — a city in space.

We arrived here to met with Erian's al-Malik patron. Our highly expensive berthing fees are being paid by this wealthy noble, whose name I had best not record here. We disembarked to discover a melting pot of people from planets all over the Known Worlds. The bustle was almost as maddening as that in the Istakhr Market. People hurried to and fro, desperate to conduct their business and be off before rivals could find them — or before their berthing fees grow too high.

Safe from monetary worry, we took our time reaching the domed city. We wandered the hydroponic gardens open to the vast night of space, lit only by rows of artificial sunlight. Here, in this chill void, humankind has erected a safe haven of light and life where even the flowers of Urth can find rich soil.

Our patron resides in a rather lavish apartment building fronted by the main avenue of the domed city. There, we enjoyed a rich repast and comfortable rest. Such a relaxed atmosphere has grown foreign to us after too many months spent on rough worlds. But here we can let down our guard and enjoy life.

* * *

I have just arisen from a good night's rest (although day and night are governed here by the League's clock, not by the rising or setting of the sun). Today, I will visit the agora, rumored to host items unavailable on many worlds. I hope to find an Obun meditation bowl, an item that has so far eluded me in many markets.

9:00 pm

What an adventure! I am lucky to be whole and with a full pouch of firebirds. Villainy walks freely on Cumulus.

After finishing my journal entry of the morning, I left for the agora. Since my comrades had not yet arisen, I decided to spend the day exploring on my own. A mistake.

The first portion of the day was as wonderful as I had hoped. I wandered many stalls, all makeshift structures cuddled together in a network of hallways vast and small. Some — the more expensive — hosted permanent structures or staterooms, where the air is more pleasant and elbow room more abundant.

But it was the smaller ones which interested me, for they carried the most exotic goods. Of course, some of these I avoided, such as those promising a taste of the dreaded zhrii' ka'a lotus or even the addictive selchakah.

After a time of careful looking, I finally found a merchant who sold Ur-Obun goods. He had two of the bowls I was looking for! While I only purchased one, it seems that when one finally finds what one seeks, it comes in abundance. Much like the Pancreator's grace.

My purchase perhaps lulled my wariness. With a smile on my face — too broad and idiotic — I turned into a tighter passage, hoping for a shortcut back to the main thoroughfare. It was here the ruffians waylaid me.

A rather large man stepped from an alcove and blocked my way, glaring down at me evily. From behind me, others gathered, chuckling low to themselves.

"What's in the bag, priest?" the large one grunted.

I hesitated, revealing my fear. "It… it is simply a meditation device used by the Ven Lohji sect of the Church, my son."

He obviously did not like the appellation I had used to address him, and showed his displeasure with a swing of his thick arm, knocking me forcefully into the wall. I clutched my Obun bowl, desperate not to break it. How foolish! I would have suffered broken bones before a broken bowl!

"Hand it over! Along with that pouch!"

My mind raced, trying to figure what stratagem I could use against them. I knew no theurgy which could help me so quickly as I needed, and my skill in arms is rather pitiful.

The large one reached his arm back to strike again when he grunted in pain and toppled backwards, pulled by his own arm. As his girth sank to the floor, his face a mask of pain and rage, I saw Cardanzo behind him, clutching the giant's wrist with his hand, twisting it enough to cause pain and force the brute to follow Cardanzo's whim lest his arm be dislocated in its socket.

I envied him his martial skill then, embarrassed at my need for his aid. But this envy passed quickly, replaced by my more rational relief at his arrival.

He pointed his heavy slug gun at the giant's compatriots, who I now saw to be but striplings. Instead of heeding his words to remain unmoving, they fled, quickly disappearing into the crowd.

Cardanzo backed out of the alley, forcing the brute to follow him, although not without some expelling of nasty words. I followed quickly, thankful to be in an open arena again.

Cardanzo bent down to whisper in the brute's ear. I could not hear what was said, but the fellow nodded quickly. Cardanzo released him and the man picked himself up from the ground and walked away at a fast pace.

I was astonished. "Why did you let him go? He'll only rob from another!"

"Of course he will, Alustro," Cardanzo replied, holstering his weapon, "He is a member of the local thieves' guild. Arresting him will only bring retribution on us from his fellows. Releasing him will allow us a degree of freedom from their kind."

"I don't understand. How is such crime allowed to run so rampant?"

"Cumulus follows different rules than most worlds, Alustro. The League has its hands full just keeping it in one piece. It cannot police it in addition."

"Then where are the priests? Cannot the Church lend some moral enforcement?"

"Ah, would you allow this? That bowl you so proudly bought is not exactly legal on Holy Terra."

I flushed with embarrassment. "How long have you followed me?"

"Not long. When I realized where you had gone, I knew you would need some help. But do not take that as an insult. Even I am wary walking these halls alone. Now that you are here, we are both better off for it."

I smiled at his transparent attempt to ease my ego. Cardanzo was a good friend, and loyal to all of his lady's chosen entourage. As we walked back through the agora, I asked: "How did you know about those ruffian's guild allegiances? Have you been here before?"

"Not to Cumulus, no," he replied. "But I've seen it's like. Before I took service with Erian's family, I was a legionnaire in the Li Halan forces. I was stationed for a while on the Hagia, a spacestation in the Rampart system. Even on a Li Halan-controlled station, I saw the corruption that finds its way into any long-term gathering of people. Of course, the station's previous owner had been the League."

"I didn't know you were in the military. I assumed you had been trained at birth to be a house guard."

Cardanzo smiled. "I am not so well born to serve so close to the lords and ladies from such an early age. I had to earn my way up. My father was a captain in the fleet, and that's how I attained my officer's status. It was my deeds in the Emperor Wars that gained me my service after mustering out. I received an offer from Count Gijan Li Halan, Erian's uncle. So, I entered the house forces and trained to guard nobles. It's very different, you know. Guarding a person rather than a ship. So many more things can go wrong. Assassins could be anywhere. You've got to assume the worst of others."

I saw no remorse on his face as he said this, although I cannot imagine living with such distrust. "How do you keep from getting bitter? You always seem of such good spirit, no matter what we go through."

"I've been through worse. The only thing I can imagine that could really embitter me is if I ever failed to protect my lady. Other than that, what else is there? Injury? I've got scars everywhere. Loss of friends? I've lost more friends during the war than most people can claim throughout their lives. Loss of property? Not even an issue. No, there's little left that I haven't lost. Best to count what one has and be glad for it."

"What about love? Is there no one who has ever won your heart?"

I said too much, for now a darkness entered his eyes.

"More than one. All unfaithful or dead. The dead ones hurt less."

I decided to change the subject and pretended to become absorbed in a craft store we passed. He saw through my attempt but played along anyway. As we walked on, I asked him about some of the things he had seen, the places he had been. I had hardly ever talked so deeply with him before; we never really had the time together. His travels were far but he rarely left the ships on which he served. What he saw of these places he only knew by the visitors who came aboard.

"What of aliens? Surely you've seen many of them?"

He smiled and chuckled. "There was a Gannok engineer on the Hagia. The Li Halan hated him but couldn't risk getting rid of him. He was the only League engineer left who knew the ship, so he got away with an awful lot. He did win the heart of the captain, however, when the Inquisition came aboard to search for illegal goods rumored to have been left by the previous owners.

"They spent weeks on board, searching everyone's cabins. But before they got to the officer's quarters, they were finally driven off. This Gannok — Kang Kang, I believe his name was — he began playing pranks on the Avestites. They started out small — rocks under the mattresses — but got worse and worse as time went on. Things like filling their ka-oil cannisters with perfume or replacing their wax candles with Brute fat.

"Then there were the cigars! The head Inquisitors had found a box of proscribed Vorox cigars. Do you know the kind? Grown from a tobacco-like plant on Vorox and heavily intoxicating. Well, this priest confiscated the cigars and no one knew what had become of them until the Gannok struck again. Two friends of mine were on routine patrol when they heard a small explosion from down a little-used corridor. Running to investigate, they came across the Inquisitor, his face blackened and burned, the butt of an exploding cigar still in his mouth!

"Well, he dropped the cigar quick and tried to claim that his flamegun had misfired, but everyone soon knew the full story. The next day, the ship was declared clean and the Inquisition left. A party was held in Kang Kang's honor, although he swore he had no idea what everybody was so happy with him for."

"So the Gannok prankster trait is not just a stereotype? They really do these things?"

"Well, you could never catch Kang Kang at it, but yes, I'm sure it was him."

I looked ahead at the stall selling alien crafts, the one with the sign showing mechanisms manufactured by Gannok. "I had considered buying one of their toys, to give to Ong. He likes wind-ups. But now I'm not so sure."

We eventually arrived back at our host's apartments in time for dinner. When offered a fine Delphian pipe after the meal, Cardanzo and I both declined.

The Rampart Plea

November 4th, 4997 (Holy Terra calendar)

I humbly thank the Pancreator for allowing me life and mind and a sound soul with which to continue my journals. Such a harrowing event did I experience that only the whiff of Empyrean's grace blew me from an ill course. I shake even now to think back upon it, even though I am safely ensconced in a noble estate in the Imperial City itself, on Byzantium Secundus where no enemy can approach unseen.

The events began simply, with a flitter journey over the Tepest Desert of the Ghast continent. I was with Canon Jophree, a respected member of our Order, who had invited me to witness the Ur ruins discovered there. With Lady Erian's permission, I set forth with my fellow priest in his own flitter (Jophree was born to House Cameton, a powerful family on Byzantium Secundus, and has access to many things most priests do not — a boon for our Order). He had learned how to fly such crafts before he took vows, and he and I greatly enjoyed our trip together. It had been a long time since I had been able to talk so deeply with a fellow priest, and he shed some light on my own strange experiences since I joined with Erian.

The ruins were... eerie. It is the only word to describe them. We did not land, but only flew over them, circling around to see them from all sides. It seems that we both had a strange sense of foreboding, and agreed not to walk among them.

After getting our fill of the strange landmarks, we turned back. I still do not understand just what happened or why, but Jophree lost control of the flitter. We spun maniacally in the sky, up and down and in circles. He fought the controls but some greater force seemed in control. I remember him yelling something about an "electromagnetic grid disturbance" and something about terraforming anomalies. But I was too hurried, fetching safety bubbles from the back and strapping them on to both of us. I had just latched the belt around him when the engine blew up.

The force must have thrown us both out the windshield. This would explain the gashes on my face and hands. I was knocked unconscious immediately. I came to on the desert floor, the plastic liquid of the safety bubble splattered over me; it had ruptured prematurely, leaving me with more bruises than I deserved and a broken survival kit. There was no sign of Canon Jophree. I prayed that his bubble had activated correctly, and would cushion his fall before bursting.

I began searching for him, but my own transmitter was broken. I feared the worst, for both of us. Without a transmitter, no one would find me in this wasteland. If I could not find Jophree and his transmitter, I was doomed.

My search took me in an ever-widening circle. By the time the sun set, I still had seen no sign of Jophree or our downed flitter. I knew my robes would do me little good against the chill desert night, and began to look for an outcrop or gully where I could light a fire safe from the winds. That is when I saw the lights.

At first, I thought it must be my friend, so I began calling. Two fusion torches came toward me. Had Jophree called a rescue party so soon? Two men approached, one wearing the uniform of a Charioteer spacepilot, although somewhat torn and dusty, made of old-style synthsilk, the kind usually inherited over generations from a wealthy family. The other was even better attired, for he wore a short cape and brooch with the crest of House Cameton.

"Greetings," I said as they came near. "I am glad you found me. Is Canon Jophree alright?"

They looked at each other quizzically and then the pilot replied. "You're a priest?"

58

"Yes. I am Novitiate Alustro of the Eskatonic Order."

They both smiled. The pilot reached his hand out to me. "I am so glad to see you, father. We've needed a priest for a long time now."

"I don't understand," I said, shaking his hand.

"Come on over to the ship. We have food." They both began moving back the way they had come, and I followed.

"Are you not the rescue party? Did Canon Jophree call you?"

"We don't have a squawker," the pilot said. "It broke when we crashed."

"Crashed? You ran into the electromagnetic interference also? How long have you been here?"

This time, the noble spoke: "It seems like years. I am Baron Arbuck Cameton, by the way. I apologize for not introducing myself earlier. We have been in the desert too long."

"Well, surely then you have people looking for you? Your family?"

"Of course they're looking for me. But this is the Tepest Desert! It's huge. Whatever caused the crash is foiling all our equipment. It is surely doing the same to our searchers' equipment."

As he spoke, we came over the rise and I saw a starship, perhaps an Explorer class vessel. It was half buried in the ground, obviously from a crash landing. Although the nose was buried deep, the rear hatch still allowed access in and out of the craft. It was to this door that they walked.

"We've got a lot of supplies," the pilot said. "So don't worry. Eat all you want. You have to be hungry after a day like you've had."

"Thank you," I replied, following him into the hatch. "I'm famished. By the way, what do I call you?"

I couldn't see his face as he walked ahead of me in the tight passage, but he mumbled his reply.

"I'm sorry. Was that Captain Kamen?"

"Kariman."

We came out of the engine area and into a common room. It

was lit by an everlight clasped to a ceiling pipe. Captain Kariman began opening tins and scooping their contents onto a plate for me. I embarrassingly wolfed it down. I hadn't eaten since well before our flitter accident.

Baron Arbuck disappeared into the forward cabin. After a few minutes, power came on, flooding the cabin with light. In the rear, where we had passed through, I heard the slight whine of an engine or generator. Kariman looked around and flicked some switches on and off, cutting some of the lights.

"Alustro," the baron yelled from foreship. "I want to show you this."

I got up and walked carefully down the passage. The ship rested at a slant, so I walked a downward incline to reach the cockpit from where the baron called.

He was sitting in a navigator's couch, moving dials and switches on and off. "I need to ask a favor of you, father. Would you bless this ship?"

"I can certainly perform a blessing, but why?"

Kariman came in and closed the door behind him, sitting in the pilot's couch.

"Because we're going to try and get this thing off the ground again," the baron replied.

"Well, I suppose I could perform a small litany, if you think it would help."

Captain Kariman spoke: "It would, father. It would, indeed."

I prepared my robes and polished my jumpgate pendant, filthy from the day's sweat and sand, and read a short litany from the Epistles of Horace. "It is done. I hope it helps."

"Hmm," the baron said. "I was thinking of something… well, more powerful. Could you perform this one instead?" He handed me a small think machine with a gospel displayed upon it.

"But this is the Rampart Plea! From the Cardano Apocrypha. Where did you get it?"

The baron shrugged. "It's always been one of my favorites, father."

"Favorites! This was deemed heretical in 4672 by the Orthodoxy. Even my Order bans it."

"I'm sorry to hear that, father," the baron said, as he swiveled around in his seat to face me, a laser pistol aimed at my chest. "But I don't condone the censure of great works. We cannot begin our voyage without it. Now, I need you to read it for me. And put some heart into it."

I was speechless. I could not even begin to understand what was going on. But faced with a deadly weapon and a threat, I complied with the baron's request. What harm could it bring? I had read the forbidden gospel before. It had been banned on doctrinal grounds only, and so was not considered harmful, just false. Once attributed to Saint Amano of Rampart, it was later deemed a forgery. I began to read:

"O Invisible Intelligences, hear my plea. Open the path to the stars and guide my feet upon it. In my travels, let me not shun the unknown regions. Show to me creations yet to be birthed. Let mine eyes scry thy true foundations, the secret thread which binds your creatures, so that I may proudly perform my duty to thee."

The baron lowered his pistol. "Thank you. Maybe now we can finally leave."

The engine sound grew louder as Kariman worked his controls. The ship shook and rattled, and a horrible grinding commenced. The baron looked up at the ceiling. "I think she's breaking apart."

"You're tearing your own ship up!" I yelled.

"Yes," Captain Kariman said. "Yes, we are." The grinding could now be heard in the rear of the ship also. I turned and fumbled the door open, expecting to feel the searing heat of a laser on by back. But as I slipped into the hall, I glanced back to see the baron staring listlessly at his readouts.

"A captain must go down with his ship, father," Captain Kariman said, flicking on every switch he could reach. "Isn't that right? Isn't that proper?"

I turned and ran, convinced that they had been driven mad by their stay in the desert. The ship rocked back and forth, the engines pushing it deeper into the earth. I had to get out the rear hatch before we were buried.

As I ran through the common room, lockers flung open with the stress and stretch of the hull. A body fell from one and smacked onto the floor in front of me. I think I screamed. It was obviously a priest. His robes and vestments showed that. But he was desiccated like an ancient mummy, and a terrible knife wound could be seen across his throat.

I leapt over it and kept moving. As I sped through the final passage in the engine room, I heard moaning sounds around me. Fearing that the two madmen had tried to kill another of their crew as they did the priest, I stopped to see where the sounds came from.

Then the flux cache hatch flung open and raw fusion energy and radiation spewed forth. Shadows lengthened across the walls and ceiling, as if something large approached from a distance, blocking the light. I dared not stay to see the source of the shapes wriggling on the walls, and threw myself against the rear hatch, now locked and bolted. I struggled with the bolt, finally throwing it off as the moaning sound grew louder.

"Ssstaayy…" a voice said from somewhere in the room.

I kicked the door and only the shifting of the ship — the hull struggling against the force of its own engines — allowed it to burst open. I jumped from the ship, which now dug a deep furrow into the ground, and struggled against the crumbling sand to reach the lip of the deepening pit. Something cold touched my ankle and I cried, making a last leap up. I grasped the edge of the hole and pulled myself out, running as fast as I could back to the rise over which we had come earlier, back to the place they had found me.

I never looked back. I myself was now mad, delirious with fear and exposure to the cold night. Two days later, the rescue team found me. Canon Jophree had landed fine and immediately called for help. Julia herself came to find me, showing more worry for my welfare than I had thought her capable of. I recovered over a number of days in a Church hospital, in the care of Amalthean healers.

I explained the incident with the two madmen and their ship, but Canon Jophree could find no such ship when he went back to investigate. And he knew no Cameton named Arbuck, certainly not a baron by such name, but said he would inquire nonetheless.

He believed the men were Ur artifact thieves who had disguised themselves as noble and guildsman to gain access to the ruins. Obviously, their ship went down, perhaps carrying Ur artifacts of a psychic nature, which would explain my hallucinations.

But I do not believe they were hallucinations. I sufferered radiation poisoning from somewhere and there is the wound on my ankle — a black, putrid bruise which required mercifal technals to heal.

November 27th

I am writing from my cabin in the Resurgent, our new starship. I have just spoken with Canon Jophree by radio. He has new information concerning my "adventure" which puzzles him just as much as it does me.

A distant cousin of his in House Cameton approached him soon after we departed and inquired as to why Jophree was interested in Baron Arbuck. It seems that a certain Baron Arbuck was this woman's ancestor. He and his crew were lost when his ship crashed in the Tepest Desert — in the year 4562. The accident was blamed on his pilot, a Captain Kamen, a suspected Antinomist. Only years after the crash did evidence come forward about Kamen's atrocities on Rampart. He is apparently a folk legend on that world, equated with evil.

After hearing this, Jophree initiated another search of the desert, near to where I had been found. He uncovered the remains of a starship, buried deep in the sand and scoured by years, perhaps centuries, of exposure. While little is left of the remains, enough is there to confirm its name: the Rampart Plea...

Blink

December 17, 4997 (Holy Terra calendar)

I had always heard about Leagueheim and its decadent ways. By what my Church instructors taught, I was lead to believe it was a veritable Gehenne of sin. I believed that once I could see it for myself, such an overblown reputation would, like so many other Church fallacies I had been taught, crumble.

I was strangely right, although in a way I never expected. Even here among the smooth ceramsteel spires and flashing lights I found a spirituality of sorts.

We arrived here in time to catch one of Erian's al-Malik allies before he left on some undisclosed mission. Before leaving, he provided us with information on an unknown lost world where the answers to our quest may await us. I will write nothing of it here, until we are closer to our goal.

In his absence, he allowed us the use of his suites. We have used this needed rest to make some additions to our new starship, the Resurgent. Julia demanded a neutrino sensor array, but the prices we discovered were outrageous. We voted against it. That's when she revealed that she knew a place where we could find one cheaper, but she would have to go there in person to arrange the sale. We all thought it promising and agreed.

"I want Onggangarak to come with me," she said. "In case of trouble. And Alustro, too."

"Me?" I said. "I know nothing of commerce. What can I do?"

"Even the most desperate thugs think twice about hitting a priest. You're my insurance against… hasty opinions."

"Wait just a minute," Erian said. "This trip is dangerous? Why didn't you say so in the first place?"

Julia rolled her eyes. "Everywhere on Leagueheim is dangerous, Erian! This is just... more so."

"Then I forbid it. I will not have Alustro put into unnecessary danger."

"Hold on, now! He'll be fine. Like I said, he's just there to sooth bruised egos and such."

"Erian," Cardanzo said, "They will be fine in Julia's care. We could really use that array."

"Then I'm coming too," Erian said.

"Oh no you're not!" Julia yelled. "They'll know you for the royal brat you are the second you step off the lift! You're staying here."

"How dare you! I can go wherever I want. Whenever and with whomever!"

"Not here, you don't. They'll jack the price up at least three times more than it's worth when they smell your privilege."

"Please," Cardanzo said, "there is no reason for raised voices. Julia is right, Erian. You and I must stay here and let them do their work."

"Why do you stay?" Julia said, looking surprised. "I could use you there."

"A bodyguard does not leave his charge," Cardanzo replied. "Besides, Ong is more than capable of providing all the muscle or threat you may need."

Julia looked annoyed but nodded. "All right, then. Let's go, you two." She picked up her belt, loaded with her blaster and all manner of tools, and headed for the door. Ong and I got up to follow.

She led us through a dizzying maze of sidewalks, escalators, tubes and cargo lifts until we reached what I believe was the ground level of Leagueheim. At least, it seemed like the ground. It was dark even though slight patches of daylight shone through openings in the soot layer above and innumerable fusion signs from hundreds of stores flashed at us from all directions. None of this phased Julia, although at times I think Ong was ready to attack something. I feared lest an unattentive pedestrian bump into him.

Eventually, Julia stopped in front of a bar called the Last Flight Out and peered inside through the grimy window. "This is it. Name's changed but the place is still the same. As long as the same owner's here, we're fine."

I began coughing immediately upon entering the place. I don't know what sort of burning weed was in the air, but it wasn't tobacco or even one of the milder narcotics.

"Yimbun," Julia said. "Cover your mouth and you'll get used to it. Smells awful but tastes great."

I nodded, pulling by robes over my nose. Ong seemed undisturbed by the smell, even though his senses were keener. I assume that the legendary Vorox resistance to toxins held true here.

Julia lead us through the crowded room to the bar and rapped on it, trying for the bartender's attention. "The owner in?"

The sweaty fellow glared at her. "Who wants to know?"

"Julia Abrams. He knows me."

The man nodded and picked up a small palm squawker. He whispered something into it, which I could not hear over the crowd's conversations. He looked at Julia and nodded, smiling. "Wait here. He'll be right out."

As we lounged against the bar, I noticed a few men looking at us from across the room. They seemed to know Julia, but were not too happy about it. As I was about to ask Julia who they were, a yell came from the rear of the bar.

"You! How dare you come into my establishment!"

Julia turned to the man and went white. "Yours?! Where the Gehenne is Lark?"

"Lark's dead," the man said, now backed up by a number of thugs gathering around him. "Left the place to me."

"He would. He never did have a good eye for character. Leaving his pride and joy to Sobol Hetch. So what now?"

"We settle up, that's what. Decide here and now who's best."

Ong began to growl deep in his throat. Sobol's thugs began to look nervous, their hands reaching for their holsters.

"Here and now," Julia said. "Let's go."

"Wait!" I cried. "There's no need for violence! Whatever your dispute is, surely there's a calmer resolution!"

Julia and Sobol both looked at me like I was mad.

"Violence?" Julia said.

"What's the harm in a game of Blink?" Sobal said.

"Blink?" I stammered. "What is Blink?"

Sobol pulled out a deck of holographic cards and slid them towards us across the bar. "That's Blink. Best damn game of chance in the Known Worlds is what."

I could see Julia's eyes roll up. "Say's you. But since it's so damn important to you, let's play. No way you'll beat me, though."

"I've learned a lot of tricks since we played last, Abrams. I think this one's mine."

Sobol went over to a table and shoved some empty glasses off it, scattering them across the floor. None of them broke. "Have a seat. All of you."

Julia walked over and sat down, but motioned for us to stay behind her. "They'll stand."

Sobol, seating himself, shrugged. "Fine. Let's play. Can your boy shuffle cards?"

"Sure," Julia said, picking up the deck, which one of Sobol's men had fetched from the bar. She handed it to me.

I have never handled a deck of cards in my life. I looked at the ones I now held in my hand and caught by breath in awe. They were stunningly beautiful. Lush, three-dimensional images leapt from the card surfaces as I peered through the deck. Impossible patterns of color and texture mixed together as two cards were connected and broke apart again as they seperated. I shook myself from the reverie and placed the deck on the table, trying to remember what shuffling looked like from having seen it done.

"They're mesmerizing, aren't they, priest?" Sobol said. "Banned on most of the Known Worlds by the Church. Your even touching them would get a reprimand from your superior and a call for confession. But here on Leagueheim, who is going to police such things? No priest with any wits would step foot in this district. Except you, and you're only here because Abrams here was looking for an element of surprise."

Julia frowned. "My confessor goes where I go, Sobol."

"Yours? Or does he belong to some haughty royal you're screwing?"

Julia stared at Sobol with utter hatred and the tension returned.

"Uhm... I think I've got them randomized," I said. "Is this good enough?"

Sobol did not take his eyes off Julia. "Fine. Go ahead and deal us seven cards each — without revealing them."

When they had the cards, I stepped back behind Julia to see what was in her hand. It made no sense to me, but I was awestruck again at the intense images. They almost portrayed something, and it was maddeningly tempting to stare at them until the image they were hiding revealed itself.

Julia hid the cards, looking at me. "Don't stare too long. That's the trick. You'll try for hours — years, even — to put the cards in the right combination to reveal 'it.'"

"It?"

"The secret they hold. The image just on the edge of consciousness. If you ever saw it, it would solve everything. Or so everyone thinks. It's all just a load of crap. A bunch of random holograms generated by a field. As long as the cards are in a certain range, they're affected by the field."

"But what generates the field? Where's the power?"

"Who knows? That's what makes them so valuable. Can't make them anymore."

"Enough talk," Sobol said. "Put down a card."

Julia looked through her hand again and placed down a bluish card with a slowly revolving vortex. Sobol quickly laid a green card with rising lines on top of it. The two images combined to create a weird effect, somewhat like a jumpgate, with lines of force radiating from a spiral. Sobol smiled. Julia frowned.

This went on for some time. About an hour into the game, Julia sent me to the restaurant next door for some food. One of Sobol's men came with me to help carry the bags.

Three hours after it began, however, it was over. Julia placed a red card with intermittant flashes on top of Sobol's yellow, pulsing mist. The effect was to destroy all the images, leaving a momentary void in the space where they had been. The effect lasted for perhaps less than a second, but I could now understand why Sobol was so obsessed with the game.

Staring at that blank moment, it seemed that something leapt in to fill it, some deep feeling of... contentment. Julia sighed and had a look on her face unlike any I had seen her wear before. For once, the tense jaw slackened and her eyes softened and she had a fleeting glance of peace.

Sobol looked like he wanted to cry, for he obviously had not received the full effect. Was it possible that it affected the winner differently than the loser? If so, what form of technology was this?

After a moment's silence where nobody made a sound, Sobol gathered the cards together, held them close to his body, and stood up. "What's it going to be, Abrams? Name your price."

"A neutrino sensor array for an exploration class vessel."

"That's it? You just won Blink and all you want is a lousy sensor array?"

"I don't want your cards, Sobol. I just came for some hardware."

"Okay. Yeah. All right. It's yours. Where do you want it delivered?"

"Charioteer Bay 33."

"It'll be there. It'll take a day or two at least, though. You understand that?"

"If it's not there in three," Julia said, standing up. "I'll coming looking for it."

Ong sensed his cue and growled a short, gruff bark.

Sobol nodded. "It'll be there."

Julia turned toward the door and began walking. We followed, although I kept glancing over my shoulder back at Sobol to see what his reaction was. I suspect this was a violation of exit etiquette for it implied that I expected a blaster at our backs. But he was slumped in the chair again and looked like a loved one had died. I couldn't even begin to fathom such an addiction.

We said little on the way back, for Julia was obviously in no mood to talk. On the lift upwards, however, I know I saw a tear in her eye. She wiped it away quickly to hide it from us.

How can it be that a mere toy of the Second Republic elicits a religious response in one who has denied it from even the Church? Such a thing is alien to me. To find faith, no matter how elusive, in a thing rather than a being is… all too human, perhaps?

An Open Mind

January 21st, 4998 (Holy Terra calendar)

Noon

I look at Sanjuk oj Kaval and wonder at the ferocity and tragedy from which her life is built. They are marked on her very skin, these stories of loss and ruin, surrounding the few tales of triumph and transcendence. Her baa'mon, her body carvings, tell all about her. I wish I could fully read them.

I know only a little written Ukari, enough to tell a clan marking here and there, and sometimes a coming-of-age mark, but little beyond that. They fascinate me, though, and I wonder if it would be impertinent to ask her to teach me the marks.

But my pondering is interrupted by the entrance of the bailiff, come to take Sanjuk back to her cell where she will await trial. I must put aside my journal for the moment....

Evening

Erian has been successful in convincing the court to hear her argument; her station does bring its privileges, even here on Leagueheim. Julia, as a Charioteer, has already been called upon as a character witness. Although Sanjuk is a low-ranking Scraver, she is still a member of the guild, and thus allowed representation.

I fear, however, that her guild is prepared to throw her to the void on this case. It is too high profile, one even they shun. I had best describe the charges for the record.

Sanjuk oj Kaval has been accused of murdering Paano HanJoirii, a high-ranking Ur-Obun diplomat in the service of the emperor. Indeed,

HanJoirii was a confidant of Bran Botan voKarm, the emperor's Left-Hand Council. Serious charges.

Sanjuk is an old friend of Erian from her days on Midian. While she is native to Ukar — she calls the world Kordeth — she spent her early years in the Scravers guild on Midian, scrounging ancient ruins under the patronage of Erian's uncle, a man obsessed with Second Republic art. She is, of course, an Ur-Ukar.

She claims innocence in this affair, and tells Erian that she was set up by rivals in her guild to take the fall — what better suspect for the murder of an Obun than his hateful cousin, an Ukar? She has too little pull to even find out who was behind this high-level murder, and has thus swallowed her pride and asked Erian to intervene on her behalf. It was mere coincidence that we were on Leagueheim at this time.

I am unaware of the full details of the investigation, but from what Erian has disclosed, there is scant evidence for Sanjuk's involvement. For one, it is unlikely that she would have ever been allowed access to the ambassadorial grounds, although she was seen outside them soon after the murder. However, she was on duty at a Scraver-run pawnshop on the nearby corner at the time.

This shop is located just outside the grounds and is merely a front, a place to arrange various clandestine activities for any adventuresome ambassador who seeks diversions from his duties. It is not the sort of work Sanjuk is normally involved in — Ukari are generally considered untrustworthy for such secret affairs — but since the claim on her recent reclamation operation had not yet come through, she signed up for any duty available. She claims that someone in her guild purposefully positioned her there to become the main suspect in a planned assassination.

Her guild, of course, does not appreciate being accused so.

Julia has done her best to find out who would have set Sanjuk up, but has gained few leads. She suspects that little word will be heard, for anyone involved in murdering an imperial ambassador would surely cover his tracks well.

Erian has arranged for good advocacy: Derrick LeFamon, a Reeve known to her uncle, has agreed to represent Sanjuk, although he believes her chances are slim. While there is little but circumstantial evidence against Sanjuk, the prejudice against the Ukari will work against her — especially that from the prosecution witness, Lorim HanPavak, the murdered Obun's brother. It is LeFamon's hope that enough doubt can be raised that the case will be dropped.

The trial is tomorrow. I will pray for our friend tonight.

January 22nd, 1998 (Holy Terra calendar)

Morning
We all gathered at the courthouse, a former Second Republic court that still serves its original function. Its huge, vaulting ceilings are higher than those of many cathedrals I know. It does seem that worship of the law eclipsed that of the Pancreator in those times.

Lorim HanPavak sits across the hall from us, watching Sanjuk. I cannot read his expression; he is well trained in stoicism. Sanjuk stares back at him, her face also a mask of calm. I wonder what she is thinking?

I wish I could say this was to be a lengthy trial, but it just is not so. The odds are against Sanjuk.

LeFamon makes his opening arguments most eloquently. He is a fine Reeve, well versed in rhetoric. But the prosecutor is even more so, a greatly experienced consul, one in imperial employ.

LeFamon tells the court somewhat of Sanjuk's life and the hardships she has had, the struggles she has made, emphasizing the sheer folly of imagining that she would throw it all away in a fit of anger against an ambassador she never met. As he tells us about her, he points to her carvings as proof of his story, showing that her life is written for all to see.

He calls upon Erian to describe her friendship with Sanjuk, and she tells of an incident in her youth where Sanjuk and she discovered a valuable sculpture from the Second Republic, marveling over it together, revealing that each was more versed in art than the other had thought. LeFamon then asks how anyone capable of such cultural appreciation could be a murderer.

Julia is called upon next, and explains her work with Sanjuk on Midian. She occasionally flew finds from Sanjuk's digs back to the Li Halan palace, and had multiple opportunities to discuss League matters with Sanjuk. She makes the point that Sanjuk would never betray the guild that provided her an escape from the clan wars on Ukar.

Our advocate then details the lack of evidence against the accused, and how her proximity to the scene of the crime is the only reason she is here in the court today. He has done a very good job of raising doubt.

And then his rival stands to speak and brings forth a list of reprimands Sanjuk has received throughout her career from her Scraver chiefs. This list is long and full of petty crimes, such as assault and theft, none enough to warrant expulsion, but all enough to paint her as a criminal.

It is clear that both Erian and Julia were unaware of these reprimands and look... disappointed. Sanjuk does not look at them as they are read; she only looks at the Obun across the hall from her, who stares back, unmoved.

And then the prosecutor calls upon Lorim HanPavak to explain why the Ukar hate the Obun and why Sanjuk would have done murder upon one.

The Obun rises and then closes his eyes for a moment. I notice Sanjuk sit back and close her's also, as if she was very tired. The Obun then speaks:

"It is true that the Ukari hate our people. But it is also true that some of our people despise the Ukari. Nonetheless, I came here to see justice done. To see that my brother's killer was tried and punished. That killer is not in this room."

A gasp of shock traveled across the chambers, and even the judge stared at the Obun in surprise. The prosecutor's jaw even dropped.

"The accused, Sanjuk oj Kaval, has graciously allowed me to read her mind, hiding none of its contents. While I must say that I find much of her past repugnant, I find her character... strong. If I had to suffer as she had, I wonder if I could carry myself as well. There is much my people have yet to learn from our long-sundered cousins."

"This is ridiculous!" the prosecutor yelled. "You cannot simply walk into the court and make such claims!"

"I have been asked to come and bear witness against the accused. I know for a fact that she is not the murderer. There are some who can hide memories from others, and even those who can weave false ones, but she is not one of these adepts. Indeed, she is nearly mind-blind.

"She is innocent and I must ask that the case against her be dismissed. I then ask that the real murderer be found. My brother's close friend, Bran Botan voKarm, desires true justice in this matter, and will not be content until it has been received. Let the innocent go free, and find the true culprit."

He then sat down, his face as expressionless as always. But those around him were far from expressionless. The prosecutor seemed not to know what to do. But the judge decided the matter for him.

"There is scant evidence against the accused. Unless you can bring forth convincing evidence, I see no reason to waste the court's time further."

"I have no more to say," the prosecutor said as he sat down, exasperated.

"Then let Sanjuk oj Kaval go free," the judge said. "And let it be known that all charges brought against her for the murder of Paano HanJoirii are dismissed." He stood and began the long walk down from his high perch.

Once he left the room, we all stood, looking dumbfoundedly at each other. We all knew that, if this was not a League-run court, such witchery as psychic mind-reading would never be allowed. Indeed, had it been a Church court, I fear that Lorim HanPavak would have been censured and removed as a witness, his comment stricken from the record.

Sanjuk seemed not the least surprised. She smiled, looking at the Obun, who nodded to her and rose to leave.

LeFamon was perhaps the most surprised of us all, confiding that he had fully expected to lose the case. This was now a feather in his cap, one he planned on spreading news of quickly. As he gathered his notes and portable think machine, he thanked us all for an exciting case and turned to leave, heading for the closest town crier.

"It's all so creepy," Julia said. "I don't know if I'd want someone like that peering into my soul."

"If you were facing the gallows, you would," Sanjuk said. "I still wonder at you humans, so virginal when it comes to mind-sight. Few Ukari grow to adulthood without suffering the mind-gaze of another — or even the mind-commands of others. That you believe your souls are your own is your great ignorance."

"I would prefer not to discuss such possibly heretical matters on such a happy day," I said.

Sanjuk looked at me and smiled. "You I could like. The rest of your order... no."

As I make this entry, the others are readying to go to a celebratory feast at a local restaurant. Erian has offered to pay (as she has the court costs), although she has not revealed to Sanjuk just how little money she has at present.

I suspect she will learn soon enough. From what Julia told me, Sanjuk may be joining our entourage when next we depart.

"She doesn't know it yet," Julia said. "Whoever set her up won't be happy. It's probably a Scraver crime family, one that won't want her hanging around. If she doesn't leave on her own soon, she may wind up dead in a sewer drain."

"But she's a Scraver!" I said in disbelief. "How could they do that to one of their own?"

"Wise up. It's not the guild as a whole that'll do it. It's whoever murdered that Obun. They may not even be Scravers. Could be Slayers. But they've got some sort of connection to the guild, one which ain't healthy for Sanjuk to be around. I figure she'll be okay if she gets off world. A few months away and everybody'll forget about her."

"Have you told Sanjuk or Erian this?"

"Not yet. Like you said earlier: Why spoil the celebration? I'm just telling you so you can help figure out where to fit another bunk on the Resurgent."

It seems that I will soon be able to broach the topic of Ukari writing with Sanjuk. There will be little else for her to do on the long journey to the jumpgate.

Fragments

Night on Hira is bright when the bombs go off. The sky is lit with the fiery, short-lived glow of munitions. The Hazat and Kurgan Caliphate forces never seem to tire of war.

But the lights and the sounds eventually fade as the night grows older and the soldiers tire, and peace settles over the broken land. The rubble of countless villages lies as a no-man's land between the forces' current embattlements, with only long-range missiles, aerial flybys and the occasional theurgic rite forming any contact between the enemies.

We are safe here for now. In the ruins of Matanto city, in the blasted basement labyrinth of the former ruler's palace, we have taken shelter to search the past for our future. This building, constructed during the Second Republic of strong maxicrete and plasteel, has lasted millennia of erosion only to be torn open and exposed to the sky by a series of direct artillery barrages.

It wasn't even looted. Once the ruling family escaped the burning town, the Hazat and Kurgan forces moved on, fighting over new lands not yet sworn to either side. Why they mutually assaulted this city, I don't really understand. My lady Erian says it had something to do with the ruler's neutrality, an increasingly rare and dangerous thing to both Hazat and Kurgan — it is a tactical mistake to let anybody live who could later ally with an enemy. Tactical mistake, perhaps, but a moral gesture, something lacking in the behavior of both sides. I am ashamed at the way one of our own, a royal family of the Known Worlds, attempts to bring the civilized rule of the empire to this barbarian world. I am even more ashamed of the Patriarch's complaisant role in this. Were he here to witness the atrocities, he would surely move to rein them in with all the powers at his command. Or so I like to believe.

I don't even know who is winning the war. From our vantage, it is impossible to tell who is gaining ground. It seems that no one is. Well, little matter. As long as the fighting does not make its way back here, our mission can proceed without interruption.

Consul Darok Rohmer is our neighbor in the palace. We did not expect to find anyone when we arrived, but he was already here, the only one in the city who did not flee when the war reached the town. His fellows in the Reeves guild surely believed him dead. A great loss, for Consul Rohmer was one of the foremost authorities on the Anunnaki, the precursor race who left behind the jumpgates. His studies brought him here, to this old Second Republic museum, once a treasure trove of Ur artifacts, then a noble palace, and now ruins.

It is our reason for coming here, too. Clues on our quest to resolve the great vision given Erian by the Gargoyle of Nowhere — a foreboding Ur artifact in itself — led us here, to this war-torn planet just outside of the Known Worlds. Something was here for us, some ancient piece in a present-day puzzle that, once assembled, would spell the fate and duty of my noble lady. Thus, I, my liege Erian Li Halan, her bodyguard Cardanzo, pilot Julia Abrams, friend Onganggorak (a Vorox) and associate Sanjuk oj Kaval (an Ur-Ukar), arrived in the Resurgent to resolve our quest.

We hid our ship under camouflage tarp in the nearby hills and set up camp in the ruins of the palace. It did not take long for Ong to sniff out Rohmer, who hid in the lowest level, evading all patrols that passed through. At first, Rohmer feared we were scavengers or Hazat conscription forces, and he led Ong a chase through the seemingly endless corridors below. But once caught by our over-eager friend and presented to Erian, he realized that we were independents, unaligned (or, at least not working) with any side in the war.

Since then, he has been gracious enough to show us about the museum in return for our aid in lifting and removing rubble, and for cooked meals. His rations were running rather low by the time we arrived; it was a blessing for him that we were well stocked.

80

Cardanzo spent most of his time patrolling the region, making sure nobody came near to our camp. On two occasions he chased away local refugees — starving bandits, by his report — who came too near. He had wisely prepared for such a role before we had embarked on this journey, and now wore Hazat military garb. Anyone who saw him feared he was a ranger for a greater force nearby.

As the others tended mainly to logistical or defense matters, Erian and I combed the ruins for the sculpture seen in her dream: an Ur mandala. This item was carved from the same alloy as the jumpgates (the copperish-purple metal no one has ever identified) and was studded with glowing jewels. More importantly, Erian believed that the mandala pattern itself was a key of sorts, some sort of clue into… what? She did not know, but we all knew it was important, part of the greater tapestry of visions she had experienced since her coming-of-age on Midian.

So we spent the days searching the museum. Rohmer had not seen the piece, but helped us search whenever he could. He had research of his own here was trying to finish, a search for the lost Anunnaki culture as revealed in their language and art. This was a monumentally hard task, for what clues they left behind are mere fragments; the whole only came together after study over far-flung worlds, and even then provided only a hazy image, a warped imperfection in stained glass.

"No, we don't know what they looked like," he told me, "but we do know something of their behavior as revealed in the myths of the Obun and Ukar, the Oro'ym and the ancient legends of Urth itself. Yes, Urth, cradle of humanity. I believe, as did the xenologists of the Second Republic, that the Anunnaki visited Urth in its infancy and guided the early footsteps of humankind. The fact that a jumpgate exists there, and the known ruins on Mars, is proof enough. But there are sites on Holy Terra itself, although they are not acknowledged as such. Ancient places where only vague traces remain, a stray rock here, a carving there."

"Have you seen any of these?" I asked. "Where are they?"

"All over the planet. If there's one good the Church has done, it's to keep Holy Terra pristine, a living museum. Certainly, many complain when their request to emigrate to the Cradle is denied, but thank the Pancreator for it! The world was once trampled with too many feet — as Byzantium Secundus and Leagueheim are now — and they kick away the footprints of those who went before."

I noticed that he was not specific in naming a site, but chose not to question him further. As he began to open up more, he would perhaps tell me one or two of these places.

"See this?" he said, pointing to a cylinder sealed behind a see-through case, lit by an everlight, glowing since its Second Republic maker set it to burning a thousand years ago. "What do you think that is?"

I looked carefully at it, walking around its case to see it from all angles. It was smooth, with carvings all over, abstract designs with a hint of anthropomorphism in certain swirls. Carved from the unearthly alloy common to Ur artifacts, it had no opening: a perfectly sealed rod. Yet, somehow, in some strange way, I knew it was hollow, that some unspeakable space was enclosed within it, an otherworldly place sharing our space, our dimension.

"A king's scepter, perhaps?" I said, noticing his look of disappointment. "Or a phallus? Perhaps a fertility sculpture?"

"You apply modern concepts to the distant past," he said shaking his head. "But don't feel stupid: your answers are the same as Crafter Oncales at the Academy Interatta. You see, there is an exact duplicate of this cylinder at that school. Indeed, I bet you could find at least one in every system of the Known Worlds. Do you know why?"

I shook my head.

"Because it comes from a jumpgate. This one was removed from the jumpgate of this very system. I don't know where the academy's is from. This one's removal, I believe, is what caused this planet to disappear from Human Space for many years."

"This? This is the reason Hira's jumpgate shut down, keeping all ships out of the system for centuries?"

"I believe so. But I don't think the scientists who took it knew. It is one of the last additions to the collection."

"Then why did the gate open again? If this item is here, why does the gate now respond to codes it ignored for years?"

"I'm not sure about that. If I were, I would be the most celebrated man in the Known Worlds, wouldn't I? The Emperor surely has need of such lore to open all the closed gates to all the Lost Worlds of Human Space. Perhaps it's like a fuse; when removed, no circuits can complete themselves. The jumpgates have already shown signs of self-repair. It is no great leap to imagine that, over the years, the jumpgate rerouted itself so that energy could flow again."

"A machine that repairs itself? How can such a thing be? That would imply life."

"The genius of its manufacture eludes us, as does the genius of all Anunnaki science. All of it built on unknown scientific principles. The line between animate life and mere matter — mind and matter — grows indistinct the more one studies the Ur races. Nothing lasts. Nothing but Ur tech," he said wistfully.

I stared in awe at the cylinder. He looked at me and smiled, shaking his head again.

"Don't go worshipping it, now. I could be wrong, you know. It may be a simple antenna, or a strut meant to help maintain structural integrity. We can't really know for sure. It's all just theory."

"Unknown principles…" I said, looking away from it. "Well, I must continue the search. Thank you for your time again."

"Think nothing of it. Any more questions, feel free to ask. By the way, what's for dinner tonight? Are you going to fix another of those Ukari dishes? I rather enjoy the way the worms squirm as you bite them."

I thought he was being sarcastic at first, but he seemed to genuinely like Ukari cuisine. I had fixed some the previous night, based on a recipe Sanjuk had provided, attempting to use as much local resources as possible rather than our sealed stores. Ukari cuisine is a subterranean dining experience: mushrooms and earthworms.

"Perhaps," I said, turning to go. "I shall have to poll the others about their responses to last night's meal…"

Erian was not where I had left her, so I went up the stairs to the level above, coming out into the night air, now still and quiet after the nightly artillery died. Erian was there, whispering to Julia and Sanjuk. I came close and coughed to announce myself.

"Alustro," Erian said. "I don't want to alarm you, but Cardanzo believes soldiers are approaching the town. We may have to evacuate."

"Now? But we haven't found the object of our quest yet!" I complained.

"Keep your voice down," Julia said. "That thing ain't worth our lives." She looked to Erian as she said this, hoping for confirmation.

"Alustro and I will keep searching. Sanjuk, will you help? There's a large room with no lights and your upbringing in the dark may help us."

Sanjuk sighed. "I have lived in the light for twenty years. Only five were spent in the dark, and even then, my clan was not traditional. I knew what a fusion torch was at two. But yes, I will help you. I'm still surely better at moving in darkness than you blind humans."

Erian frowned but said nothing. She was used to Sanjuk's manner by now, and knew better than to press royal rules of intercourse here. She turned to the stairs, and Sanjuk and I followed. Julia remained above, watching for Cardanzo and Ong's return from their patrol.

The room was indeed dark. Our fusion torches seemed to penetrate only slightly into the gloom, and a thin mist could be felt and barely seen in the air. Consul Rohmer, who had joined us on our way down, coughed.

"Eternair…" he muttered.

"Excuse me, consul?" Erian said. "What did you say?"

"It's Eternair. Eternal Air. A preservative atmosphere devised by

Second Republic archivists to use when sealing things in cases. It's meant to keep those items unchanged over time. It's near miraculous. A canister must have broken somewhere in the room. With little ventilation, the stuff stays in the air here."

"Is it dangerous to breath?" I asked.

"I hope not," he replied.

We continued on into the room, navigating the cases and shelves. This did appear to be an archivist's room, for many items were displayed on tables with tags clearly showing that they were not yet ready for public display. Most of the items were reproductions of actual Ur items, made from extensive drawings and holograms. A few items were genuine, however. Consul Rohmer's obvious interest in these told me which were real and which fake.

"You know," Sanjuk said from somewhere up ahead, unseen in the darkness. "I really think we should set up some of the camp lights down here. We're not going to find anything in this light."

Erian sighed. "You are right. We will set them up during the day tomorrow, once we've heard from Cardanzo about the approaching troops."

"If the troops don't get here first," Sanjuk said.

We left the room and returned to our camp in the servant's quarters on the first level of the palace. This section was in the rear of the building, its back entrance now blocked by rubble. Those entering would have to come through the main hall, where we could see them well before they saw us. Cardanzo had led a search through the upper levels, now open to the elements, and had identified a number of sniper points he could assume if necessary. One of these, the remaining high tower, part of the original architecture, we used as a watchpost. Looking up at it from the street below, I could barely make out the old museum sign, now partially covered with the local ruler's torn and dirty flag: "Museum of the Ancients, Estab—" I wondered what date it read.

Cardanzo and Ong had returned from their patrol. The approaching troops were rangers, teams from both sides of the conflict. They each entered the market section of town, a few miles from us, and left soon after encountering each other (with no shots fired, apparently).

"I think now that each knows the other was here, they will move troops in force, each believing the other is trying to claim this ground," Cardanzo said. "With luck, it'll take them two days to get back here. We need to be gone by then."

"We will spend another day searching," Erian said. "Then leave."

"No later," Cardanzo said, looking into his liege's eyes. "We still need time to escape atmosphere before any fighters take to the skies."

"That's all we need!" Julia said. "A dogfight between Hazat and Kurgans. Oh, yeah, I can fly through that no problem!"

"Point taken," Erian said. "We leave tomorrow evening then. No later."

I was relieved to know we'd be out of danger soon, but nervous that we would leave without our prize. As I prepared dinner (chorro steaks, courtesy of Ong, who came back from his patrol with a catch, saving us from another Ukari dinner), I cast my mind into the museum and walked through every room I knew, trying to divine where the curators would have kept the mandala. The smell of burnt steak woke me from my musings, and I consented to have the spoiled meat for my plate while I paid greater attention to the others' preparations.

As I served the steaks and finally sat down to eat myself, a loud chiming sound broke the silence. Everyone looked at me.

"Uhm… sorry," I said, placing my plate on the scuffed table and running to my bags nearby. I pulled the small, hand-held think machine from its pouch and touched the power stud, shutting off the chimes.

"Why does that thing always go off?" Julia said, glaring at me. "I hate it. Can't you tell time like the rest of us?"

"It's not for telling time," I explained. "And that alarm was to remind me that it is only a number of hours till Renewal Day, the anniversary of Zebulon's healing by Saint Amalthea."

"That's nice and all, but what's it got to do with us here? There's far better uses to put a rare think machine, you know. Can't you just pray at dawn like most priests?"

"Dawn on Hira is not dawn on Grail. My think machine is set to automatically begin a recitation of the Thankful Exaltation, the Latin chorus as delivered by Zebulon to Amalthea, on exactly the proper moment: when dawn breaks over Mount Siddik."

Julia rolled her eyes. "And what the heck does it matter if you miss the exact moment? I'm sure Saint Amalthea will forgive you; she's certainly forgiven much worse."

"That's not the point. I am an Eskatonic; the energetic correspondences are very important. By opening a channel in our hearts and minds at the proper moment, we cast our light back to Grail, and it is in turn reflected back to us. In this way, we partake of the divine moment as if we were on Grail itself. The theurgic significance is incredible."

"Whatever," Julia said, finishing her steak and then rising to stretch. "Just don't let that racket wake me before my watch!" She left for her sleeping bag in the garret directly above us.

I checked the program again to be sure its clock was correct and set the liturgy to play upon the appointed hour. After cleaning and storing the cookware, I crawled into my own sleeping bag by the kitchen.

That evening, I did not dream. This is not unusual except that I had dreamed every night since we arrived on Hira, dreams of ruins and combat.

We spent the following afternoon searching the darkened room. We moved all our portable lights there and found the illumination enough for a cursory search. Consul Rohmer idly examined the Ur artifacts and replicas.

"I had hoped to make my fortune here," he said. "To build my life. I doubt anything can come of this now. I don't dare alert anyone, or the Hazat will storm in seeking war-tech. Best to leave it be for now until I can get others to come. So little of this can be moved."

"Can't we just remove the artifacts from the cases?" I asked.

"Have you ever tried cracking one of those things? Near impossible, not without shipyard grade tools. And the cases themselves are likewise immovable, meant to deter thieves in an era where such criminals had high tech means to steal. No, most of this will remain here as it has for centuries."

"But that means… If the mandala is in a case, we'll never get it out!"

He looked at me sympathetically. "Well, we can always take holograms of it. I have a camera with me."

Sanjuk came over. "A holocamera? That must of set you back a few firebirds."

"Not really," Rohmer said, continuing his idle search. "I took it in return for a bad debt, in my younger days in Collections. The debtor paid up eventually anyway, but I kept the camera."

"There is nothing here!" Erian said from a few shelves away, frustrated. "Surely we would have found it by now if they kept it in this room."

"Perhaps we should try elsewhere," I suggested. "There's still the back wing…."

"It's strictly Diaspora era," Rohmer said. "I checked when I first arrived."

"What if the mandala was discovered then?" Erian said. "Wouldn't it be kept there?"

"Well, I suppose it's possible," Rohmer said. "I wasn't looking for it in my search, since I hadn't met you yet. It's at least worth another look."

"Sanjuk, would you come with me?" Erian said, heading for the door. "Alustro, please keep searching here, just in case."

"But I'd like to see some Diaspora artifacts!"

"Just dioramas mainly," Rohmer said. "Images the Second Republic believed were true of life during humanity's first spread to the stars. Rather boring, actually."

Erian was already gone, so I resigned myself to a continued search.

I had worked my way down the far left aisle and was ready to traverse the back wall when a rumble shook the building.

"They can't be shelling this early," Rohmer said, confused, looking at the ceiling as if he could see through it to the skies above.

"I think we should leave, consul," I said, moving toward the door. "If they are shelling, it may mean troops are advancing already."

He sighed. "Alright, but let's go back through the east wing. I want one last look at—"

The air exploded and the ceiling collapsed, burying me under a pile of tiles. I coughed, singed from the fire that had momentarily engulfed me. The Eternair must have ignited, I thought. But the mist still swirled around me, so it had not all gone up.

I pushed the tiles off and crawled to my feet. Half of the room was gone, blocked by a wall of rock, dirt and furniture from the levels above. "Consul?" I yelled.

"Here…" a weak voice answered. I worked my way over to him across the sliding tiles and rock. Consul Rohmer was half buried under a maxicrete strut, his head bleeding, his hand clutching his chest.

"It's finally over…." he moaned.

"I can heal you!" I cried, trying to lift the maxicrete that pinned him. "But we have to move this strut!"

"No…" he said, his eyes glazing. "It doesn't matter. Your faith can't heal plastic."

"What? I don't understand," I said, trying to raise the strut but failing completely. It was too heavy. If Ong were here—

"Don't… don't bother." He coughed blood. "My heart… it's cybernetic. My third. The others failed. I knew this would, too. That's why I came. To make something of myself, to complete my work."

"But… maybe we… Julia… can fix it," I stammered.

"Leave me here," he said, weaker, barely audible. "Among… the Ur. Close… the door… on your way… out. Air will… preserve me." His eyes closed and a final breath escaped his body.

I now understood his respect for the artifacts around him. They were the only things to last in a world of entropy. Everything died — people, culture, even the stars. But the Anunnaki had crafted with their unknown principles things immune to the laws of decay.

I felt for a pulse but could find none, then placed my hand on his false heart, tears welling in my eyes. I said the Prayer to the Departed, asking the Pancreator to draw Consul Rohmer's illuminate soul to its reward, to protect it as it traversed the dim and dying spaces. And then I switched off all the camp lights in the room and closed the door, leaving him in the peaceful, preserved dark.

I looked about, trying to get my bearings in the aftermath of death. My survival was important now, and I feared for my liege and companions. Had they been buried, too? The hall was a mess; my way was blocked on all sides. Only a thin ray of light from atop a pile of stone (a later addition to the palace, not a part of the original structure) promised a way of escape. I climbed and began to pull dirt and rock aside. I soon had a small hole through which I could squeeze. It was tight but I was soon on the ground floor again.

I stood, scraping dust off and surveying the area. The walls no longer existed, and gaping holes into the museum could be seen the length of the palace. I had no idea where I was standing. Was it the main hall or the dining room?

The sun was setting on the horizon and it was growing dark very quickly. As I stepped forward to search for my liege, praying she was still alive and well, a footstep sounded behind me. I turned and stared into the eyes of a Kurgan ranger, his rifle pointed straight at me.

He should have shot me on sight. But something was wrong. I could see fear in his eyes. Not fear of me, but fear of death. His arm bled profusely, although it still seemed usable. His face was one of near shock, a man too long on the front lines.

But courage returned, and he slowly raised his rifle to aim.

Then the Prophet sang.

He paused, confused. From nearby, under a thin shale of tile, came the chorus of the Thankful Exaltation. My think machine. It was now dawn on Grail: the divine moment had arrived.

He looked at me and then at the sky, as if shocked to realize the time and the day. He slowly lowered his rifle, looking into my eyes to see what I would do, and brought his hands together in prayer.

I joined him. We both closed our eyes and answered the chorus.

"And the light that burns, burns away poison.

"And the hands that heal tend the flame...."

He knew the Latin words. Our cultures, separated by time and the gulfs between the stars, still each remembered the deeds of the Prophet and knew them to be holy. Tears ran down my face as I answered the chorus line-by-line, unafraid, for I heard his voice singing, too.

When the program ended, and silence fell, we each slowly opened our eyes and looked at the other. Before anything further could pass between us, he stood and clambered over the stones. He was out of sight before I could think to yell to him, to offer to heal his wound.

I stood there for a time, thinking upon the wonders revealed amid the horror. Eventually, Onganggorak shook my shoulder, startling me. He had crept through the ruins silently, a great Vorox hunter.

"Alustro, are you well? I smell no injury," he said tenderly.

"I am fine, Ong. Where are the others? Is Erian okay?"

"She is wounded, but will live. Cardanzo guards her at the Resurgent and Julia prepares to leave. I came to find you, little confessor."

I smiled. "That was foolhardy. Kurgans are here. You could have been caught."

"Hmmph. We cannot leave without you. Ong's life is little next to yours," he said, tugging me to leave with him.

I made to disagree but finally assented and went over to the pile of shale that hid my bags and my think machine, the device that had saved my life today. "I'm ready."

"Where is the consul? I cannot find his scent. He should leave with us," Ong said.

"He... died," I said. "He rests with his artifacts."

Ong nodded and made a grunting noise, a statement of some sort in his own tongue, but before I could ask what he meant, he turned to go, motioning me with one of his four arms to follow.

As we began our trek to the ship, the sky thundered and glowed. Bombs flew once more. The flickering light of the deadly fireworks lit the area, and I saw the remains of the high tower, now scattered across the ground. The ruler's flag was gone and the museum sign stood bare. I could now read it:

Museum of the Ancients. Established 3973. "And the Anunnaki fashioned their individual shrines, the 300 younger gods of heaven and the Anunnaki of the Apsu all assembled."

I stood in shock, staring at the sign. "Ong!" I cried, and he came running, sniffing the air and casting his eyes all about. "There!" I pointed to the sign.

Underneath the ancient quote from some long-forgotten Urth text was a beautiful mandala.

Our mandala.

I rushed over to the sign to examine it. It was the very same seen in Erian's dream — copperish-purple alloy, four images quartered around a central star. "This is it, Ong. Our artifact."

I tugged at it, and it snapped right off its base. We both stared at each other, chills traveling up our spines. Of all the Ur artifacts in the museum, why was this one so easily removed? I looked at the base it had rested on and realized that it had taken a direct artillery hit. The ceramsteel was melted and pitted, blackened every place but where the mandala had rested. The metal and magnetic glue had given out, but the artifact was unblemished.

I decided that enough was enough. Placing the mandala in my bag, we headed off to the ship. Ong blazed the trail, taking small paths through the ruins. I heard voices from afar, and radio chatter, but Ong's path avoided all patrols.

We finally arrived at the ship. As I entered the hatch and Ong closed it behind me, I heard Erian call to me from her cabin. I ran quickly and saw her lying on the bed, her leg wrapped in red bandages.

"My lady!" I yelled, and immediately set to examining her wound. Cardanzo put his hand on my shoulder.

"She is fine, Alustro. I staunched the blood flow."

Erian looked tired but she was awake. I reached into my bag and produced the artifact, holding it up to show her.

"The mandala!" she cried, trying to rise to her feet. Cardanzo and I both rushed to keep her down, slowly lowering her back into bed. She gazed at it wondrously. "Where did you find it?"

"The sign. The museum sign — covered by the flag. The one on the tower. All this time, right above us."

She looked at me and I felt a rush of pride. "Well done, my priest. Well done."

I nodded and rose. "Get your rest, lady. We can examine it later." I left the artifact with her as I headed to my cabin to change out of my filthy clothes. I would tell her about Consul Rohmer later, when there was time to reflect on a life now past. I felt the rumble of the engines and knew the ship was taking off.

As I entered my cabin, I heard Sanjuk and Julia talking in the cockpit.

"I can't believe he found it," Sanjuk said. "Of all the dumb luck."

"I knew he would," Julia said. "It's not luck. The boy's got a track record."

I smiled, knowing that her comment was not meant for me to hear.

The next few hours were rough, as Julia encountered two squadrons of Hazat troops demanding we land to be examined by their military generals. Of course she denied all requests in Erian's name, knowing our ship would be conscripted if it fell into their hands, and flew us out of the way of most conflict. Our ship's shield easily deflected the few shots we took.

As I write this, we have not yet reached the jumpgate. Julia intends to hide behind the last planet until the jumpgate is clear, or until the few ships there engage enemies coming or going. Then we'll slip over as quickly as possible, activate the gate, and be gone from this place.

I am confident that we will encounter little problem. We have come too far, and the fates have been too kind. Why would they mean us disaster now? The pattern is clearer now, fragments assembled by some principle whose meaning is as yet unknown.

Tangled Web

I pray that I never again experience a Night of Fire. The Inquisition's flameguns burn not only wood and straw, they boil the blood and singe the soul.

The town of Ravican, in the barony of al-Bazan on Criticorum, was last night's target for Inquisitorial fervor. The rumors had spread throughout the marketplace earlier that day: a Symbiot had been seen by Yeoman Dar in his apple orchard, creeping about in the trees. There is no telling just what his initial description of the thing had been, for by the time word spread in town, various descriptions were given, with the creature growing larger and more malevolent as the shadows from the sun grew longer.

We ignored the rumors at first, for we are all well used to such superstitious panics among commoners. This was meant to be our rest time, a month far from the bustle and politics of the big cities. We deserved this time away from responsibility. As our liege, Erian Li Halan, pondered our next step in the quest, we relaxed and roamed the idyllic hills and meandering streams of this pastoral region.

Our peace ended just after nightfall when the Inquisition ship landed in the fields near the shire reeve's home. Cloaked and hooded priests — mainly Avestites, but some Orthodox priests among them — stamped from the ship and into the town, immediately demanding that no one leave. They summoned the local lord, a retired knight, and demanded that everyone in the town subject themselves to Inquisitorial questioning. Unable to deny them lest he be suspected himself, the old knight acquiesced and gave them free reign to find the Symbiot they had heard was hiding in Ravican.

The priestly team split up and marched down the streets, lining up the citizenry, eyeing them for any signs of inhuman behavior.

Erian, her bodyguard Cardanzo, and I were in a small pub on the far side of town. A farmer ran in to cry the news about the Inquisition, and the other drinkers and diners immediately abandoned their meals to flee from the town to their hovels in the surrounding hills. This was no sign of guilt — no one willingly subjects himself to Inquisitorial scrutiny. Even I, a priest myself, know that the accusing monks are wrong more often than right.

We decided to slip away ourselves. Our starship was in a field not too far from here. Julia, Sanjuk and Onggangarak were there now. By the time we passed two streets, the smell of smoke was already in the air. Somewhere a hapless fool said the wrong thing or tried to run when he should have halted, and flameguns had roared as a result. The sky was lit with the flames, started in one building perhaps but now obviously spread to more of them. The whole town would probably be cinders by the morning. I almost hoped the rumors of Symbiots were true, to at least justify the cost.

As we neared the pig sty near the small path that would lead us to our ship, we heard voices approaching: "I saw movement here, brothers!"

We leapt into the dark doorway of the hovel and tried to still our breathing as a group of the robed fanatics rushed past and down another street. Our quiet allowed me to hear the sobbings in the room behind us.

I peered into the gloom and saw a man slumped to the floor, his head in his hands, his body wracked with sobs. I moved to him and bent down, my hand over his head. "Don't fear; I am a priest, but not like those outside."

The poor fellow looked up at me, his eyes pleading. "They killed my children, father. They burned them. My poor, poor children." Tears streamed down his face. I didn't know what to say. How do you console a man who has just lost his beloved children to the flames of priests?

I moved my hand to his shoulder but recoiled in sudden fear and disgust, unable to control my instinctual reaction. From out of his shirtless torso grew four thin, segmented spider legs. He didn't seem to notice at first until he heard the intake of my breath. He looked at me and then at himself in surprise. He then leaped to his feet with amazing speed and scuttled up the wall to the rafters above, his new legs clinging to the ceiling.

"By the Pancreator!" I heard Erian yell. Cardanzo drew his blaster and aimed it at the rafters, trying to discern the creature in the darkness.

The thing spoke: "Please, father, I beg you. I mean no harm. I was a priest once, like you."

Cardanzo, seeing the creature, pointed his gun and prepared to fire. I leapt forward, knocking down his hand, yelling: "No! Wait!"

Both Erian and Cardanzo looked at me like I was mad. I explained: "Let me hear him. I... I don't know why, but please. Let me hear him."

They didn't move, and the thing bent down further into the dim light coming from the doorway. "I was an Illuminatus grade monk on Stigmata. I fought Symbiots, and believed them to be evil and demonic. But then I was changed, converted by a stray spore they had spread months before. They came for me and taught me who they really were. They aren't like we think. They are a good people, living closer with nature than you can know."

As he spoke, he slowly came down from his perch, crawling down the wall and looking at me earnestly. "I remembered more of my human memories than most converts. I still know the litanies and exegeses drilled into me at the Naos. I still revere the Pancreator and Zebulon, but I see that their message is broader than even Pallamedes knew. The Holy Flame is not restricted to humans. All beings share its spark. Each world has this fire, which empowers all living things."

He stood up straight on two human legs when he reached the floor, moving closer, his arms gesturing as he made his case. "Because I still knew human ways, I was sent back to the Known Worlds to learn about the new Emperor and his plans against the Symbiots. I changed my form to look like anyone I wanted to, and spent time in the main capitals of many worlds, pretending to be many people I was not. But I tired of it, and longed for the peace and tranquility of my old home, the town where I had grown up.

"I returned to Ravican and started a family. My wife, who knew of my secret, loved me the more for it. She died last year of the Vantokos Sickness. But our children lived. They are human, like you. I cannot and would not convert them even if they asked. I love my Symbiot brothers, but prefer my human family. Do you understand?"

I stared at him, not knowing how to respond. He spoke so passionately, his tale came from the heart. His grief over his lost children seemed so genuine.

"I… I'm so sorry," I stammered.

"We do not need to be enemies. We share the same dangers. The light of the suns fade for us all. There is a saying among the Phazûl: Weaving webs around the sun."

"What?" I said, surprised.

"It means to support the Lifeweb, to renew the light."

He paused for a moment, as if trying to figure out how to say something difficult, something hard to translate from one tongue to another, when a sword thrust out from his chest. He stared down at it in shock, and Erian, standing behind him, withdrew her rapier and quickly slashed it across the air. His head rolled forward and thumped to the floor. His body's spider legs twitched momentarily before the body collapsed.

I stared in shock.

Cardanzo stepped forward and emptied his blaster into the body, turning the carcass into an ashy husk. Summoned by the blaster fire, Inquisition troops bolted down the street and through the door. As soon as they saw the scene and the sizzling body on the floor, remnants of its spider legs still apparent, they nodded quietly.

Erian wiped her blade on a nearby sack, and the Inquisition leader stepped over to her. "Well done, my lady. May I know your name?"

"Erian Li Halan," she replied coldly, as if speaking to her social inferior. "And this is my entourage. Cardanzo, my bodyguard, and Alustro, my confessor."

Her attitude worked well, for the Inquisitor, cowed somewhat by a noble and her brave deed, bowed slightly. "I thank you for catching the Symbiot menace and sending it to Gehenne. We will clean up the remains."

Erian, without any delay, walked out the doorway. Cardanzo followed, but I was still too stunned to realize that this was our cue to exit. I stood looking down at the body, my thoughts in turmoil.

One of the priests placed his hand on my shoulder. "Its evil is done with. It cannot harm you now."

I must have looked at him like he was mad; he completely misunderstood the cause of my confusion. But the startled look on his face brought me back to my senses. I bowed my head. "Yes. Yes, you are right. I was... unprepared."

He nodded with sympathy and I walked through the door. Erian and Cardanzo had not waited for me, but walked slowly so that I could catch them. As soon as I came to them, they increased their pace, and Cardanzo whispered, "Hurry before they think to search us for taint."

As we moved through the woods past the sty and toward our ship, my consternation was clear. Erian looked at me with worry. "It's all right, my priest. You see the best in men, and not their lies."

"But... the web. The web in the sun. It was in my vision. What does this mean?"

"I cannot say. Are not lies seen as a tangled web? Perhaps your vision warned you against his deception."

I nodded, but I knew that was not the answer. There was a deeper meaning here, and I feel our prejudice and fear silenced the answer before I could ask the question.

Volume Two: Provost

My Quest

To: Archbishop Marcus Aurelius Palamon, Cathedral of Saint Maya, Holy City, Galatea, Byzantium Secundus

Dearest Uncle,

It has been long since I last wrote you. I apologize for not doing so sooner, but the dangers involved were too great. I'm sure you will scoff at such a remark, but I tell you it is true. How dangerous, I hear you ask, to write to the Archbishop of Byzantium Secundus? No one would dare delay delivery of such a missive, and none would dare break its seal to read it.

As you know, trusts and confidences can be betrayed under intact seals. My liege, Erian Li Halan, has many enemies, not the least of which is her brother, a hateful man bent on destroying her. To that end, he has inflamed many of his allies against her, some of whom are involved in the highest levels of information gathering. I could not risk even a letter to you, lest it reveal our whereabouts before we had moved on.

Such cloak and dagger lives disgust you, I know. I wish I could live otherwise. I yearn for the life of simple contemplation I left behind on Midian when I eagerly joined Erian on her mission to the stars. My hunger for new sites and experiences could not be sated, and the cold walls of the monastery seemed a prison. Ironic that it now seems a warm den of rest and safety, after so many years on the roads between the stars.

But I am not writing for pity or justification. I simply explain my situation so that you understand the long years between my correspondence. I wish so much to speak with you in person, to walk the corridors of your great cathedral and hear you orate the virtues of the Prophet's disciples again, in your commanding voice that was once a pillar of faith for me. It matters little that I betrayed your own faith by joining the Eskatonic Order rather than the Orthodoxy — both our sects share the words of the Prophet.

I digress. I must put aside reflection and state the matter about which I write. My liege readies to travel again, this time on a new path, one full of possibility and danger. I am to go with her, for our fates are one. I am her confessor, and spiritual guide besides. No longer is this role just in her service, however — it is also in mine, for I have been gifted with dreams and visions leading me toward an uncertain but important future.

I wrote of the Gargoyle of Nowhere in my last letter, that monolithic relic left behind by the Anunnaki, they who wrought the jumpgates and tamed the heavens before our kind was raised from the muck by the hand of the Pancreator. The vision it gifted us then — the maddeningly vague clues that lead us from world to world in search of ever more clues — only now begins to take shape.

To explain this shape, I must first explain where we have been and what we have seen. The Known Worlds are huge, sprawling across the nightscape of the dimming stars forty worlds strong. While this is a paltry sum compared to the hundreds of worlds once known to the Second Republic, it is still a testament to humankind's unity that even so many worlds as these have stayed together, connected through the jumpweb now under the rule of Emperor Alexius.

I have been to many of these worlds — nearly all of them, in fact. How many people can claim that? Most never leave their hovels, let alone their provinces — and to leave one's very planet is a momentous step indeed. From there to travel to more than three worlds is a jaunt even most Charioteer star-pilots never achieve. But to travel like Erian and her entourage — unimaginable.

And yet we have done so. We have broken all bonds of place and come and go from hither to yon as birds migrate through the seasons or as leaves travel the aether or float along the stream. What's more — we are not alone. More and more people of brave will and good constitution awaken from a long night of captivity on their homeworlds to escape gravity and go outwards, to worlds once known only to their grandparents or more distant ancestors in the past. The Emperor Wars kept everyone penned in, trapped behind enemy lines in their own homes.

But that dark time is over at last. Alexius is ascendant and the jumproads are open once more. The cage is broken and the beasts have slipped through the bars.

Yes, I mean beasts. For every man and woman of good heart and purpose who now travel between the worlds of the Empire, two or three scoundrels of black heart and base desire also go forth. For this reason, only a fool travels alone, and those of good intent are best served by their own kind. I do not follow Erian because feudal duties alone decree it — I do so because in her service I am among others of good heart, some with strong arm and hand to defend us bodily from the harm others intend. I can attempt to sooth a soul with words of scripture, or even seal a wound with prayer, but I can do little to prevent injury in the face of evil.

Cardanzo, Erian's bodyguard, is a capable man and goodly tactician. Of even greater might is Onggangarak, our Vorox friend who has elected us members of his angerak — his blood pack. No better soldiers could one ask in the quest for right.

And no better pilot than Julia Abrams. Although her demeanor is caustic, her heart is strong and deeply tied to ours. She is the engine of our escape and a hearty companion on the road — a true follower of the first disciple, Paulus the Traveler, he who guided the Prophet on his sojourns.

In your response to my last letter, you warned me against associating too closely with the Ur-Ukar aliens, whom you, like many, distrust for their seemingly primitive, clannish ways. I have learned to look beyond the expected, and seen the truth that lies in people's hearts. Sanjuk oj Kaval is a woman of supreme courage. Her travails on her harsh homeworld of Kordeth, in the subterranean caverns of her clan, have only strengthened her bravery. While she is as yet largely ignorant of scripture, I have made a pact with her — for every legend she tells me of Ukari culture, I read to her verse from the Omega Gospels. In such a way does understanding between two different peoples grow. It is just such an interchange that must take place on a galactic scale, to overcome the centuries of ignorance and hate fostered between fiefs and territories.

The Church teaches us of the good in our souls, and yet acts as if people are mean and evil unless taught otherwise. The rod of rulership must fall heavily on humanity and its alien brethren lest they rise up to do evil. Or so the widespread belief — justification — goes. I know otherwise. I know that even the most oppressed men will share their only foodstores with suffering strangers, even if such strangers be from strange locales and other worlds. Yes, distrust and suspicion is rampant, and some are more likely to be greeted by a lynch mob than an invitation to dinner, but this is by no means as universal as we are all taught.

Perhaps during the Emperor Wars and its aftermath, distrust was the lot of humankind. But with each new starship that comes from afar bringing goods undreamed of before; with each new person who comes bearing news of distant and long-forgotten family on other worlds; with each new knight that comes from the Emperor bringing law to the lawless regions, understanding and hope grows.

When men have hope, they begin to cherish their dreams once more. No matter how dark the suns may fade, the light of hope cannot be fully extinguished.

The fading suns. I have tried often to forget them, for their dimming light fails to show the way forward, only the way back. I no longer want to look back. I want only to go forward, to solve the dilemma of our impending ruin, to reignite the stars that have for so long only portended our doom. Heresy? To hope to change what the

Pancreator has wrought? But you yourself preach that it is not the Pancreator that darkens the day, but the demons who haunt us and hover before the light, casting their mournful shadows over our stars.

Why not act against them? Why simply sit and wait for the end, assured that judgment will come swift to all. What if that judgement depends on our acting? If we fail in this, how will we be judged then?

Go back to the Prophet's words and read them afresh. I believe with the deepest sincerity that he was not speaking for the people then, but for now. He spoke of a "dark between the stars," and the demons that dwell therein. He spoke of the evil which would descend on us and the ways that we might fight it. Yet when he said these things, were not the stars shining bright? Did not humankind have its greatest moments yet before it, in the founding of the Second Republic that was to come?

Then why was he so ill at ease and dark of heart? Why in an Age of Miracles did he alone see danger? I tell you he did not see with the eyes of the present but with the future — to our present, to our time and its rising darkness. He set down words which we would need now to survive against the chill end of time.

All his deeds, all his acts and words that enriched us, did so in the hope that we would not simply look to them as artifacts of a better past, but as examples of a greater future. It is for us now to become as his disciples and follow their steps toward the stars, to Quest, Defend the Faith, Right Wrongs, Seek Justice, Heal the Injured, Aid the Needy, Seek Wisdom and Look Within.

If Paulus could do so, why not we? If Mantius and Lextius, Maya, Amalthea, Hombor, Horace and Ven Lohji — why not we?

I know your answer. Heresy. We are not saints, and we dare not elect ourselves so. I agree. I am no saint. But I can try to be. I can muster all my will and faith toward walking as one who can make a difference, one who can change fate for the better.

Worry not that the Inquisition will hunt us for such hubris; they already have. I have dodged more flameguns and brown-robed fanatics over the past years than I thought could possibly exist. There are so very many who desire to punish others for reaping benefits they themselves fear to ask for.

We have surely sinned in that we travel in a starship. Is not this the sort of technology they spew sermons against? I am not ignorant of the dangers of such tech, for the Second Republic proved what science without faith can produce, and its mewling horrors are not easily forgotten. But I will not stand against all technology because some of it was misused.

I digress again. I meant to tell you of our travels, of the sights I have seen since last I wrote. I have sent you in separate letters copies of my journals of the past three years. While they tell of my deepest thoughts and our entourage's trials on many worlds, I want here to tell of the things I could not enter into those journals, because the hectic pace of our lives prevented it. I want to impress upon you what I found, how things are not as we are told, and why I seek to go even farther.

My thoughts first turn to Malignatius, that frozen hell of a world, gulag for so many suffering under the whim of House Decados. No better served were the people, however, when House Li Halan ruled the world before the Emperor Wars. I know the Li Halan well, having lived in their service all my life, and I believe I can thus see their faults clearly. Never are the common folk under them allowed to rise, no matter how they prove themselves otherwise. But the virtue of the Li Halan is that neither do they mistreat their charges, unlike the Decados. While surely even the lowliest Decados peasant may rise to better status for committing any number of heinous deeds that please their lords, most are trampled under foot.

This world is renowned for its religious schisms and the many charismatics who have risen to guide people on to bizarre spiritual paths. Such loud men and women have branded the world fanatic, and this is surely how the Orthodoxy sees it. But what if I were to tell you that, hidden in the ice caves under the surface, there are many monks of astonishing enlightenment? I met one, a Friar Ged, who treated me to such a dialogue of scriptural questioning that I had not had since my first exposure to Magister Tarsus, my Eskatonic examiner. I came to realize that no matter the political situation in a place or the tenure of its people as a whole, there are always unique individuals worthy of encountering.

And there are wonders, too, visions of beauty and natural awe. I can never forget my undersea swim on the world of Madoc, a planet whose surface is mainly ocean and archipelago. Using breathing suits provided us by a wealthy guildswoman — technology of which I'm sure many in the Church disapprove — our entourage swam deep down to examine the ruins of that planet's previous culture, a civilization that had fallen even before humans left Holy Terra.

Off in the far distance, fearful to come near us, I saw shadowy figures flit in and out of the coral ruins, watching us with their large eyes. One wore sparkling armor of sea shells and another bore a luminous staff — these were no simple sea creatures. They were Oro'ym, the fabled amphibian sentients of that world. I wished so much to approach them and speak with them, hoping they knew our language, but they fled whenever I drew near.

Even more enigmatic than the Oro'ym, however, were the Vau. Ah, I wish I could see the look of shock and indignation on your face when I tell you that I have met a Vau. I even shook its hand, although it seemed bemused by the gesture. It was on Manitou, that border world where the Church itself treads only lightly for fear of raising the ire of the Vau rulers. Here many of the outlaw dregs of humanity have collected — not its pirates and murderers so much as its thought criminals, those who follow different gods or indulge in pastimes harmful only to themselves but which are punishable by death in the courts of the Known Worlds.

I will not tell you why we were there, for you would greatly disapprove. I will simply say that, while wandering the agora and marveling at the wealth of black market goods, an emissary from the local Vau mandarin approached us. He appeared to be of their worker caste, a lowly position among his kind but still far and away more prestigious than our serf class. He seemed curious about us, but afraid to show it. Nonetheless, he came up to Erian and smiled, a gesture alien to his kind but one that he had obviously practiced for our sake. She greeted him, unsure what to say or do, and I offered my hand. He took it. And then he left, as if he had already gone further than he was allowed.

I still don't understand the matter, but I am impressed nonetheless. Perhaps my liege is destined for greatness, and the Vau somehow know of this. It is said that they have machines that foretell that future, and ancient prophecies given to them by the Anunnaki. Who can say for sure? They remain removed from humankind, protected by their superior technology.

The Ur-Obun also seemed to favor my leige, and believe she is destined for something, although Julia opines that they were simply "sucking up" to a human noble. Our stay on Velisimil was short, but most relaxing. While Erian made alliance with many Umo'rin members, I spent a meditation retreat in a humble Voavenlohjun temple. I was the only human, but they welcomed me as if I were one of their own. They do not separate involvement in the Church into sects as we do; all who follow the Prophet's teachings are sacred to them. Of course, they see all religious system as sacred in a way, although they certainly do not honor them equally. They recognize prereflective faith and postreflective grace, fear not.

I will shock you again with an admission concerning the Ur-Ukar — I have sat in a cavedark ceremony on Istakhr. It was not a true cave like on Kordeth, but a deep basement. Nonetheless, it was pitchblack. I joined the others, Sanjuk and her family, in reading the deed carvings of their ancestors on the wall. I only know a little Ukarish, and missed much of what was written, but Sanjuk's recitation aided me.

A barbaric practice? How so? It brought them together and united them in blood and a shared past. That Sanjuk allowed me to join in was a great honor and a sign that she considers me as trustworthy as family — a powerful trust for an Ukari.

What I found most enlightening about the reading, however, was the history of the Ukari gods. While Sanjuk sneers when I mention the common human belief about the truth of their gods, I still believe it so. How can any deny, after hearing the legends of the Ur-Obun and Ur-Ukar, that their deities were any other than the ancient Anunnaki? That this powerful race grandfathered these younger races in their early days hints that perhaps they did the same for us, on old Urth.

The xenoarchaeologists of the Second Republic thought so. Is this not why they named the Anunnaki after the old gods of Urth? What if these gods of our prereflective ancestors were from the stars? And what if they took our ancestors with them on their journeys? What would have become of such humans? Do they still exist among the stars?

These questions are impossible to answer as yet. I hope to do so one day, however.

But let me not leave out opinions on the Merchant League and noble class. You'd surely be most disgruntled at my omission — if you've bothered to read this far. I know you have been to Leagueheim, for your disproval of its "Republican sympathies" was most apparent to me even at a young age. But even you were somewhat awed at its spires and cities, one of the few worlds that still resembles the Second Republic at its height. I have walked those spires, and ambled the sky lanes from building to building, traveling leagues without ever touching ground.

As I walked, flitters would hover near me with guildsmembers offering me rides, confused that I would willingly choose to walk when I could ride for free. But I knew their kind offers were not truly free, for I would surely be subject to a sales pitch of one kind or another should I choose to ride in their gravity-defying chariots. It is indeed true that everything is for sale on Leagueheim, including allegiances.

How refreshing then, to meet those for whom allegiance is a

matter of honor, not firebirds. I mean the Hazat — those nobles of a most martial bent whose hot-headed fury has shaken up the Empire on many occasions. Erian has allies in the house, and we have visited them often. On one occasion, on Aragon, we were witness to that most famous of noble pastimes: the duel.

Erian was to be Baron Allejandro Campeiro Justin de Justus's second in a fight. This means that, while she would not fight herself, she would hand him his weapon and watch for treachery from the baron's opponent. We all gathered to watch, and I was ready to mend any wounds taken by either side.

It was a short but vicious fight, with terms of surrender alone. Whoever gave in first would be the loser. Such a duel between Hazat nobles is usually to the death, but the baron's opponent was an al-Malik dandy, Sir Jacob Saladin al-Malik, whom we all doubted would choose death before honor. He was an expert swordsman, though, and had first blood on the baron in mere seconds. But our friend ran him through moments later, thanks only to a malfunction in Sir Jacob's energy shield.

Nobles rely on these shields to protect them from the worst harm, although they don't stop relatively harmless blows from landing. It is these small wounds that add up over the course of a duel, however. In this case, the shield failed, and a mortal wound was delivered — or would have been mortal if not for the miracles of faith. My Eskatonic training allowed me to call upon the Pancreator's mercy to heal his wound, thus saving his life.

Instead of triumph, the baron was mortified, for he had no intention of winning a duel in such a way. Sir Jacob, who had been his enemy at the start of the day, became his friend by the end, for so gracious and generous was Baron Allejandro to his wronged opponent that he spared no expense in making things right. He invited the lord to recuperate at his mansion, in as much opulence as he could withstand. For his part, Sir Jacob was more than relieved at being brought back from death's door, and he pledged to tithe heavily to my order when

111

next the chance arose.

I tell this tale not to impress you that I move in the company of nobles, but to mention the odd sense of honor they display. Sometimes, that is; not everywhere universally. There are nobles who are far from honorable, those who shame their very class by becoming tyrants. I speak of Duke Granzil Hassan Keddah, a lord on Grail who mistreats his people terribly. Even the Etyri of his fiefs have fled, flown on to other territories in high eeries rather than suffer his decrees, even though it is illegal for them to have done so. He has called a hunt on these avian sentients, but one that has been thankfully ignored by fellow nobles of his house, who have denied these hunters entry onto their fiefs.

And so I come, through long digression, back to the heart of the matter: the shape of my destiny in Erian's company. My lady has taken a great step forward and allied herself to the greatest power in the Known Worlds: she has taken pledge as a Questing Knight, in fealty to the Emperor himself. She now places his needs over those of her own house, although we both pray they never come into conflict. By this act of fealty, she is empowered to Quest.

To such happy news I add this: I, too, have taken an oath, one that places me in even greater fealty to her and her lord. I have become an Imperial Cohort, the new office opened by Alexius for those who wish to aid the Questing Knights but for whom such rank is closed. Since I am not of noble blood or landed rank, this chance to aid my lady with the full support of her lord is a welcome opportunity. Cardanzo, Julia and Onggangarak have also pledged themselves as Cohorts, and so we all form a knightly company now in Alexius's service. We, too, can now Quest with the full support of a great lord — our destiny nears completion. The riddles posed years ago by the Ur can begin to be answered.

I hope that this act of mine pleases you more than my previous decisions. My refusal of orthodoxy hurt you, but perhaps my new fealty to the shining star of your diocese on Byzantium Secundus will assure that my deeds will from now forwards be in the name of universal justice and law.

I know that you did not fully approve of the emperor at first, but his regular appearance in your cathedral for services has warmed you to him. I know this because I saw it myself. You and he, his Imperial Eminence, chatting together like old friends after the service, surrounded by bodyguards on all sides.

Yes, I saw this, for I was in your cathedral yesterday, witnessing your service from the high balcony. I so wanted to come down and greet you, to pray in the first pews before you. But I did not dare. Too many eyes are upon you, and your reaction to my presence would have alerted Erian's enemies, even if word took time to reach them.

My lady prepares a mission of great import and I go with her, as always. I know not where or what our pledge leads us toward, for it is not yet revealed to us. We leave, however, tonight. I had hoped to visit you in your personal quarters, far from prying eyes, but it is too late. I delayed too long, and duty pulls me away to another world, perhaps even to barbarian space, for many Questing Knights have been dispatched there of late.

I will see you again, uncle. I will kiss your hand in recognition of your high station and because you are my mother's brother. Fear not for me or my liege. If I should die on the reaches far from home, the Pancreator's light will still find me and guide me back, as it will all of good heart and right hand.

Farewell.

Your nephew,

Provost Guissepe Alustro

Loyal Service

The old general stared out across the fields as if yearning to join the farmers working there. He shut his eyes for a long moment, and then shook off his ennui, turning to greet me with a smile. His movements were graceful and measured, practiced many times before in countless courts, but given an unusual edge by his years of military training and martial practice.

"Ah, Erian's young confessor," he said, gently cupping my hand in both of his, a gesture of familiarity normally reserved only for family. "Come, sit. I was preparing to take tea. I think today it shall be shava tea, in light of your visit from afar. Like you, it comes from Midian."

I bowed and took the cushioned chair he offered me. He reserved the hardwood stool for himself, spurning soft, physical luxuries even now, years after his last campaign. His age ensured that there would be no more battles for him.

"Thank you, my lord," I said. "I am pleased you consented to see me."

He nodded slightly. "Your liege is very dear to me. What concerns her, concerns me. Until yesterday, I had not seen her since her ninth natal day, yet ever has she remained dear to me, a luminous reflection of her mother, my dearest sister."

I waited for him to invite me to relate the matter upon which I had come, but knew that, as is Li Halan custom, such weighty matters would wait until he was ready to hear them. The servant arrived with a tray and teacups, and poured us each a steaming cup of the suffused exotic leaf. General Hanmei Usaki Li Halan sipped slowly, his attention again amidst the fields. The sun's noon heat rippled through the humid air and the thrumming sounds of insects filled our ears. After nearly five minutes of such quiet contemplation, he turned to me and spoke:

"What concerns you, holy man, and how does it involve my favored niece?"

"Her rivals, my lord," I said. "As you surely know, her brother was most insulted by her refusal to stay in her father's home once it had passed into his rule. He fears she plots some method of overthrowing his inheritance. A most ridiculous and uncivilized assertion, but it stands nonetheless. He has sent agents against her many times, and has spread lies and deceit to his loyal allies, poisoning their minds against her."

"Yes," the old general said. "The masks of decorum occasionally fall from noble faces even in the Courts of Divine Mandate. The Li Halan, like so many others, preach a doctrine even they rarely hold."

I didn't know what to say to such a frank admittance. I was embarrassed, and unsure if he was testing me for a sign of disloyalty or if he had simply forgotten to whom he spoke. I have served his family for years, but I was not one of them, and thus not used to being privy to family criticism. I remained silent.

He smiled as he watched me, and then continued. "I know of her brother's campaign against her. He tried to initiate me into it. I refused. A simple thing, since I am so far removed from the courts." This last was said not wistfully, but with a startling righteousness, as if he had earned the right to exile. He looked at me and waited for me to speak again.

"Last night," I said, "my lady confided in you and told you of our plans, about how we are preparing to leave Byzantium Secundus for Leminkainen and then Hargard, and from there travel deeper into barbarian space in service to the Emperor. She said this trusting fully in your confidence, knowing that you would never reveal to others our mission."

"And yet?" he said, staring at me pointedly.

"Her brother has somehow heard of our plans. A leak among the Questing Knights, perhaps. His allies are here now, although I know not who or where they be. I do know that they will try to stop my lady from leaving, although how far they will go to achieve this end, I know not. But I fear it will be far…"

I saw the general's anger for the first time. It was not a loud thing, but a simmering heat radiating from behind his eyes. I thanked the Pancreator that he did not direct his gaze at me, but inward in contemplation of some deed, act or person that ignited such a rage.

"And you seek protection from me for Erian? You need not speak it. It is her's, and always has been. I would muster all my armies for her, or receive myself the sword aimed at her breast." He stood and moved closer to the balcony, staring fiercely out at the fields and into the deeper distance, at the Ventridi garrison town. "I have sat too long in this manse, rubbing wounds and replaying lost strategies. I had not heard that Inami's allies were here. The old man naps while the cats slip into the garden to steal the golden carp. How did you know this?"

"Cardanzo saw a familiar face at the inn late last night, a former bodyguard of Erian's father whom he had served with before. He knew this man to be disreputable and long-suspected to be in Inami's employ even before his father's death."

"A loyal man, Cardanzo. He truly understands the role the Pancreator has given him; his loyalty to Erian is his loyalty to the Pancreator. And I, too, am loyal to both. This man of Inami's will not make a move while Erian is my guest; he will instead cloak his actions, perhaps hiring locals to act for him. He will do this only when she is in town, away from my manse."

"But she is in town now! She insisted on overseeing the provisioning with Julia." A black hand clutched heart. Fear and panic overcame me, and I stood, wanting to run to the town. "I should not have gone to Saint Maya's! Oh, selfish errant priest! I should have come to you first!"

"Fear causes the jackrabbit to rush before the wheels of the chariot," the general said, gripping my shoulders and seating me again. "We must act with surety in the time the Pancreator allows." He clapped thrice quickly, and a guard appeared from a hidden alcove I had been completely unaware of.

"You heard?" he asked the guard, and when the man nodded, the general spoke again in a tongue I did not know. It was surely a secret Li Halan battle tongue, a unique language used to hide communications from listening enemies on the field of war. The guard then turned and disappeared into the manse. "A general does not grow to great age without inspiring loyalty. Go now, there is a flitter waiting on the lawn to take you to Erian. But wear a mask as you go: your part is the innocent shazzle, unaware of the forces moving through the woods around him. Do nothing to alert Erian's enemies, and be assured that all is well; none will move against her without first encountering my displeasure."

I bowed, and hurried down the hall to the front lawn, where the driver who had brought me here prepared to fly me back to the garrison town. Halfway to the car, I halted and forced myself to walk calmly. I must appear undisturbed, as if nothing had taken place but a pleasant conversation. I climbed into the car and sat in the back, my hands twisting and almost tearing at my robe in frustration and anxiety.

Soon the flitter landed in the square before the town gates, and I rushed out, hurriedly seeking sign of Erian or our friends, forgetting Usaki's advice. The place was full of soldiers, most of them imperial legionnaires recently arrived for a quiet retirement from Stigmata. While they were still a standing army, they had little to stand for here in Old Istanbul. Nonetheless, the imperial capital world must keep soldiers ever at the ready. Among them thronged mercenaries and soldiers from other armies — even a Church contingent — sharing uncomfortably the largest garrison town outside of the Imperial City.

It was market day in Ventridi — the reason Erian had come— and merchants yelled over the low rumble of diverse conversations. I threaded my way through crowds, nearly scattering a pair of dice on the ground as I accidentally trod through an impromptu game of odds. Two burly and scarred veterans on their knees in the mud looked angrily up at me, but I kept moving and was soon out of their sight.

I cried with relief when I saw Ong in the crowd, his head reaching above even the tallest soldier. I waved and yelled to gain his attention, and his keen eyes quickly darted in my direction. He smiled as he recognized me, and moved forward through the crowd as I struggled to pass a band of Hazat veterans.

"Little father," he said when we reached one another, "I thought you went to see our lady's uncle."

"Erian is in trouble!" I said, as low as I could, fearful now that someone might overhear. Ong's keen ears had no trouble understanding what I said, and he stood to full height, his eyes searching for our lady. He apparently saw her and practically leapt in her direction, startling a group of beggars and scattering them in all directions. I followed in his wide wake.

Erian was standing outside a merchant's stall, Cardanzo by her side, while Julia haggled with an old crone over the price of what appeared to be old canned goods. They all looked at Ong as he came, and Cardanzo's hand instantly shot to his pistol, his eyes scanning the crowd for the source of Ong's anxiety. As I ran up, I saw his eyes tighten into hard slits and his pistol slide from its holster to point at a target to my left.

I had failed to notice the crowd clearing to the left for reasons other than our Vorox friend. A group of grimy mercenaries gathered there with clubs, maces and bats, all staring at Erian and our entourage. The leader stepped forward, boldly ignoring the blaster aimed at his eyes.

"Eh, you there! Li Halan!" he yelled.

Erian shot him a contemptuous glare and ignored him; he was well below her class and she was well within her rights to pretend he didn't exist.

"Don't turn from me!" he said. "You're the one that cheated us out of our pay. Twenty-five men dead — all because of you! The rest of us abandoned on that field, bleeding and crying for evac. But you couldn't be bothered. What are a bunch of liege-less mercs to you? But we did our duty, and now we're going to take our pay out of your hide!"

Erian looked aghast. "I've never hired mercenaries in my life!"

I scanned the rest of the crowd. They were moving away, refusing to get involved in what they deemed a matter of pay between a mercenary group and a disloyal noble. No one here — all soldiers and veterans, surely wronged themselves at one time or another by a noble's whim — would defend Erian, a stranger to them. I moved to Erian's side. "They work for your brother, my lady. This is a trick."

She looked at me with shock and then at the mercenaries. "You dare hide your affiliation to my brother under lies?! Step forward and fight me then!" She drew her sword and stepped clear of us.

Cardanzo moved in front of her. "They have no intention of honorable dueling, my lady. Step away. I will defend you."

The mercenaries fanned out; they intended to take us all. Even with Ong's strength and speed, and Cardanzo's skill, they posed a risk to Erian. I cried out to the throng: "Can't you all see this is about a noble vendetta, not about wronged soldiers?" No one responded.

I moved in front of Cardanzo, to stare in the mercenary leader's face. "If you intend harm to her, you must then harm me first."

He smiled. "All right, priest," and then swung his club. Too startled to resist, I felt the hard wood crack into my skull, and I sunk to the mud. The world seemed distant and like a magic lantern picture show. I could watch but not act. My limbs didn't respond to my thoughts.

A blaster bolt tore into my aggressor, charring his fatigues and knocking him back. But his men surged forward, weapons swinging. They did not reach Erian. Soldiers from the crowd appeared between them, slashing expertly left and right with katana blades. The mercenaries turned to defend themselves but could not stand before the equal but better-trained numbers that assaulted them.

As I recovered my senses and tried to rise, I saw the uniforms our allies wore, emblazoned with red hawks swooping over a field of bones. I knew who they were, and I whispered a prayer to the Pancreator for General Usaki's aid. The Red Hawk Company, third regiment of General Usaki's Scarlet Legion, were renowned veterans of the Emperor Wars, now retired like their lord. While most had returned to the Garden Worlds of the Li Halan, some had retired here, on the general's lands, to be close to their beloved lord.

The short battle lasted mere seconds, with the false mercenaries routed, many disappearing into the alleys of the garrison town but most dead in the mud of the makeshift market.

Ong helped me up, and Julia tended the wound on my head. "A little blood, but it's not that bad. You'll have quite a knob for a while, though." Cardanzo gave me a "whatthe-hell-did-you-think-you-were-doing" look, but I just shrugged, unsure myself of what came over me.

Erian examined my wound and smiled. "My brave defender appears to have survived. But from now on, he had best perform the role of medic and not wounded soldier." I nodded but smiled.

One of the Red Hawks addressed Erian. "My lady Li Halan, I have been asked by my Most Notable Commander of Crimson Conflicts to escort you to his manse, where you may rest safely away from such rabble as tried to accost you today."

"I thank my uncle for his timely aid, and you for your valiant service. I accept his offer and will return with you to his estate."

The Red Hawks stood in a formation, waiting for sign that Erian was ready to depart. As soon as she saw we were together, she walked toward the gates, surrounded regally by this force of disciplined soldiers. As I walked among them, guarded on all sides by their regimented march, I saw that all were older than any of us. Indeed, there did not appear to be one of them under forty years of age. I marveled at the loyalty engendered by the general to keep such troops standing in his name even years after their days of glory in the Emperor Wars had passed.

My head hurts and I tire of writing. My letter to my uncle has already been given into the hands of Usaki's servant, with strict orders not to be delivered until after we depart tonight. Once aboard the Resurgent, I think I shall sleep for a week.

I will be safer than before. One of the Red Hawks, Lieutenant Chinzi Gosado, begged Erian's uncle to be allowed to accompany us into barbarian space. With Erian's permission, he agreed. He knows the soldier well, and vouches for her. There is no place for this woman of war on Byzantium Secundus, but among the Vuldrok and Kurgans, her tactical lore may do us much good, and she begs to be of assistance once more to her noble lord.

I witness her untiring devotion to a cause, even one that threatens her life constantly, and wonder at the nature of faith. I follow the call of the Pancreator's service, and I know now that people such as she do the same, even though their path is carved with blood and mine with words.

Margins of the Wild

The margins of the wild seem much closer here.

I couldn't help but feel pity for the stray mongrel from the woods that stared at me, its ribs shockingly apparent on its starved torso. It eyed me with a mixture of wariness and desperation, wondering if I was the sort to kick it or feed it.

I opened my satchel and withdrew a strip of dried meat, part of the travel rations we had purchased in Elfhome before making our way into this Pancreator-forsaken country of Jyandhom. Hargard has proven every step of the way that it is not one of the Known Worlds. I threw the strip at the mongrel's feet; it leapt backwards before realizing what it was I had offered. It lunged greedily at the meat and gobbled it in an instant, and then looked to me for more.

I sighed and turned away, looking into the thatch hovel where Erian and the rest of our group held converse with the local matron. We sought a meeting with the infamous star-thane, Haldon Boldeyes, in the hopes of acquiring his patronage as an escort and guide deeper into Vuldrok space. While the idea of allying with one of the raiders who routinely pillaged Hawkwood space was initially abhorrent to me, it's necessity is now obvious after weeks of failure to obtain jumpkeys to other Vuldrok worlds.

Our lack of knowledge about these planets and their people proves a constant hindrance as we betray our ignorance to the locals with every word we speak. What little information was provided us by fellow Questing Knights and Cohorts has taken us this far and provided us with a number of potential guides, along with some murky idea of what other worlds lie further beyond Hargard's gates. But it has proven terribly incomplete, full of hearsay and bigoted opinion relayed as fact.

I felt something tugging at my satchel and looked down to see the mongrel had advanced upon me from behind and now held my bag in its teeth, attempting to wrest it from me. I yanked it away, crying "No!", but it clung tighter and growled evily. I pulled again and freed its jaws, but the beast, emboldened by its taste of meat, leapt at me, barking.

I jumped back, afraid it would bite me and bring a host of infections, but it whimpered and ran, quickly disappearing into the nearby woods. I recovered myself, wondering at its sudden cowardice, and turned to enter the hovel — only to run straight into Onggangarak, my Vorox friend. He had silently come from the hovel upon hearing my cry to stand behind me. No wonder the mongrel had run off.

He chuckled and smiled, shaking his head. "A lesson about wild beasts: if you feed them, they will see you as food."

"Well, I... it didn't seem completely feral. I mean, it did approach me. Surely it's been around the people of this village long enough to become somewhat domestic."

Ong smiled. "I know something of 'becoming domestic,' and it is but a thin veneer over a surface of instinct. Some would say it is not worth the effort, but I disagree, appreciating greatly the wonders of civilization. I can thus see the lack of contrast between the two more clearly, perhaps, than you, little father. You have lived long among those schooled in morals."

"Is not certain morality inborn? While dire circumstance may try even the best of us, does not even a cub understand and seek love?"

"Perhaps. It is hard to remember what I thought before I was taught to think in the known manner. It is an argument without ready propositions."

I laughed. "Ong, you could argue theology before the Metropolitan of Kish! Most men are not so familiar with our own language as you."

Julia interrupted us as she exited the hovel, followed by the rest of our party. "Enough philosophy, you two. We've got to head into the valley; there's a fortress where we can supposedly find this fabled Vuldrok we're looking for."

I turned to Erian, who looked perturbed. "My lady, did you get all the information you needed?"

"No," she sighed, tired after these weeks of frustrating attempts to pretend the Vuldrok informers she interviewed were not peasants but equal peers. She had quickly discovered that her typical noble airs aroused only hatred here. "These people know how to hide secrets from the Hawkwyrdedda, as they call us. But the woman swears that Haldon's steading is in the valley below — if he's not away raiding Hawkwood fiefs."

She marched past us toward the woods, to the thin trail that wound downwards. Cardanzo quickly moved past her to take the lead, and Ong dropped to all sixes and bounded into the trees to the right side of the path, scouting our flank and remaining hidden in case the need for surprise arose. The rest of us, I, Julia, Sanjuk and Lt. Gosado, followed behind our liege.

Lt. Gosado is still new to our company, but her military discipline has served her well in our strange surroundings these past weeks. Her presence among us has calmed Erian, for she is a soldier sworn to Erian's uncle, General Hanmei Usaki Li Halan; it is almost as if the old warrior were here himself, so well does Lt. Gosado know his proverbs and tactical wisdom.

It was a cool day, but not as cold as it was rumored to get in this region. I pulled my robes tighter, but had no need for anything thicker. As we marched through the woods, I found time to reflect on the immediate environment and took some pleasure in its peaceful beauty. Green conifers dominated, but the occasional open meadow displayed brightly colored flowers, with the slight buzz of insects about. Birdsong rang through the trees from various distances, undisturbed by the sounds of any human-made thing — there was no whine of flitter or skimmer, no jangling even of horse-tack or horse-drawn wheelcarts.

While this is not unusual even in the Known Worlds, it was new to me to experience this nearly uninterrupted for weeks. Even the poorest fief in the empire has some form of craft or tech to eventually disturb the silence.

We soon came into the valley, and the trees opened up to reveal a broad meadow with a trickling stream cutting through its center, its source revealed as a thin cascade from a rising mountain chain on the far side. In the middle of the field was a stone fort, supposedly built — according to our recent village informant — years ago by the earliest Vuldrok settlers. It was an old ward station marking the boundary of a now extinct thanedom. The only sign of modernism to it were the ceramsteel planks bolted to serve as shutters on its windows, stolen, I surmised, from some spaceship hulk.

Children ran and played in the stream and mud ponds around the fort, excitedly pointing at us when we broke through the trees. Their commotion summoned bored-looking soldiers from within, who immediately gained some energy upon seeing us. They called for more of their kind, and waited patiently but glowering by their home as we approached.

Five of them moved forward as we neared the door, each handling his or her (there were women soldiers among them) sheathed or slung weapons, an assortment of swords, axes and even a blaster-axe, much notched and scorched but probably in fine working condition.

Erian greeted them and explained our goal, promising Imperial riches and rewards to Haldon Boldeyes if he consented to see us and guide us to other worlds. They seemed unimpressed, but sent a man inside to inquire of their chief. He eventually returned, this time smiling, and gestured for us to enter the fort.

The interior was surprisingly cosmopolitan, its walls hung with fine hangings and fine art paintings — loot from Known Worlds holdings. A short passage opened to stairs on both sides (upwards to the left, down to the right) and forward, into a main chamber, where a hearty laugh greeted us.

A man in a worn but well-kept Charioteer jumpsuit opened his arms and smiled at us. His chest was studded with patches and badges, both Merchant League and Vuldrok, and an array of weaponry (blaster pistol, dirk and skinning knife) and tools hung from his belt — including a key ring with at least 12 jumpkeys.

"Aha," he cried. "Julia Abrams! Little Jules!"

Julia stared aghast at the man, and finally stammered out a reply. "Gordon Samothrace? It can't be you!"

"It is! It is! In the flesh and healthier than ever!"

"But the travelwaste disease! You were dying of radiation poisoning last time I saw you at the Academy on Leagueheim. Pancreator's mercy, that was nearly 10 years ago!"

"A lifetime. Time enough to be born anew. I have put weakness behind me and live with gusto, Little Jules, my best pilot in the whole squadron!" He turned to Erian, as if she were but one among many of us, not the obvious noble she was. "Nobody took to tax collection maneuvers like Jules! The Reeves were ready to graduate her then and there as long as she signed on with the fleet. But not Jules! She had her own gig going already! What was it? A contract with the Li Halan worlds for a Rampart-Kish mercantile route was it?"

"Something like that," Julia said, not wanting to talk about her past sour contracts. "What the hell are you doing here? How did you get here? How long have you been here?"

"Oh, going on seven years I suppose. I wanted to go out fighting, Jules, not die in some sickbed racking up Apothecary bills. I hired on with a Hawkwood noble seeking revenge against some Vuldrok raiders. It was a suicide mission for all us, but I had nothing to lose."

Erian coughed. Samothrace seemed to remember where he was. "Ah, what a host! C'mon, sit down." He gestured to the benches surrounding a large throne, what looked to be a captain's chair torn from some starship deck. He sat on a fur-covered ottoman beside the throne, while we spread out on the benches.

"To continue my tale," he said, winking at Julia. "I came here to

Hargard intending to die in a glorious space battle against barbarian hordes. Well, we got boarded instead. I was knocked out cold and woke up captured instead of dead. Sold as slaves, we were separated and sent on deeper into Vuldrok space."

Erian again coughed. Samothrace smiled. "To make a long story short, I worked my way into the trust of our ship captain — helping steer the ship after its own pilot got himself shot got me many kudos. I was eventually freed and offered the position of pilot on Haldon Boldeye's ship. Those were hectic times. So harried that I almost forgot about my disease. It seemed to disappear. I learned that I loved this new, reckless life, with no idiotic bureaucratic authority from on high to tell me what to do. I haven't had a disease symptom in three years. The life of a raider has cured me."

Julia shook her head, staring in wonder at him. "Amazing."

I prodded Julia. "You seem to have an awful lot of old acquaintances scattered across the stars. Are you going to properly introduce your friend to our liege?"

"Oh! Uh, yeah. Sorry about that. Commander Gordon Samothrace, this is Lady Erian Li Halan, currently serving in the Emperor's service."

Erian nodded at the pilot and began to speak, but he cut her off. "Another Questing Knight? Been a lot of you guys around here lately, poking around, asking questions, all trying to get to the Vuldrok heartworlds."

"My mission of diplomatic embassy is a noble one, commander," Erian replied, hiding her annoyance well. "Is it so wrong to greet one's neighbors with visits?"

"Considering that these neighbors — including me — have been pillaging your Emperor's holdings for some time now, yeah, it makes some of us suspicious."

"And what of Haldon Boldeyes? Do you speak for him? Or does he hide behind pilots, fearful to meet us himself?"

Our new friend frowned, not a look of anger, but disappointment, as if a dinner guest used the wrong fork. Before he could continue, one of the soldiers who had brought us in spoke, stepping further into the room.

"Fear? Haldon fears no one and no thing! He has spat in the eye of Satrar himself, and screamed in rage at his power when others broke down like milksop boys seeing their first bare woman's breast! No, he does not hide, but neither is he stupid enough to announce his presence before strangers who have earned no rights by him."

Erian stood and bowed to the man. "I meant no insult, star-thane. But impatience can prove to be a virtue, as it has here."

The soldier stared warily for a moment and laughed. "What an odd way to speak! I like it. Too many of your kind demand things or beg them. Few speak honestly of them." He walked past us and spun around as he dropped onto the throne. So this was Haldon.

"You are persistent," he said. "My people have watched you and sent word of your seeking me these past weeks. I told them to delay you, to test your resolve and demeanor. So far, you have proved yourselves able enough. Perhaps you would not be so annoying on a long star journey as I at first though, eh? Gordon, how say you to their request?"

Samothrace smiled at us, looking longest at Julia. "I say honor it, thane. There is much to be learned on both sides."

Haldon nodded. "It is done then. You want me to guide you into the Vuldrok Star-Nation. I want you to tell me of your emperor and pay me 25,000 firebirds."

"What?!" Julia cried. "That's robbery!"

Both Haldon and Gordon roared with laughter. "You think I got my jumpkeys for free?" Haldon said. "They cost me in blood and broken tech, and they'll now cost you."

"A high fee," Erian said. "One we shall pay. On one condition: our portion of any raids you involve us in goes towards this fee."

Haldon was shocked. "Ah, I'm seen through. How did you know I intended to raid with you aboard?"

"You can't afford to travel far without stopping for booty. If we're with you, you'd surely expect us to pull our fair share of the duty."

Haldon nodded and narrowed his eyes at Erian. "Aye, I would. And if you turn against me, to protect one of your own kind, the deal's off and I leave you in the void."

"Conditions accepted," Erian said, smiling slightly.

I was astonished. I could not believe my lady intended to engage in piracy to achieve her goals. I looked to Cardanzo and saw that he was not surprised at all. Surveying all my friends, it appeared that only Ong was equally surprised, but he smiled at the prospect of action while I paled at it.

"We leave for Khotan at the end of the week then," Haldon exclaimed. "And then on to Frost."

It appears that the margins of the wild are not only close, they have engulfed us.

Obligations

I am on a starship traveling a strange journey into unknown spaces. My liege, Lady Erian Li Halan, presses us further into greater and greater danger in pursuit of her quest. Our fate has now led us into barbarian space, escorted by a Vuldrok pirate lord through jumpgates unknown to the empire — lost worlds that we hope to find again.

I have much time to write here in my cramped cabin. My journals are caches of my reflections on our travails, on our hopes and fears. I often send copies of them by trusted courier to my childhood friend, now chartophylax at the Vermillion Repository on Midian, who sees that they are published and distributed among allies. For this reason, I have not yet transcribed our leading goal here among the barbarians.

But danger is ever preying upon us, and I fear that we may not all survive this adventure. For this reason, I feel it best to record our goal. If we cannot accomplish it, then it is a lost cause. If we do, then I shall burn this entry and leave no evidence of our quest.

It was on Byzantium Secundus, where so many plots and causes are hatched, that fate chose to chain my lady to new obligations. She had only recently taken her vows as a Questing Knight, and already we prepared to tread new and dangerous paths for reasons given us in visions by the great Anunnaki Gargoyle of Nowhere. So as not to insult our host during our stay, we partook of his grand parties at his villa outside the Imperial City.

Boring and tedious affairs for the most part, my lady did find them amusing at times, for she knows the thrusts and ripostes necessary to thrive in such atmospheres. I, however, have no mind for even petty intrigue, and found myself on far too many occasions drawn into social conspiracies without my knowledge or consent, only discovering the truth of these matters after I had excused myself for the evening and discussed my meetings with Erian.

Such was the status quo on this night. Rather than be suckered into yet another attempt by some bold noble compatriot to pass messages to a lover or co-conspirator — why are priests considered such good envoys for such things? Are we that naïve? — I slipped from the hall to wander down a side passage near the servants' quarters, finding myself deep in contemplation of the proper response an Eskatonic provost should give to such frivolous social entreaties as met me on nights such as these.

A servant quickly exiting from an open door nearly knocked me over. He was in a rush and I was lost in thought; we barely avoided a painful smack. Before he could get his wits about him, I heard a yell of pain in the room. Reacting on instinct rather than wisdom, I stepped into the room to see who had cried so.

On a straw bed lay a soldier, his tunic and the straw beneath him stained in blood. A horrendous gut wound was apparent, one to which another servant was doing his best to administer. But he was no chirurgeon, and I wondered why no physick had been summoned. Harshly, I stepped over and snatched the blade and gauze from his hands, kneeling down to examine the wound. "Fetch hot water," I said.

The servant immediately leaped up and joined the other, and both left the room in a rush. I hardly noticed. My attention was completely drawn to the wound. It was grievous. The man was dying, and it was amazing he had not already passed on. I calmed myself and spoke the litany taught me years ago by Mother Kalpa, calling upon the divine fire in my breast to seal the torn flesh. The skin grew taut and the edges of the wound — from a sword, I presumed — reknitted somewhat. But it was not enough.

The man was looking at me now. He had awakened from his temporary delirium and stared into my eyes with an intensity I had never before encountered. Who was this soldier to have such a general's glare about him?

"Leave it, brother," he said, sighing. It seemed he was in a place beyond pain. "I am dying, and there is nothing your rituals can do about it."

"Who are you?" I asked. "I am a confessor. I can hear and absolve you."

"Of what? I bear no sins, but for pride perhaps. Regret, maybe…"

"Can I help?" I said as I soaked the blood from his wound. It did no good. My rite had not closed the wound entirely.

He then looked at me with that stare, one which commanded complete respect. "I need a Questing Knight, brother. Not a brat on tour away from father's fief, but a real knight."

"Then I shall fetch one," I said, standing. I could not hide my smile at the amazed but skeptical look on his face. I stepped out of the room and saw the servants returning, each ferrying a pail of steaming water. I took one from the lad I had nearly collided with earlier, and said: "Go to the main hall, quickly. Fetch Lady Erian Li Halan."

He stood there for a moment, doubtful, looking into the room. The soldiers' voice came: "Go, boy, do as he says. But quietly!" The lad was immediately off, moving as quickly as he could yet taking pains to appear like a normal servant on no mission of import.

I stepped back into the room and dipped the gauze in the water, rubbing it over the wound to cleanse it. The man dropped in and out of consciousness. I momentarily thought he had died, but a fierce will within him kept him here.

Erian Li Halan came into the room, a look of concern on her face. When she saw my charge, her jaw dropped. "Warlord Sentaku…" she whispered in awe.

His eyes fluttered open and he looked at her. "Who?"

She dropped to a kneel and bowed before him. "Lady Erian Li Halan, daughter of the Seven Petaled Rose lineage. You served with my father in the Shansei Conflagration. You saved his life. I remember sitting on your knee as you told the tale before the Matrons."

The man smiled. "Can the Pancreator be so kind as to bring you before me now? Quickly, young rose with thorns, are you indeed sworn to the Emperor as this priest says?"

"I am."

"Then I ask this one thing of you: Travel beyond all the maps we know to a barbarian world called Sky Tear. There, in a bunker, is hidden a relic important to the empire. Fetch it and give it to its rightful owner."

Erian looked dismayed. This was an insane request. I shook my head, signaling that I believed the man to be delirious.

"What you ask is… difficult," she said.

The man parted his collar, and revealed there an amulet carved into the shape of a fiery lotus.

Erian shuddered and nodded. "The Burning Lotus. There is no greater military honor from my house."

"It was given me by your father."

"Then I shall do what you ask, if it is in my power. But I have a quest of my own, you must know."

"He who gave me this ring…" the man said, struggling to remove a large ring of copperish-purple metal, "…takes precedence." Once he'd freed it from his hand, he held it out for her. "It is Second Republic manufacture. It knows the makeup of my body, and I now set it for you. Take it." She did. "Hold it here, where I can reach." He touched it and a slight sound emanated, but nothing more. "There. None can now bear this but you, and it is a sign that you are my chosen. It carries the lore with it that you will need. In return for the quest I have set you, the owner of this ring shall render to you a service of your asking."

Erian looked puzzled, waiting for him to reveal the patron.

"Look on the inner ring," he said, his strength beginning to fail him.

Erian gasped. "The Phoenix Seal of Vladimir. Only one man can rightfully use it…"

"It is he," the soldier said. "Now I am through."

And there he died.

And here I now sit, in a starship somewhere making its way to the mysterious world he named. Our guides know it, but they only laugh when we ask about it, and say that we will know it when we ingest it. And then we will "know everything." I have no idea what they mean, but I suppose we will find out.

We did not speak of the incident to anyone, for the servants declared that the soldier demanded secrecy. Our host was an ally of his, and he had appeared at the gates wounded, seeking aid from someone he knew would keep his secret, but he gave the servants no explanation. By the time our host arrived, Warlord Sentaku had died.

Our host was greatly troubled and would not speak of it, but he did notice the ring on Erian's hand — his raised eyebrows were hard for even him to hide. He seemed to have some unspoken idea of the debt wearing it entailed, for he was ever more respectful of her from then on. It seemed to me he treated us all as if we were leaving for a war from which we would not return.

It appears that the heavy hand of obligation makes martyrs of us all.

Strange Communion

Madness. Utter madness.

The inhabitants of Sky Tear are afflicted with a brain rot from which none seem to escape. Even we feel its effects. Only Haldon Boldeye's assurances — that time and distance away from the orb heals all its ills — gives me the calm patience to write this now.

Curse this lawless space! Never before have I lost a journal book, but my most recent accounts of our time in barbarian space was reduced to ash by the hot plasma of a raider's blaster. It seems our guide has enemies here, as well as the friends for whom we hired him. I shall have to recreate our journey through Hargard, Khotan, Frost, Wolf's Lament, Fingisvold and Epiphany at some later time, when the stress of escape is no longer upon us. We only stayed any length at Wolf's Lament, anyway, passing through the space of those other worlds but not touching upon them. We were in too great a hurry to come here, to this stark world with its patches of eternal night.

Eight jumps from Byzantium Secundus through unknown, hostile territory. Many here do not like Questing Knights, even though the majority have never met one — rumor alone precedes us, most of it lies. However, there are enough people here who welcome us, curious about our customs. Indeed, some even look upon us with a sort of reverence, relics from their legendary past come to walk among them.

Our mission is certainly a vexing one. The data ring that Erian wears only divulges necessary information on a "task required" basis — we must trust it to reveal important facts before we make fatal errors in our search for the secret relic its memory guards. Once upon Sky Tear, in the frigid dome of Cydax Station, it finally awoke to give guidance, informing us that we would have to leave the Vuldrok settlement and travel to another continent. It only spoke in latitudes and longitudes, but Julia was able to translate these onto the continent of Gervais.

Our guide's local friends here chuckle and shake their heads. A "fool's errand," they say, for Gervais is a vast jungle, unexplored except by savages — and this was a barbarian speaking. What sort of degenerate must one be to earn the title "savage" from such a thug? Here Haldon failed us, claiming that he was hired to simply take us here, not to go thrashing through a jungle waiting for the Muazi to chew on his brain.

Cardanzo demanded to know what the hell he was talking about, and so the Vuldrok of Cydax Station gathered to tell us the campside horror stories about Sky Tear. Terrible accounts of men driven mad simply by breathing the air on the world, or worse, of the bizarre sentient fungal aliens that whisper into a man's sleeping consciousness, driving him to insane acts. Ong was getting nervous, as was Sanjuk, and even I began to fear, but Cardanzo smiled as each story got wilder and wilder. I began to understand that they were intentionally trying to scare us.

Nearby, watching but not taking part, was a man in animal-skin robes, painted sloppily with odd markings, similar to those we had seen on Wolf's Lament — the alleged Anunnaki script called runes. I am skeptical about their mythical powers, but recognize that the Vuldrok revere the runecasters and speak carefully near them. I assumed this quiet watcher was a runecaster, or perhaps apprenticed to one.

"Excuse me, good sir," I asked him. He simply stared back, meeting my eyes in acknowledgement but refusing any further sign. "And what can you tell us of this world? Is there any way to survive such perils as your comrades tell?"

The Vuldrok storytellers grew silent and sullen, but the robed man smirked. He came forward and sat in a chair immediately vacated for him by the lead storyteller. He stared at each of us, but Erian in particular, and Ong also.

"It is as they say, but not always so. They tell the worst, for they thrive on danger and feel that no trip is worth taking without a sense of adventure. But you are different. I can tell. You have purpose, and no time for drama. What do you seek?"

"I tell you truthfully that I do not know," said Erian. "But I have sworn an oath to retrieve it."

"Ha! Searching for the unknown with threat of dishonor. A brave quest if ever there was one. How will you know this thing when you see it?"

"A voice will tell me," Erian replied. "A voice from the past."

The man stared at her for a while, then nodded. "I can believe this... spirits are strong upon you. A rune dances on your forehead, but one I have never before seen. It is faint, otherwise I would have these warriors bind you while I studied it."

Ong growled at this, and earned a look of approval from the runecaster. "Yes, mighty beast, I would risk even your ire to gain such lore. But it is clear that it is not meant to be. Not yet... the rune evades me purposefully, and even I am no fool to raise the anger of such a thing."

I had no idea what he was talking about, but everything I had so far surmised concerning Vuldrok religion seemed true here. That they were animists, believing that even stones and trees have intelligence of sorts, or at least indwelling spirits. It seemed this one believed that ideas or thoughts had a similar life.

He said little after that, only commanding the nearby warriors to aid us on our quest, telling any who accompanied us that a chance for destiny was at hand. This carried much weight, for we soon had five volunteers to help us navigate the wilds, one of whom owned a flitter, taken, he proudly informed us, from the "milkfed Kurgans on Ananoxia."

There is little worth reporting about the following day's provisioning activity, or even the flitter trip across continents, except that our pilot avoided the "night regions," flying us five hours around one. These places, where clouds of crystal loom in the skies, often see no light for years, except for the stabs of lightning shot down from the heavens like spears thrown by an angry god. Ah, too much time among pagans afflicts even my imagination with their imagery.

As we approached the reported site, the ring once again awoke and chimed forth information, this time a detailed description of an old Second Republic archaeology bunker abandoned in the jungles below, besides the ruins of an old alien civilization. When Erian asked about these aliens, it droned forth a truly ancient report about them, in a long-dead voice from the Second Republic. It told us little, though, except that they resembled insects and were apparently not Anunnaki. They were a mystery shown only in ruins even to the first human explorers to this world.

We landed in a clearing six kilometers from the site — the closest we could get through the dense foliage — and trekked forth, leaving behind the flitter pilot and one other to guard our only escape from this place.

As we traveled, Cardanzo became quite surly, even snapping at Erian — something she had never experienced before, as evidenced by her shock and hurt. I begged him to tell me what was wrong, but he refused to even speak to me. Sanjuk also was not herself, shivering and staring at the jungle, obviously afraid. While I had seen her fearful before, never like this — she was a mouse expecting a cat to stalk her at any moment.

One of the Vuldrok warriors, seeing my reaction to my friends' behaviors, came and whispered to me, "The madness begins, my friend. No one escapes it for long." I shuddered, and hurried on, hoping we would be done before nightfall and away from this world before another week had passed.

The bunker itself was completely unimpressive. It was a block of maxicrete unceremoniously dumped on its existing spot by its unimaginative makers long ago. Since then, the jungle had swallowed its exterior, lending some degree of vibrancy to its long abandonment. The doors were sealed with a sophisticated lock, but the ring spoke again, demanding to be placed before the lock's "eye," where it could silently transmit codes. A rumbling within was heard and the door slid open a crack before a loud explosion came from somewhere deep within.

The ring chimed out: "Error. Internal power plant failure. The door must be forced."

At least it had opened far enough for us to squeeze a tree branch in, and use it for leverage. I say "we," but it was Ong and the Vuldrok who did the labor. No locking mechanism worked against us now, only the weight of the doors. The branch broke after the doors had been moved enough for Sanjuk to squeeze in, but we thought it best to try again before she risked going alone. A second branch did better, and this time the doors were fully opened.

No lights could be seen within, so we lit lanterns and activated fusion torches. Corridors led to old offices empty of anything — whoever had worked here took their think machines and files with them upon leaving. The ring guided us to a set of stairs and bid us travel to the bottommost level three stories down. At various places along the walls, cracks had allowed wet earth to seep in; I assumed we were near to some underground river or stream. Molds and oddly-colored mushrooms sprang up on some of these spots, emitting an ugly stench.

We finally arrived in what I assumed to be an old archive chamber. Crates were scattered about the room, sealed sometime during the Second Republic and unexposed to air since. It was apparently one of these which we searched for. The ring asked Erian to hold the shipping manifests before it, and it somehow saw their contents, comparing them to its own records.

I looked about the room with Ong, who sniffed and wrinkled his nose at the stench, greater now in this room than the stairwell. The Vuldrok looked nervous, so I went to the one who had confided in me before and whispered a query at him: "Why so edgy?"

"The fungus," he said, trying not to look at it as he said so. "It isn't normal. It is Muazi. Hsst! Do nothing to acknowledge it. Get your thing so we can begone from here."

I went to warn Cardanzo, but the angry look in his face stopped me short. I felt a burst of betrayal and a sense of shame that he would act like this, but then I noticed the sweat on his brow, sure sign of the great effort of will working within to hold back an even greater tide of rage. We had to leave now, relic be damned!

I grasped Erian's ring hand: "We should go, my lady. This very minute."

"We have not come all this way not to search every crate, Alustro," she said, her look acknowledging my fear and worry but telling me it was unimportant next to the goal of the quest.

"Damn your quest!" I yelled. "Are we but pawns for the Eye?! We'll meet our deaths here!"

Julia moved to pull me away from Erian before Cardanzo could fully draw his sword, but we were all startled to hear the ring speak: "100% confirmation. Open this crate."

Erian snapped the hinges on the crate before her, and the slow hiss of air seeped out. After a minute, it was safe to open it, so she carefully reached for the lid. She was gently pushed aside by a silent Cardanzo, who reached instead to open it first, still performing his duties even when gripped by a madness none of us could explain.

I cannot convey enough our extreme initial disappointment in what we found. A stone carving rested on a pillowed shelf, displaying the odd carvings of the aliens who had once built cities here. A grasshopper shaped entity could be seen, but the other markings made no sense. We had traveled all this way for a piece of stone.

I cried out in rage. Reader, realize that I was not myself at this point. I moved forward and grabbed it from Cardanzo's startled hands, smashing it to the floor in frustration. The stone shattered, scattering across the perfectly smooth maxicrete. Cardanzo's fist impacted by jaw and the next I knew I was lying among the broken carvings. A glowing crystal was near my hand, something I had not seen before.

Small chunks of stone revealed that it had been inside the carving, at its core.

Before anything else could transpire, I heard a Vuldrok yell: "Get out of my head!"

And then I remember little but heaving floors, quaking stairs, spiraling molds on the walls, and the melting yet continually reforming face of Ong as he carried me. And this one, curious thing above all: a feeling of confusion not my own, changed to relief and then regret, all mingled with intense memories of my vision of the Gargoyle of Nowhere.

When my sense finally cleared from what I now know to be the fungal-induced hallucination, we were all once more aboard the flitter on our way back to Cydax Station. Erian held the glowing crystal in her hand, soaked in blood — not hers, but that of the Vuldrok who tried to take it from her, a renegade even his comrades did not mourn. Only she and Ong had remained unaffected, Ong because of his Vorox constitution, and she due to an antidote injected by the ring — which had apparently possessed foreknowledge for all that had happened.

Our relic appears to be a soul shard, one of the famed makings of the Anunnaki. Each has unique properties of its own, and I would dearly love to investigate this one's, but Erian's ring reminds us that it is the property of he whom we serve in this quest, and that is enough to quell my curiosity.

We are once more in space, almost to Sky Tear's jumpgate. Captain Gordon Samothrace tells us to expect trouble on the other side: Kurgans riled by our previous jaunt through the system when we ignored their calls to communicate with them.

I don't know when I'll get another chance to write again, or to replace the lost journals, but I hope to have many things to say by then. Poor Cardanzo flinches every time he sees the great bruise on my jaw, but I smile to tell him it causes no pain (a lie, but one he needs to hear). More than that, however, he needs to hear my council, and I hope he will soon accept my offer of it. His confidence is wounded, for he prides himself on iron control. We both suffered from contact with Sky Tear, and perhaps an alien mind.

I realize now that my mind had been touched by the Muazi intelligence present in the room, one which had feared us until it encountered the memory of my vision, which seemed to accord us some respect. When I told this to the others, after hearing their tales and piecing my own conclusions together from them, I earned a name from the Vuldrok: Alustro Muazi Friend. I'm not sure I like it, but it does reflect somewhat my strange communion.

Approbations

Never did I conceive such wonders as I have seen of late. Amidst the violent cruelties of barbarian space I witnessed strange beings and saw that, even far removed from the core worlds, humanity survives and thrives in manners all its own. Though my ribs still hurt when I draw breath and my leg shall ever walk with a limp from the wounds I sustained there, these maimings have been more than paid for by our patron's gratitude. Our mission — whose aim and ends must still remain secret — held importance for this nameless lord.

And yet wonders still present themselves, one greater than any that occurred on that long star sojourn into barbarian space from which my companions and I only just returned. On Byzantium Secundus we finally came to rest, three days ago, delivering the prize we had sought, found, and fought hard to retain on the perilous journey back to the Known Worlds. My wounds are still too fresh, even weeks after their delivery, to write overmuch of their getting — or the wounding I delivered in return. My soul still bleeds with sorrow from the deeds I committed in that far place, the dark void of space where bandits prowl heedless of all threat.

As I write, my Lady and her bodyguard meet with our quest liege, and surely great shall be the honor gained in his eyes, although she must wear it cloaked and silent. Julia, Sanjuk and Ong traveled to the Port Authority, hoping to immerse themselves in its cosmopolitan goings-on, so long denied them in those places from which we lately came. Lt. Gosado sought old friends at the Li Halan garrison, where she can reveal her newly won scars and tell the tales of our glory among Vuldrok pirates.

But I sought only solace and healing, and so wandered to the

Holy City to rest in its chapels and meditate in the incense scents of sandalwood and jasmine. Walking unsteadily from circle to circle, borne on the cane I still find unfamiliar and damnable, I stopped at whatever shrine or cathedral took my fancy, and there prayed again and again, hoping in such wise to purge my guilt.

Finally I came to the Pelunia Gardens, in Corona Secundus, over which looms St. Maya's Cathedral, on its perch on the upper and final circle of the city. I sat by a willow tree on a stone bench placed by Patriarch Halvor during his service as Regent of the Known Worlds. A simple carving, now forgotten by most priests, it brought me solace with the memory that here, in times of trouble, Chia Wen, the Patriarch's sister, would come and watch the gentle spring that runs past, delivering the fallen blossoms from the far end of the garden to a pond around the bend, hidden by trees. Here I sat for a number of hours, working over and over in my mind how I might have performed my actions differently, and thus saved men their lives. A useless exercise.

So deep in thought I was that I failed to notice the complete stillness that fell over the gardens, for no passersby had come for some time, as if barred from the place. When I noticed the strangeness of its complete silence, I stood and looked about, wondering the cause.

Then I saw the Mandarin. On the broad lawn from the front entrance the Vau came toward me, his (her?) robes flowing about him as the wind swept gently through the trees, causing them to shiver and stir. We were alone but for his guards — Vau Soldiers bearing short staves — which I could now see at the gateway, keeping all others from entry.

He came near and stopped, nodding slightly, a faint smile on his face. I was too stunned to act at first, but then remembered my manners, and so bowed to him. His smile grew larger, and he watched me as one would a friend long sundered.

For many a long moment we stood thus, simply watching each other. I noted the intricate carvings of his headdress, which extended over his shoulders and part of his chest, decorated with strange, indecipherable glyphs. Colored a dark brown, it looked more like a piece of wondrously shaped driftwood than the result of a technology beyond human ken.

Finally, he spoke: "I had hoped to deliver my invitation solely to you and your company, but your wounds do not permit your going at this time. A pity, for your insight would have served your kind well. May the glyphs turn and allow for such a moment to again occur. Then perhaps you shall meet with us in gardens of our own sculpting."

He bowed fully to me and turned to leave.

I barely knew what to do, awed at the attention this being had given me. How could this be? What supernatural means did the Vau employ whereby they would know me, from among so many others of my race?

"Please wait," I said, perhaps too hurried. "How is that you know me?"

He turned his head, his smile still there. "I have read your journals. It is wise that you chose to publish them."

He walked back whence he came as I stood dumbfounded and feeling somewhat the idiot. My journals are anything but supernatural and available to many who can read. I am nonetheless amazed that they have come to the attention of such as the Vau.

I watched the Mandarin leave the gardens, his escort behind him, and stood once more alone in the stillness. I tried to follow, but collapsed to the ground as my cane gave way beneath me. The exhaustion of my day-long walk had been too much for my weakened state, and the shock of my encounter perhaps too much for my turmoil-wracked mind. I passed into unconsciousness as a fever warmed my brow.

I awoke not on grass but in a bed, a large cushioned one fit for a lord or rich merchant, judging by its size and the gilt on its four-poster hangings. Looking about the room, I saw a fire crackling in a small chimney, before which was an empty reading chair, positioned to catch light from a closed, ornate window. From beyond a door, now slightly ajar, I could hear the coming and going of people, servants by the sound of them.

I slid from the bed and noticed my cane leaning near. Clutching it, I stood and tried to quietly move to the chair, but could not do so without emitting a pained grunt — my broken rib complained overloud. A boy stuck his head through the door, saw I was up, and rushed to help me sit.

"Where am I?" I asked him.

"Worry not, provost," he replied. "You are within the quarters of Bishop Yost. Rest now, and I shall fetch him who ordered you brought here." He slipped from the room before I could say ought else, and so I sat, staring at the fire and trying to remember if I knew the name he had given. I did not.

It was not the mysterious Bishop Yost who came quietly through the door, but my uncle, the Archbishop Palamon, the highest spiritual authority on this world.

I bowed my head to him but was too startled to give the proper address.

He placed his hand upon my head and tilted it upward, so that he could see my face. I wondered at the look upon his face, for it was so like that given me by the Mandarin — the expression of one who has long missed looking upon a friend. Tears welled in my eyes, for I so deeply missed looking likewise upon my uncle, who was once as a father to me. He bent down and embraced me with genuine ardor, but also, I suspect, to relieve me of the shame of my tears. I quickly wiped my eyes and gently pulled from his hug.

He called out to a servant: "Bring me a chair." In a moment, the boy came again, this time carrying a light chair, certainly not one fit for an archbishop. But my uncle took it without complaint and set it across from me, tilted slightly toward the fire. He waved the boy away, who quickly left the room, closing the door behind him.

We sat in silence for a few moments, listening to the pop and crackle of the flames, each wondering where to begin. I, of course, waited for him to speak first.

"When I received your last letter," he said, "telling me of your journey beyond the Known Worlds, I feared you would soon be dead. I believed it to be foolhardy in the extreme, and knew not what madness could have driven your liege to lead you there.

"And today, my priests followed a contingent of Vau emissaries to the Garden of Respite and found you, lying fevered on its lawns, within sight of my very bedroom window. I could scarcely believe the news, and came myself to see. There you were, unconscious and pained by a wound-fever no priest should ever know. I had you brought here, to the home of Bishop Yost, a retired yet revered local. Your coming is unknown by any but those loyal to me, and so you need not worry about your secrecy. Oh, yes, I heeded well your comments in your letter about rivals and enemies. What noble does not reap such from their sowings?"

"Thank you," was all I could say.

He turned from the fire and looked upon me again.

"Fear not my ire, nephew. It was extinguished by the cold that gripped my heart when I imagined you dead on some world far from the Church, but is now replaced by the warmth of seeing you again, weakened but still whole. I forgive you your transgressions against an old man's fear, for I ever resisted your following a questing path, the most regretful of the Prophet's admonitions to one whose duty it is to raise boys into adulthood, only to see them travel far from their hearths.

"Your letter laid upon me finally the burden of acceptance. I accept your duty, and your quest. And by my intelligence, I know that it has now led to perilously high acclaim."

My eyes widened, but then closed. Of course, I realized, if any on this world know of our recent patron, it would be my uncle, whose eyes and ears hear and see much that the Faithful do here. "Then you know. I beg you not to speak of it."

"I?" he said in surprise. "To whom would I tell? Is there any whose alliance I need court? Not I. Although he who was your liege in this holds goals different from those I foresee for the Church, he is yet true to the Faith and acts in accord with it. I can gainsay him nothing in this, nor you for your role in his mission."

"I know you, uncle," I said. "And your word I trust. But I also know that you would not have me leave this room without revealing something to you of my encounter with the Vau, and so I shall tell it—"

"No, tell me none of it," he said. "Although I have ever demanded to know all of your doings, even one as old as I can still learn, and I perceive that what this being told you was for you alone. Let it stay that way for now, until you meditate further on the wisdom of revealing it."

"You amaze me," I said. "I almost fear you are not real, but a fantasy of my fever, which I thought was abated."

He laughed at that, and stood up from his chair.

"You are surely wide awake, nephew, but must not remain so for long. Rest you need, and here you shall have it, safe from all intrusion. Your friends will come, for I have already dispatched messages. However, I ask this: Do not mention my role in your rescue to them, at least not yet. They would fear the hand of politics come down upon them, and I would not burden them so."

"I am tired," I said, but rose from the chair. "Yet I cannot allow myself to sleep. I have too many questions concerning my visitor earlier."

"Ah," he said. "Few answers will be forthcoming, but I can tell you this: The being traveled to the second circle and there waylaid an unsuspecting noble and her entourage. He gave to her an invitation, an emissary mission to Vril-Ya, and then departed to a starship outside the Holy City. The noblewoman, whose name I shall not reveal — for she deserves privacy as much as you and your Lady — is already the talk of the high court. No clue can be found as to why she was chosen for this honor; it is seemingly a random choice.

"One more thing will I tell you, a thing most people do not

know as yet and may never come to know: This noblewoman and her entourage were not the first so chosen for ambassadorial duty to the Vau. Others throughout the Known Worlds have been so gifted of late, and their choosing is seemingly just as arbitrary, unless they all withhold intelligence of deeper doings. And so a strange sampling of humans go to meet the Vau, and none dare prevent it for fear of losing insight into those aliens' inscrutable ways, regardless of the consequences of allowing them to pick and choose from our kind."

He went to the door and turned to me once more before he opened it. "You are lucky, although I know you do not think so. If the Vau had chosen you, greater danger would have threatened you than you have yet imagined. Your very soul would have been tried by whatever plots the Vau hatch with this scheme. You have but late been delivered safely from evil; pray seek it no more."

And with that he left, closing the door behind him. I went to the bed and lay down, thinking on the transformation of my uncle's attitude toward me, but came to few conclusions before I fell once more into deep slumber.

I dreamed. There I stood in a hall unknown to me, for its make was strange and inhuman, the markings on the walls and floor forming patterns that made little sense. The Mandarin from the garden appeared in a doorway that did not exist before, although whether this was but the logic of dream or some vision of actual Vau architecture, I know not. He smiled at me, and made an odd noise, his mouth forming a trumpet shape. He extended his hand and offered me an item that looked to be a portable think machine.

I gazed at it and saw, swimming in streams on its screen — flat, but yet seemingly with infinite depth — many glyphs, changing into different glyphs as I watched. Then they gathered together in a spiral and formed one large, complex shape that I could not look upon. As it formed, my mind reeled, and I surely knew what it was like for a dreamer to hit the ground after a long fall — something oneirists claim shocks us awake before impact. And yet still I dreamed, and was now

149

in a cage formed from the glyph, so tightly that I could no longer see it whole, and was thus spared further pain. I was desperate and grabbed the bars of my cell, shaking them with all my strength, but they did not yield. I saw past them to other cages wherein stood my companions, talking through the bars to one another as if unaware of the enmeshing glyphs.

I cried out but they heard me not. In despair, I uttered a prayer to the Empyrean asking for deliverance, and a light appeared, so strong as to shine through the bars, revealing them to be insubstantial and unreal, a mere illusion. They melted away and I stepped forward into the light, where I saw a shadowy silhouette of a robed man awaiting my approach.

I then awoke to the sun-filled bedroom as a chirurgeon bent low over me, testing my brow for signs of fever. There were none. Awake now, I requested paper and pen, and so recorded this account. I know not whether my dream was fever-induced or visionary, but I must admit that it matters not to me at this time. I have returned to the hearth of my uncle's regard, from which I traveled far, and have been welcomed home. Even though my feet shall wander again, my heart shall ever have a place here.

All For One

"And as the stars shine in their multitudes and yet are aspects of the One Flame, so are you now a multitude who are one — angerak mates! Friends until death claims you. Loyal to one another beyond all other ties. Only three oaths are more binding: those to the Pancreator, to the Emperor and to your liege lords. So it is ordained in the Empyrean as well as the Gray Realms of our bodied existence.

"Where before you had but six limbs to devote, now you have 26. Never turn one against the other, but instead clasp them together. Combined, you are mighty. Use your strength of brotherhood to lift great weights from your own souls and those of others who are weak and alone. You shall never be lonely again, for your souls are one even though your spirits be many.

"Clasp hands and walk together into the Light!"

And so we did. Onganggarak led us as we stood in a circle, backs to one another, holding hands as we moved as a group from the shadows of the cathedral into the shaft of light descending from the apex. I blinked as its intensity hit my eyes, and also to hide my tears of pride.

Ong howled in joy and tugged Erian and I toward him, gripping us in a gentle but encompassing hug. Julia, clinging to my left hand, stumbled as I was drawn in, tugging her forward. Sanjuk, clasped to her, also stepped up, as did Cardanzo, holding to her left hand as his left held Erian's right. Erian completed the circle with her left hand clasped to Ong.

The burly Vorox released us and leapt amidst us, hugging the others now as they released their holds on one another. I clapped and the others followed my lead.

Howls and bellows erupted all around us as Count Galagadang's

Vorox angerak cheered the union. The count himself laughed heartily from the dais, standing beside Philosophus Wing San-chi, who smiled as he closed the book from which he had read the Angerakaal, the ceremony of adult bonding for civilized Vorox, as devised by Archbishop Man-shao centuries ago.

It was a profound honor that Onganggarak had asked us to be his angerak, his bond mates in the most sacred oath a Vorox can make. We had traveled before with a similar privilege, as his angruwa, or closest friends. But now he formalized that bond and made it greater and permanent. An adult Vorox's angwal, or adult bond, is his most important, the one which will last the rest of his life. His asking us to be part of this bond is a sign of his complete trust and loyalty to us — incredibly rare among humans. How could we refuse?

I looked at Erian and knew that this meant a great deal to her. She had traveled far with Ong and had come to trust him greatly; many times had he saved each of our lives. What's more, she had no vassals but us. For Ong to request this of her was the best of compliments and confirmation of her leadership abilities.

Not all Li Halan — or Known Worlders for that matter — see it as such. To them, this union would surely be considered a joke, a barbaric custom that should have been ended long ago. They understand little of the strength and power the angerak holds for a Vorox. Although it is but a formal ceremony for us, for Ong it is the tying of his soul to ours. I must strive to respect that with all my being. I owe him no less.

As I write this account in the evening, full of food and wine after the feast Ong provided us, I think back on when we met this unique friend.

Was it really five years ago? We had come to Ungavorox seeking Captain Maria Sao-Lui Li Halan, an officer who had once loyally served Erian's father. She had heard of Erian's disenfranchisement and her brother's enmity, and sent word that she was safeguarding an heirloom that had belonged to Erian's mother. She had instructions to carry it until the day Erian would need it. That day, she told Erian in her message, had come.

Erian, Cardanzo, Julia and I came to Ungavorox in the Hardball, an explorer lent us by Charioteer Director Hendrix on Midian. Actually, he had contracted its use to Julia for certain specified mercantile operations. Ungavorox was not one of the specified destinations. However, we assumed our trip would be short enough that our scheduled trip to Criticorum would not be long delayed. Additionally, Julia's planned purchase of rare Ungavoroxian spices might even prove profitable.

We did not intend to get shot from the sky. As we approached the planet, a pirate vessel assailed us, damaging our maneuver jets. Julia managed to evade them and brought us in for a landing. Unfortunately, it was in the wild jungles, far from our destination of New Kowloon.

Everyone is raised with horror stories about the dangers that Ungavorox's jungles contain. Indeed, even breathing on the world can prove hazardous, as spores and insects lodge themselves in your breathing passages uninvited. Or so we'd heard. That last was exaggerated, but the dangers of predatory plants and animals were quite real.

As we disembarked to examine the damage to our small ship, we each wore breathers and full suits, too paranoid to touch anything. That's when we discovered that the ship was slowly sinking into some primordial mud from which I could not even dislodge the stick I had used to prod it.

Julia and Erian began arguing. Erian was convinced we'd lost our ship and would have to walk through who knew how many kilometers of jungle to reach even an outpost of civilization.

That's when the sharprats attacked.

Or they would have had it not been for Onganggarak. The Vorox's timely arrival to investigate the downed ship saved us from the beasts' assault. He had crept through the spiky grass and surprised their leader before we even realized we weren't alone. The other beasts squealed in surprise and ran back to their den, while Ong casually wiped his bloody glankesh sword on the blades of grass and introduced himself most eloquently to my lady: "What brings a fine lady like you to a swamp like this?"

The well-chosen words and humor were so incongruous I think we all stared in shock and surprise for a moment while Ong's smile (showing no teeth) grew the wider. He knew he had scored one on us.

After introductions, he offered to help us prevent our ship from succumbing to the dagmush — this mud wasn't mud at all, but a lifeform intent on slowly digesting our hull. He disappeared for a time into the jungle and came back with massive loops of thick vine that resembled hopelessly tangled spider webs wound into a single line. He tied the vines to our ship's cone and then, with Cardanzo's help, tied the other ends to a nearby tree. This, he assured us, would keep the ship from sinking further while we repaired the engines.

As we waited for Julia to fix the damage (only she knew how to tinker with the arcane materials), we spoke at length with our unusual guest. By strange happenstance, he knew of Captain Maria Sao-Lui and could lead us to her in New Kowloon. He was himself a householder for Baron Emilio Cesarus Li Halan, a local lord serving as a liaison between certain Vorox lords and the court of Prince Flavius on Kish. Onganggarak, or Ong as we came to know him, had recently been serving as a go-between for his lord and a group of nomadic ferals who had moved into the wilds adjacent to the lord's fief.

What we did not learn until later was that he was not yet an adult, and had thus not chosen his angwal, or adult angerak. While he pretended that this did not bother him, it was clear that he was lonely. Otherwise, it is doubtful he would have been so friendly to strangers such as us.

It did not take Julia long to patch systems well enough to launch us to New Kowloon, where more extensive repairs could take place. Ong agreed to accompany us, for his lord was visiting the city and he could make a report on his recent time among the ferals in person. First, however, he introduced us to Captain Maria Sao-Lui, who commanded the garrison of Li Halan troops protecting the city.

She spent the next few days reminiscing with Erian about her family, and her mother especially. The details of their talks do not concern my account here. I spent the time with Ong, for he proved an excellent guide of the city. I accompanied him as he reported to his liege, and in doing so raised the curiosity of Baron Cesarus.

He had heard of my lady and her troubles, and after a long tea ceremony, confided in me that the pirates who attacked our vessel were not mere raiders. They were agents of a certain Baron Cornado Li Halan, an ally to Erian's brother. Baron Cesarus knew for a fact that Cornado sought to capture and deliver Erian back to her brother, where he could keep her in sight.

At the mention of Cornado, Onganggarak growled low and menacing — the first such sign of his bestial instincts I had yet encountered. It unnerved me greatly, and he was immediately apologetic and ashamed. Baron Cesarus asked Ong to leave us, and then explained to me that Cornado was Ong's original lord.

"He captured Ong as a cub in the deep wilds," the baron explained. "He treated him brutally in a crude attempt to civilize the young feral. I was ashamed to witness it, for I feel that the manner in which the Li Halan treat the Vorox reflects on our soul mirrors. If our own compassion is tarnished, then so will be the Pancreator's compassion towards us.

"I made my disdain clear to Baron Cornado and he challenged me to a duel. It was an uneven match, for he was a renowned fencer and I was but a diplomat with only the barest of formal sword training. Nonetheless, the Pancreator intervened and won me the day when Cornado's foot slipped on a patch of zrux slime and he fell right onto my blade, awarding me first blood.

"Our terms, however, were not simply for honor. I demanded aforehand that, should I win, he would transfer Onganggarak to me. Cornado angrily allowed the transfer of loyalties before the gathered group of nobles and priests, and stormed away. I am sure the man stills bears a grudge, but one directed more against Ong than me."

He sighed and sipped his tea before speaking again. "I have become quite fond of Onganggarak. He is a model example of what his race can achieve in their climb from savagery. I shall now reveal my reason for relaying this tale to you: I would ask your lady if she will allow Ong to accompany her off-world, to remove him from Baron Cornado's ire. He can offer in return his loyalty and protection, should Cornado pursue her further. Ong would be a great aid in anticipating Cornado's tactics, for he knows him well.

"Onganggarak's angwal, his adulthood ceremony, is still a year away. In return for transferring his fealty to your lady, I request that she become angruwa to him, a companion and sister, teaching him of the human worlds while he protects her from her brother's assassins."

I thought the idea most interesting, for I had come to like Ong greatly. I told the baron that I would propose his idea to my lady. She, of course, readily agreed. She had also come to enjoy Ong's company, and felt that any ally she could gain against her brother was a good one.

Captain Maria Sao-Lui admitted that she knew Baron Cesarus to be an honorable man, but knew little of Cornado. "One would at first suspect Cesarus's reasons for surrendering a valuable vassal, but he surely cannot intend Ong to be a spy; the angruwa bond would provide too great a conflict of interest. Vorox take such oaths most seriously. Perhaps it is truly the case that he cares for Ong and wishes to remove him from Cornado's vengeance."

Only now do I realize other reasons Baron Cesarus had. I knew too little of Vorox then, but I now understand the tragedy of Ong's early life. Over the years I have been able to learn from him, as he has been ready to tell it, his true story.

He was not taken from the jungle as a raw cub but as a youth who had already undergone his kabaljal and angerakaal. His angerak mates, who had grown up with him from infancy, were killed in a battle between Li Halan and Decados forces for control of a patch of land. This was during the later years of the Emperor Wars, when the fighting was at its fiercest and most meaningless, with forces opposing one another less for tactical reasons than as retaliation for past losses.

Only Ong survived the conflagration that swept the jungle, but he was caught and caged by Baron Cornado, who decided to make Ong a model example for his own ideas on how his house should conduct the Vorox civilizing process.

He was only with Cornado for a few months, but they were enough to scar him deeply. Only Baron Cesarus's kind and disciplined rule calmed him, and this only after he escaped and attempted to rejoin his feral tribe. They would not have him, however, suspecting that he was a civilized spy, and they threw him out. Dejected, with no tribe or angerak, he returned to the only place he even remotely associated with home. The baron forgave his leaving and raised him well, teaching him letters and good speech. Over time, Ong learned to control his wild manners even better than others of his kind.

And so he came to join our company. I think back on the happenstance that delivered him to us at our time of need in the jungle and marvel at where it has brought us today. The odds that such a boon friend could be met in such a manner are staggering, enough to throw doubt on the existence of coincidence in favor of a more ordered matrix to our meeting.

I am told that a Vorox who loses his angerak is a terrible creature, alone forever. And yet, Ong has overcome any instinctual depression and built his life anew along human principles. Perhaps he is less than a true Vorox because of it, but he is fully a part of our group. Indeed, after this evening, we are also a part of him.

He is no longer alone.

Ghost Stories

"You, priest, surely you've heard worse tales," said the man with a scar descending down the length of his left cheek, its chalk-white, puckered trail reaching to his neck. His eyes bored into me, seeking both a challenge and an answer to his hopes.

I cleared my throat. "Oh, yes. Far worse."

Cardanzo, sitting to my left, smiled and sipped his beer, and Sanjuk, to my right, raised an eyebrow. The scarred man, one Lt. Harbald Drax of the Muster, leaned across the table, attentive.

"Do tell, friar," he said, his eyes still on me as he motioned behind him to his comrades, summoning them over. I took a sip of beer myself as I waited for the mercenaries to pull up chairs, each of them eyeing me suspiciously.

Once they had settled, I put my mug down and stared intently at the wood grain of the table, as if seeing some augury there.

"It was dark that night on Midian during the crop-gathering season. Peng-Lai, the Woman in the Moon, did not come out that night to play her lyre. Only torches lit the edge of the lake where the men gathered to administer justice...."

The room grew quiet as ears turned to listen attentively. Smoke from a dozen different weeds from half as many worlds floated over our heads, misting the wan light from the lanterns hung by each table. The room was full of silhouettes, with few features discernable from over an arm's length away.

"Their captive struggled against his bonds, but they were drawn tight about him and made of strong-threaded hemp. If he could only reach his wireblade, he would be free. But his weapon, along with the rest of his devil's gear, had been taken from him, distributed among the vigilantes who carried him, kicking all the way, to the lake's edge.

"The old headman, leader of the village gang, turned from the dark waters and regarded the captive. He nodded to the men and they began wrapping more cord around the bound man, these ones tied with stones and rocks of varied sizes.

"The captive, frantically trying to dislodge the stones, cried out to his accusers: 'This is illegal! I demand you cease immediately and free me! How dare you even lay hands upon me! When my family discovers your crime, you shall all be killed, and your children sold into slavery!'

"The old man looked on, no emotion on his face. 'I reckon it's no worse than what you'd do to us if we didn't take justice into our own hands. You're an evil man, Baron Michaelo. The Pancreator will judge what's wrong and right here.'

"'You have no proof for your accusations!' the criminal cried.

"'Don't need it. This ain't no Reeves' court. You killed them children with this here Republican sword,' he said as he held out the criminal's wireblade hilt, 'and carved horrible symbols and signs into their flesh before dumping them into the lake. I don't know who you tried to sell their souls to, but I tell you they are the Pancreator's children — they're in a better place now, not that hell you intended for them.'

"The criminal quit his struggling and an ugly grin stretched across his face. 'Do you know what I wrote into their skin, old fool? Compacts and deals, sealed with blood. Agreements that cannot be broken by your petty justice. Do what you will to me. I shall wreak my vengeance upon all of you one by one. Your own avarice shall be your undoing!'

"'Throw him in!' the old man yelled, and the vigilantes lifted the criminal — writhing in their grasp — and flung him into the lake. The stones quickly dragged him into the dark depths. A few air bubbled broke the surface but their coming eventually slowed and finally stopped.

"The men dragged their tired bodies to the nearby village and each returned home, lighting a small candle to burn through the rest of the night.

"Over the coming weeks, the village returned to normal. What children still lived were allowed to play outdoors once more. With each day, they were allowed to roam farther and farther from their parents' sight, until they once more played like all children do, roaming far and wide over the nearby hills and dales.

"But it was not the children the villagers had need to fear for. All those men who had participated in the murder of Baron Michaelo came to calamity, one by one. First, there was the butcher. He had kept the baron's fine hunting dagger for his own, and used it to skin what deer others brought to him for preparation. One day, while skinning an ontagont with the knife, he slit his own throat with one well-determined swipe. Others soon found him, his blood mixed on the floor with the split innards of his butchered animals. They assumed it was suicide, anguish over his lost child.

"Next, however, died the tanner. He had kept for himself bottles of the powerful beverage the baron carried with him, a vintage from some far world none knew where. He used such bever to console his guilty soul on the many nights that had passed since he had helped to throw the baron into his watery grave. One night, he drank three whole bottles. His wife found his body, and the local apothecary discovered that one of the bottles held not wine but sweetened poison from the glands of a vicious Ungavoroxian beast.

"More vigilantes soon died, each helped along by some item pilfered from the dead baron: his synthsilk rope used to hang the wrangler, his travel rations to choke the baker, his velvet cape to smother the weaver. Soon, the only one left alive from that night was the headman who had personally condemned the baron.

"He fled the village, believing it to be cursed and haunted, and took to the hospitality of his family in the city. Surely here, far from that damned lake, he could escape his fellows' grisly fate.

"Among his gear was an item of great worth, one he meant to sell once he reached the city, for it would make him rich for the rest of his days. After his cousins showed him his room, he curled up on the bed, exhausted after the long ride. He clutched his treasure in his hands, fearing that his own family would pilfer his bags seeking loot. Nothing would prevent his selling the thing on the morrow.

"He awoke as the sun crept through his window, casting its accusing light upon his eyes. He stretched and yawned and immediately doubled up in pain. He stared at his body and the blood welling up over the bed sheets — his nightclothes torn to shreds, deep, precise cuts all over his skin. His body was laced with symbols and images arcane and unholy, not unlike those the baron had carved upon his young victims.

"The headman stared aghast at the unreadable text of his flesh and groaned as his sight fell upon his hand, which he now realized still clutched the treasure he had so passionately guarded before falling into sleep. He moaned in horror and released the hilt of the wireblade. It slipped from the bed and rolled across the floor, coming to rest in the corner of the room.

"He leapt from the room and ran into the streets, screaming for a priest, for a healer, for anyone who could save his soul flame. A trail of blood followed him, for his wounds could not seal — so perfect had been their cutting, there was no edge where flesh could adhere to flesh. He died by the time he reached the next block, his blood having run completely from him.

"The Church authorities were summoned to investigate. Upon seeing the flesh glyphs, they scoured the headman's gear, searching for any signs of the man's killer. They found the wireblade on the floor, and recognized the crest carved into its pommel.

"Three days later, a young Eskatonic investigator called upon the Michaelo mansion and was greeted by a servant. Led into a vast library, he waited only a few minutes before the baron arrived, fresh from his lunch, its strong smell pervading his clothes. The noble apologized for his appearance, claiming to have suffered a long illness that caused his flesh to become pasty white and his skin to heal wounds but slowly.

"The Eskatonic, nauseous from the smell, produced the wireblade and asked if it were his. The baron claimed it, and said he had lost it when his boat capsized in a lake to the south, well over two seasons ago. He had thought it long gone beyond his reach.

"The priest, too sick to interview the man much longer, forgot the urgency of his mission in his desire to once more breath fresh air. He bid the baron farewell, found his own way out, and mounted his horse in the courtyard.

"'If there's one thing I cannot abide,' he said to his horse, 'it's the smell of dead fish.' He then rode back to the city and went about his daily prayers, thinking no more upon the matter."

I sat back and took a long sip of my beer, watching the faces of those who leaned near.

Scarface crinkled his brow in thought. "What happened then?"

I shrugged. "I don't know. I heard this tale when I was a young novitiate on Midian. Priests in my order swore that the baron still existed in his mansion and sometimes rode out at night on missions of retribution against any serf who dared to stand against the nobility."

One of the mercenaries spoke up. "I don't buy it. It's too much like a morality tale. Keeps the peasants in line." Others grunted assent.

A smallish mercenary, older than the others and sitting in a booth against the far wall, spoke: "I've seen him. This Baron Michaelo. I worked for him once. It's true — his flesh stank of the rotten sea."

The mercenaries grew silent. "Yeah? Doesn't have to mean he was a warlock. Maybe he had a remote control for the wireblade, so he could operate it at a distance to chop that guy up."

The old merc leaned forward: "What about the rest of his stuff? You think his knife and cloak were remote-controlled, too? There's things out there no guild scientist can name, boys, and it'll get us all in the end."

Scarface smiled and guffawed. "Ah, it's just a ghost story, colonel. It don't mean nothing. Just a story to scare good folk is all. Might work on peasants, but not toughs like us. Right, guys?"

"Gehenne, no!" one merc yelled, and another added: "You gotta try harder than that to get us, priest!"

The mercs got up and went back to their tables, scattering again into small groups. Scarface looked at me. "Good try, friar. But next time add a haunted starship or something. You know, something that could actually happen!" He stood and stumbled to the bar, bellowing for a refill.

Cardanzo looked at me. "Was the story true?"

"I really don't know. But I do know one thing: I still can't stand the smell of dead fish."

Witness

Erian Li Halan and I walked through the Resplendent Dew Gardens, both of us amazed at its marvels. Sculpted hedges mimicked animals from across the Known Worlds — mastopliants from Artemis, gorduvants from Grail and even a pod of leaping slu'meevee from Madoc. In some areas of the vast estate, the leafy creatures growing from the ground had existed only in legend, such as the mastadon, a folk monster of old Urth.

"Fascinating," Erian said, stopping to stare off the path at a collection of pack animals made almost real by the well-sculpted hedges. It helped that we walked in the late evening, when silhouettes shadowed mundane details, helping to evoke the myth of form. "They are exact duplicates of the maned wolf hedges on my father's estate."

I looked at them but they were unfamiliar to me. "I have visited that place many times and I do not recognize them."

"They hunted only in the family's private garden, off limits to those not of the immediate blood. I wonder how they came to inhabit this place, so far away from their home."

"I understand that often Li Halan ambassadors who are placed here to serve the Imperial Court bring with them tokens from their own lands, to ease the pain of separation. Perhaps one such ambassador once knew of your family's gardens and sought to imitate them here."

"Perhaps," Erian said, moving on. The path curved to the left and revealed an open lawn sparkling with many miniature ponds and tiny streams, each crossed by tiny bridges. "And yet, I still wonder. Those wolves bring back ill memories. A strange event in the garden, when I was… oh, I must have been no more than nine years old."

I listened quietly. I knew my lady well enough to realize that she needed to reminisce aloud without interruption.

"My father held a party. I'm not sure why. There were always parties for one reason or another, either ours or someone else's, where we children were taken off to distant estates and left alone with our nannies while the adults socialized in grand ballrooms or serene pavilions.

"This one was different, for it seemed more celebratory. I think it was my grandmother's birthday, perhaps? Or some other important anniversary of her's worth celebrating. My Uncle Vicardo was there."

I frowned, but knew Erian did not see my expression, for I still walked behind her. I knew the name. And the rumors of his demise. This memory was becoming familiar to me, also.

"We don't talk about him much, today. He was said to have been involved in… revolutionary thoughts and deeds.

For a long time, I didn't understand what they were. I heard the rumors and gossip, of course. Most people believe he was involved in some sort of pro-Republican conspiracy, an attempt to place someone on the Imperial throne who would then declare a Third Republic. Of course, this was in the middle of the early Emperor Wars, so such plotting was perhaps even more dangerous than usual."

We stepped over a stream and entered a grove, ringed with Urthish yew trees. In the center was a small plinth with ancient markings, long worn by harsh weather. I suspected it had come here from its original home — wherever that was — already in its present state. These gardens saw much rain, but were protected by ancient Second Republic nanotech filters, wondrous devices that ionized the dangerous particles of Byzantium Secundus's acidic rain.

Erian placed a hand on the monument, contemplating for a moment its origin and possible meaning, and then sat down on its ledge.

"There were famous men and women from all over Midian there that night," she said, continuing her story. "Even some from other worlds. I recognized a few: Duke Shou Zan, the famous general, and

Countess Sa, considered practically a saint even then. Others, too, most of whom I do not remember.

"As usual, I was ushered in to stand nearby as the guests came, part of the illustrious host's shining family. I was not to speak or even murmur, but to stand straight and smile always. Once this was over, I was taken back to my rooms and not allowed to see the goings-on. However, this was our estate, not that of a stranger, so I knew well how to sneak away from my vigilant nanny and spy on the socialites from the top of banisters. I even knew a few hidey holes once designed for our family's secret guard.

"But I quickly became bored with watching people bow and smile and speak venomous lies to one another in honeyed words. Even then, I could recognize the cruelty of the court. My brother, old enough to stand by my father's elbow but still too young to be allowed to speak to guests, saw me on the stairs and scowled. Fearful he would report me, I slipped away into the garden and played in the groves and streams while the sounds of conversation could be heard over the walls from all directions.

"I heard voices approach from nearby, and wondered who would be walking in the private gardens, one of the few places forbidden to guests this night. I crept through the underbrush to get a peek and saw my Uncle Vicardo walking and talking in whispers with a courtesan. They giggled now and then.

"Too young to enjoy such voyeurism, I began to crawl away when I heard a sharp intake of breath behind me, the sound of someone startled and in fear — too afraid to even scream. I crept back and saw a robed figure standing before the couple. He wore a large hood and a mask underneath it, and had apparently stepped from out of the hedges across from me. The maned wolf hedges.

"He spoke: 'Baron Vicardo Chou Ssu Li Halan, you are guilty of conspiring against the prince!'

"Poor uncle stammered, deathly afraid, 'No!' he cried, 'You don't understand!'

"The hooded, masked figure drew a rapier and said, 'I understand too well!'

"He then stepped forward in a flash and thrust his sword at my uncle. But instead of poor uncle, his blade pierced the courtesan. She had leapt to save uncle and took the blow meant for him. Uncle Vicardo stood staring at her with horror, and she choked out a final message before dying on the end of the blade: 'Remember the dream that was our ancestors'!'

"The masked assailant seemed confused, as if he had not expected this. He acted very much unlike an ominous and sinister force, and withdrew his blade almost lovingly, as if he feared to stain the dead girl's dress. I was deathly silent. I don't think I even breathed.

"My uncle bent down to cradle her in his arms. 'It does not matter now,' he said. 'My dream is dead. Do with me what you will.'

"The masked man seemed to think a while and then acted swiftly: He stabbed my grieving uncle through the heart. He died without a sound.

"I must have then gasped or cried out, because the masked figure wheeled and stared at me, crouched on my hands and knees under the hedges. He (or she? I am still unsure) did not seem to know what to do. That's when my nanny arrived. She gasped and took in the situation immediately. She waved her hands at the masked one, as if warding him from me. Even in my terror, I almost giggled at the odd gesticulations she made, so unusual for my prim and proper nanny.

"But the masked figure bowed to her and then slipped back into the maned wolf hedges from where he had come. Nanny grabbed my hand and hauled me up, dragging me painfully back to my rooms by a route I'd never seen before or since. Once there, she harangued me viciously, making me swear never to tell a soul what I had seen on threat of death for the both of us. I began to cry.

"She went to her locked cabinet and withdrew a large chocolate bar, the kind I was only ever allowed to eat on birthdays. She hushed me and fed me sweets the rest of the night until I fell asleep. I knew by that gesture alone that what had happened was truly important and that my silence was equally important. Nanny never broke the no-sweets rule. Until that night. She never broke it again. Even today, I associate sweets with conspiracy."

I had been standing quietly and respectfully throughout all of this, but now felt the need to speak.

"I have heard of your uncle. Many people have. A jealous lover was said to have killed him. Others, however, whispered that the Hidden Martyrs took him. I see now that the latter version is the truth."

Erian looked at me but I could not read her expression in the darkness. "I only discovered that years later, after learning about the Hidden Martyrs and their ways. I often think about my poor uncle and the crime he had been accused of. Perhaps he was a pro-Republican, but if so, it was for love. When his love died, so died his ideals. He quickly followed them into death."

I nodded and sat down next to her. "And why do you tell me this now?"

Erian sighed. "I don't really know. Absolution, maybe? I have carried this with me for so long."

"Carried what?" I said. "You could have done nothing."

"No. Untrue. I could have cried out and brought guards or guests running. I could have saved my uncle, maybe even his lover."

"And what then? You would have been watched by the Hidden Martyrs for the rest of your life, if not killed by them."

"How are you so sure they don't watch me now?"

"I'm not, but rumors says they work mainly within the Garden Worlds, rarely without. It has been a long time since we were home."

"Yes, but my brother will surely have tried to contact them and turn them against me."

"I suspect that, if that were true, you would have seen them already. They may be fanatics, but they surely aren't so foolish as to follow your brother's twisted crusade against you."

I saw her smile; I could tell by the glint of her teeth in the moonlight.

"I hope you are correct." She stood and smoothed her cape. "So, my confessor: I have told you my crime. What is my penance?"

I leaned back and look up at the sky. The stars were dim, clouded by the screen of nanites above our heads. "You are to pray to the Pancreator for solace each night of the coming week at the hour in which you witnessed your uncle's murder. Thenceforth, do not remain silent when witnessing crimes, but speak out and rectify them. The little girl you once were could do nothing; let her forced inaction be a lesson for you to act upon your own will at all times."

"I shall do so," she said, head bowed. When she lifted it, I could see her smile again.

"Come, Alustro. We have walked too long alone in the garden. Let us join the others and be joyous!" She stepped out of the grove and headed back to the manse, where the rest of our crew were resting, waiting for us to return.

I followed behind her, glad to witness the bold steps she took as she sallied forth into her future, away from her past.

Volume Three: Illuminatus

Aeolus Solaris

It's not easy to think straight with a gun pointed at your head.

My every muscle was tense, holding me perfectly still — but for a quivering in my legs — as the Inquisitor's right arm circled my neck while his left held a slug gun to my temple.

His attention, however, was focused not on me — except, perhaps, for a taut awareness of any movement I might make — but instead on my liege, Lady Erian Li Halan, who stood glaring at him with iron determination, her unwavering rapier poised to pierce his ribs. This standoff had already lasted nearly a minute, with no word spoken or gesture exchanged. Only their glared intent communicated the coiled conflict ready to burst forth at the slightest move any made.

Caranzo, Erian's bodyguard, began to slowly — almost imperceptibly — move to my left, but then halted at what was surely some sign of recognition from my captor, perhaps a flick of the eye or tilt of the head. I couldn't see it from my vantage.

I tried not to notice the subtle checks and counterchecks being made around me. I instead attempted to pray. As I said, it is hard to collect one's thoughts when a cold steel gun barrel is impressed upon one's temple. Nonetheless, I endeavored for a moment to let go of the world and open myself to the Pancreator's grace, silently reciting the litanies that had been so assiduously taught me in theurgic seminary.

It was not easy. The rite I attempted normally required that I recite the litany aloud, accompanied by a series of gestures. Without these components, the proper enactment of the rite was not assured.

As the cadence of the rhyme culminated, I released my internal, mystical flame with an exhalation of breath — so slight I hoped it would not garner the attention of my too-attentive host. With the rising and release of the flame, the rite was complete. As I felt the buoyant, airy jacket of divine protection wreath me, I lunged forward and away from the gun.

It fired. The bullet sparked against the immaterial field of force that surrounded me, ricocheting across the room. The Inquisitor's arm released me and I ran forward as fast as I could, escaping any further attempts to snare me.

I turned and saw the robed fanatic crumple to the floor, Erian's rapier buried to the hilt in his torso. He had released me only because his arms had become too weak to hold me, robbed of vitality by the sword thrust into his heart.

I said a prayer for his departing soul, hoping that its light found its way back to the Empyrean. I feared, however, that the weight of its own anger and intolerance would keep it mired in this universe, a ghost hungry for both vengeance and release.

I drew the sign of the jumpgate in the air, thanking the Pancreator for his grace and the theurgic secrets that had protected me from harm.

"Are you all right?" Erian asked, looking at me with some concern as she withdrew her rapier, now slick with the Inquisitor's blood.

I nodded. "Yes. You don't need to worry about me. I'm sorry I let that happen."

"Don't be," Cardanzo said, moving past us to examine the passageway from which the Inquisitor had come. "He was quick. But I don't see any more of them. If he had companions, they're somewhere else in the complex."

"Then we shouldn't waste any more time," Erian said, heading to the passageway. "The sooner we reach the control room, the quicker this ends."

Cardanzo slipped into the darkness ahead of her and she followed. I fell in behind them, feeling my way along the dark walls, following the faint sounds of their footsteps and breathing. I felt safer now, cloaked in grace, but knew it was no guarantee that we would survive this foray into the past.

A faint light came from somewhere ahead, from down a side passage. We followed it. It soon led us to a circular room lined with glass windows, now empty of any electric life. The glow came from a weak everlight hung from the ceiling, an orb set to burn a millennium ago by its Second Republic makers. It still performed that duty, lighting the room enough for us to see the desks and control panels that promised access to the think machine entity buried beneath the complex.

Two other passageways led from the room, each into more darkness.

Erian spoke into her whisper pin. "Julia? I think we found it. Can you backtrack and follow our scent here?"

I couldn't hear the response; the speaker was hidden in her ear, its words whispered only for her.

She nodded. "Okay. Don't be surprised at the body." She then looked at Cardanzo and I. "They're coming. Ong should have no trouble picking up our scent."

"I can't figure out how to restore the power," Cardanzo said "It may mean going down into the generator."

"We don't have time for that," Erian said in exasperation. "Besides, that's probably where the rest of the robes are. Let's hope Julia can figure it out from here."

By "robes," I knew she meant more Inquisitors. I looked around the room, hoping to find something I could do here. Until the think machine's power was restored, however, I had nothing to lend.

The rest of our crew arrived within 15 minutes. Onggangarak was the first into the room. He had traveled the low-ceilinged passageway on all sixes, but stood on two legs at his full 10-foot height once he entered the room. The Vorox nodded and bowed to Lady Erian as he did so.

He was immediately followed by Julia Abrams, who simply nodded at all of us and immediately got to work examining the terminals, her tools already in her hands. As a member of the Charioteers Guild, she was qualified to operate and repair all manner of high-tech devices.

Entering behind them a few minutes later was Sanjuk oj Kaval. An Ur-Ukar, she could navigate the darkness better than most of us, for she had spent the first years of her life in the dark caverns of Kordeth. "I think there's someone coming," she said. "I'll go back and find out who."

Erian nodded to Ong, who dropped once more to six legs and started to follow Sanjuk. The Ukari stopped and shook her head at him. "You're too big. There's no way they won't hear you in these halls."

Ong turned to Erian again. She nodded and motioned to another corridor. "Perhaps you'd best keep watch on one of the other passages." He was there in seconds, disappearing into the darkness. I turned to watch Sanjuk again, but she was already gone.

"Got it," Julia said matter-of-factly. "The circuit breaker was hidden under this panel. Give it a few seconds and the power should start cycling."

Almost immediately, lights began to flicker and glow across the panels, and the glass screens flared with life. We could see passages displayed on the some of the screens, places we had been and others I didn't recognize. On one screen, the darkness was filled with a glowing red bulk, an odd shambling shape. "What is that?" I asked, my voice displaying perhaps too much of my nervousness.

Everyone looked concerned at the image until Julia laughed. Her chuckle was a strange thing here, echoing through the dusty chamber. "It's Ong," she said. "That's an IR camera. It's watching his passageway." She motioned to the passageway Ong had gone down. "At least we can keep an eye on him, in case anything happens."

"All right," Erian said. "Let's get to work. Can you bring up Doramos's files?"

Julia sat down at one of the swivel chairs and began typing at one of the terminals. "Let's see... It shouldn't be too hard. I mean, this place was meant to monitor his work, after all."

"Yes," I said, "but the files we want won't be so obvious. If they were, they would have been distributed in some other cache or datafile before now."

"Well, c'mere then," Julia said. "A lot of this is in Latin, and I can't read it."

I came and looked over her shoulder at the file names. I was no stranger to data libraries — the Church maintained quite a number of its own — but this one seemed unique, designed to baffle the casual reader. File names were in Latin, with ostentatious titles — clearly codewords of some kind or other. We didn't have all day to decipher them.

"Alustro," Erian said. "Sanjuk tells me there are five more Inquisitors in the first foyer. If they follow our trail, they'll be here within 10 minutes."

"I understand," I said. I had to figure out Doramos's codewords in a scant few minutes — surely impossible; no other Second Republic figure was so arcane as Doramos, the World Architect whose terraforming skills had reshaped the Known Worlds. Here, in a long-lost complex buried beneath Pentatuech's Megiddo Desert, he had hidden a number of important files, keys to his methodology that any guilder — or Eskatonic priest, for that matter — would surely contemplate murder to get. That's why the Inquisition, who followed the same leads we had, were out to prevent anyone from finding it. Their irrational hatred of technology extended even to the work of a man the Republican patriarchs considered to be a saint. They would kill to ensure that nobody got it.

I had to get back to basics, review what cosmology Doramos had worked from, and hope to find a clue there to his naming conventions. We couldn't open every file, hoping to find the one out of hundreds that we needed. Julia was awakening them as fast as she could, only to discover simple and well-known terraforming programs (well-known within those technical schools, that is; rare elsewhere); we couldn't waste our time with them.

I knew that Doramos had used codes based on the Omega Gospels, the collected sayings and stories by and about the Prophet and his disciples. The file we searched for promised — according to all the sources we had followed — to reveal some of the secrets of Pentateuch's wild weather patterns. Hence, a title displaying some weather event from the Omega Gospels would be most appropriate.

I asked Julia to engage another monitor, so I could perform a separate search. She lit the one next to me and I scanned its file name list. There — about half way down: "Aeolus Solaris." It was from Paulus IX, the chapters concerning Saint Paulus, the Prophet's starship pilot. The Divine Starwind, the invisible wind that blows through the void, enlightening the wise, guiding the lost and damning the sinful.

I awakened the file and read the Latin text — a whole tome hidden in electric pathways. "This is it," I said. "It must be. There are words I don't understand, but it's definitely meteorological."

"Which one?" Julia asked. I told her its title and within seconds she had a data-crystal copy in her hand. "Let's go."

Ong suddenly burst into the room, panting hard. "Golems! Coming this way!"

Erian looked confused, staring at the monitor that watched his passageway; it was blank. "I don't see anything."

Ong growled. "They're coming! They shot at me!"

"They've probably got IR baffling," Julia said, heading for the passageway we had arrived from, pulling Erian with her. "The camera won't read them."

Cardanzo motioned me to go first and then fell in behind me, with Ong guarding our rear. We didn't even shut down the machines.

"Go right!" Julia yelled.

"But that's not where we came from," I said, barely able to see their moving figures in the dim light that now receded behind us.

"Sanjuk says the Inquisitors are almost here; she advices going right," Julia yelled back.

I followed. We made two more turns, leaving me not only in the dark but completely lost. I jumped when something brushed past me, only to breathe a sigh of relief when I realized it was Sanjuk.

She tsked and whispered: "All too blind. I'll have to teach you some dark steps, so you don't trip over yourself."

"Where are they?" Erian whispered to her.

"Behind us. They're heading for the control room." A distant blaster shot echoed its way to us. "And I guess they've found Ong's golems."

"How appropriate," Erian said. "Let's use the diversion to get out of here."

"This way," Sanjuk said, moving past Erian and Julia to lead us through the darkness. She had spent much of our time here mapping passageways; I was amazed how quickly she had come to know them. A true Scravers Guilder.

As we moved on, the roar of slug guns joined the high-pitched whine of blaster fire. I didn't know whose weapons were which, but I certainly did not want to confront Second Republic-era Protector class golems to find out. It was ironic that those who hated technology were now confronting its vanguard.

I said a prayer for them and hoped that, if they survived, they would gain a bit more respect and awe for the works of our ancestors, and not so quickly move to destroy things that could fight back.

We had our treasure, our datafile. Our patron would be glad to get it, and his rewards would fund our passage onwards through the stars, ever seeking the culmination of Erian's quest, delivered in a vision by the Gargoyle of Nowhere. A quest whose very goal is still unknown to us but whose shape is constantly revealed in clues and mysteries as we seek it out, buoyed and buffeted by the Aeolus Solaris.

On Wings of Prophecy

Spacestation Cumulus, April 15, 5003 (Urthish calendar)

"You there! Priest! Have you seen the Twisted Man?"

I recoiled from the snarling face and the frap stick the man so carelessly swung, which caused even his own mob to shy away from him. He was unshaved and unbathed — a not unusual condition for a longtime resident of a space station — but his reek rose above the level of even the worst Byzantium Secundus bog stench.

I shook my head. "I don't know what you're talking about."

"The Changed! There's one of them bastards aboard and we aim to catch him and show him the ass end of an airlock!" He smiled with a mixture of lust and cruelty, his words backed up by yeas from the mob that had gathered around him. They carried a motley assortment of makeshift weapons, from security batons to diner forks taped to broomsticks. Truly lethal weapons weren't allowed on Cumulus — at least, not openly. These locals, most of them stevedores and mop urchins, couldn't afford real weapons anyway.

I looked them over with a feeling of disgust and pity. Even as recently as a year ago, I might have intervened, told them to return to their cabins and leave policing duties to the League security forces. I would have admonished them with scripture and appealed to what sparks of decency might smolder in their overworked breasts. But no longer. I was wise — hardened? — to such gangs as this erstwhile inquisition. If I bore a bishop's miter, they might listen. But I only had an Eskatonic's cowl and a cohort's badge — enough to impress them with thrilling tales in a bar, but not enough to cause them to put aside their witch hunt.

I am not losing my faith; I am simply less naïve. I didn't know this poor wretched being they hunted (and doubted such a creature even existed, here on a spacestation where all entry is watched), but my loyalties were already with him, even should he turn out to be the monster they believed him to be.

"Oh, yes," I said. "I heard. There was a commotion on the deck above. Someone said it went into the ducts."

"The ducts?" the mob leader snarled. "Damn, that means dirty work for us. C'mon, boys, let's find the hatch and flush him out!" He hurried off down a hall, his mob obediently following, some of them nodding thanks to me before they raised their weapons once more, eager to use them.

I had heard of no commotion or anything about ducts. I figured that keeping them slithering around in tight, oily tubes and passages would perhaps eventually still their ardor for the chase. I shook my head and continued my way, looking for the berthing hanger of The Crimson Talon, the escort whose captain we were to meet with (on matters which I dare not even write in this journal; perhaps once our plans have come to fruition, or we are away from prying eyes once more…).

A whispered "hsst!" startled me from my thoughts, and I looked to the side passage from whence it came. Sanjuk hid in its shadows, looking tentatively to the left and right, as if wary of someone. "Are they gone?" she said.

"Yes, I sent them into the plumbing," I said. "What are you doing here? Erian asked you to help Julia with the supplies."

"Yeah, yeah," she said, coming out of hiding and walking with me down the hallway, but still looking over her shoulder now and then. "Julia can handle things on her own. I want to see this mysterious captain. There're all sort of legends about Captain Kor'uk; I want to see what he really looks like."

"Nobody sees Kor'uk," I said. "Those who do, die. For death follows Kor'uk, like a lover seeks her husband gone to sea." I said this with intentional dramatics, repeating the folk legend mantra.

"Yeah, right," Sanjuk said, chuckling. She wore a pair of fine silk pajamas, not the kind for sleeping but the sort one wears to informal al-Malik garden parties. She saw my wondering scrutiny of her outfit and grimaced. "Look, I haven't had time to change," she said. "I went with Erian to our patron's soiree last night and he insisted we wear these. It's comfortable, at least. And I get less stares, if you can believe it."

"It makes you look... close to power," I said. "I'm sure people assume you're attached to a royal house."

"Whatever works, all right? As long as those mobs don't get frustrated at not finding their prey and decide to beat up on an Ukar instead."

That was certainly a risk. I felt a wave of shame that my kind would treat another race so poorly. Sanjuk had been looking over her shoulder ever since she was born.

"Hey, this is it, isn't it?" she said, pointing to an iris-valved door marked 12B.

"Yes, this is the number." I pressed the stud but nothing happened. "It must be locked. That's odd; the captain was supposed to leave it open for us."

Sanjuk spun her head and crouched low, an instinctive reaction. I, too, now heard the sounds coming from down the corridor, from where we had just been. The mob was returning.

Sanjuk deftly pulled a device from her satchel and connected its trodes to the door. I could see it was a scrambler pad — a thieves' tool, designed to break past electronic codes. In seconds — faster than I could imagine the device working — the iris valve receded, opening a portal into the hanger. Sanjuk disconnected the trodes in one deft yank and leapt through the door, motioning me to follow. As soon as I was in, she hit the stud on the interior wall and the iris sealed behind me.

The sounds of the mob were cut off — the walls and the door were too thick to allow them to pass through. The room was completely dark. I couldn't even see my hands, but I could hear the slight rustle of Sanjuk's silk pajamas as she walked about, searching for a light switch. I could imagine her feeling her way by touch as easily as a dog follows his nose, for she was raised in the midnight pits of Kordeth, and had not "come into the light" (as her people say) until she was of age.

She found the switch. I had to cover my eyes, startled by the sudden brightness. Then I heard an odd whistling and chirruping noise from the center of the hanger, and I squinted to see what it was.

Church folklore and passion plays speak of the image that confronted me, but they hardly prepared me for the true grandeur and chilling foreboding that travels up one's spine when seeing it for real.

The first thing I saw were the wings, huge and outspread, ready to lift their owner into the air if necessary. Then I saw the eyes, staring right into my soul's flame, seeing my secret aura laid bare. Below these was the beak, sharp and tattooed with intricate symbols. And then the full picture became clear: the large, hawkish Etyri bent low over a body sprawled across the hanger. The body had been neatly cut open and its entrails laid bare, glistening in the bright light. The image was an icon from a stained glass window: the Etyri prophet of death foretelling doom from the bodies of the dead.

Except that the body was wrong. It was that of a man, no doubt, but the guts were abnormal. Instead of intestines, they were lungs, at least four of them in a radial pattern. This was not a normal human being. I realized with a sick lurch in my stomach that he was Changed — a mutant, surely the one the mob outside clamored for.

The Etyri took its hands off the entrails and stood. He towered over me, standing perhaps seven and a half feet tall. He spoke, and I once more heard the chirruping sound that had first attracted my attention. I couldn't understand a thing he said. But I did notice the tabard he wore, and the symbol emblazoned upon it. He was a Questing Knight. Behind him, looming in the large hanger, was an escort-class starship: The Crimson Talon.

I spoke, although stammering. "I... I... I am Provost Guissepe

Alustro of the Eskatonic Order, sworn to Lady Erian Li Halan of the Questing Knights."

He nodded and spoke Urthish, with an odd accent and a strange pitch. "Greetings, provost. I have been waiting for you. Captain Kor'uk at your service."

He spun and drew his sword upon hearing the sharp intake of breath somewhere behind me and to my right.

"Wait!" I cried. "My companion, Sanjuk oj Kaval, also sworn to the service of Lady Erian." I turned to see Sanjuk rising from behind the crate behind which she had hid.

"An Ukar..." Kor'uk said, his head cocked quizzically, as he looked at her with a sideways profile, much like a bird, although his eyes were binocular, like mine. He sheathed his sword.

"You're Kor'uk?" Sanjuk said, approaching slowly. "Holy shit, I never would've figured it out. It makes sense, though: 'the friend of death.'"

Sanjuk and I had come to the same realization: The Etyri was a priest of his race's strange Death Gaze rites, and this had created the legend of his close ties to death. It also explained why he was rooting through the entrails of the dead Changed.

"He was one of mine," Kor'uk said, looking down at the body. "My crewman. I rescued his body and took it here, where I could interview it and discern the cause of his death."

"Your rites told you who killed him?" I asked wonderingly.

"Yes, and I shall now kill that person. I am sorry; it will delay our meeting, but this is a matter of honor."

"They will not understand that," I said. "He was Changed; in the eyes of the law, anyone can kill him."

"There are many laws, including those of retribution."

"You endanger yourself to do so!" I said.

"Danger does not halt for necessity," he said. "I go. I will send a message to your lady as to when we might meet again." He quickly stepped over to the portal from which Sanjuk and I had entered, opened it, then was gone.

Sanjuk and I looked at one another, worried that we were about to lose an important key to our mission. We needed Kor'uk to accomplish to next stage in our endeavors. I rushed into the hall, hoping to halt the mob from attacking him, but found no one there. The mob had departed and there was no sign of Kor'uk. He had clearly taken his hunt to other decks.

Sanjuk and I returned to our lady's apartments immediately, and told her what we had seen. She was annoyed and worried, of course, but there was nothing we could do. We dare not tell anyone of Kor'uk's identity, for it is clearly part of his mystique and a means he uses to serve Alexius. We had to wait and hope he would contact us soon.

Over the next few days, rumors grew across the station that Death himself had come to Cumulus, manifest as a raptor, preying on sinners. Three men were found dead over those days, torn to pieces. No one witnessed the actual deaths, only the bloody remains. When no more deaths occurred, tensions eased, and the word spread that Death had had his day, and no more judgments were ordained... for now.

A week later, we heard once more from Captain Kor'uk. Not personally, but from one of his crewmen. The captain had been injured and had taken time to heal his wounds, but was now recovered and ready to meet with us and plan the next stage of our journey.

My Lady Erian and he finally met when we returned to his ship's berth. He was a gracious knight; if it were not for the sling his left arm rested in, one would never assume that he was the predatory spirit that had just haunted the station.

As we made our introductions and prepared to tour his ship, he stopped me at the entry hatch and looked into my eyes.

"I thank you for your warnings, earlier," he said. "Your concern, even when you did not know me, speaks well for your soul flame." He then squinted at me, a low warbling hissing coming from his throat. The hairs on my neck raised. I have been a practitioner of theurgic rites long enough to have an idea of when invisible powers are at play. He then opened his eyes again and cocked his head at me, as if deciding whether to speak further.

"Tell me," I said, "Speak the oracle, oh heavenly messenger, spread your feathers across the future." This last was a quote from The Annals of Misery, a famous Church play written by Friar Maul G'ent on Grail, home to the Etyri.

Kor'uk blinked, surprised, but then lowered his beak, a gesture I took to be similar to what passes for a smile among humans. "Beware the whispers of the past spoken in the tongues of ecstasy. They speak wisdom, but also folly. Heed not all that they say."

"What does that mean?" I said.

Kor'uk shrugged. "I'm not sure. But these voices are in your future."

"Then I shall prepare for them, and remember what you have told me."

"If, when the time of fulfillment comes, you do indeed remember, then you shall have achieved more than most of those gifted with a prophecy. No matter how forewarned we be, it is our doom to march unknowing into the abyss of what is to come."

I frowned. He seemed awfully pessimistic for one who engages in prophecy. He shrugged again and entered the ship. I followed behind him, marveling at the size of his wings and their plumage, and wondered if there was a connection between the ability to fly to heights and look down from them and the power to see what lies ahead.

Hidden Faith

"Don't touch that!" Illuminatus Jefers cried.

Startled, I pulled my hand back in, but too late. I had already pressed the glowing stud.

A brilliant, prismatic array shot forth from the projector, and Doramos, the World Architect, Shaper of Planets, loomed huge above me. He looked straight through and past me, to whomever he lectured those many, many years ago when he recorded this holovid. It took my breath away.

I had, of course, seen many images of Doramos, but always in pictures, never a live moment like this. He swept his arms to the side, indicating a formula he had written in the air with a light pen, but it seemed to me with his great size that he motioned to the entire universe, beckoning us to see in it what he saw— a spark of the divine embedded in the material. His genius still has no equal these many centuries since his death.

Jefers reached past me and turned the device off.

"I'll ask you to keep that little gem a secret, eh?" he said, winking at me as he ambled back to the vast shelf he had been searching on my behalf.

"Of course," I replied. "I apologize. It was... magnificent, though."

"Oh, yes. Doramos is always impressive to watch, even when projected at the proper size. Even more impressive to listen to."

He must have sensed the yearning in me — or knew it too well among our kind, and so anticipated it.

"No, you can't listen. Not to that speech. It's special, you see. Meant for the ears of his students alone. You wouldn't understand half of what he said, and the half you did get would awaken questions of faith you're not ready for."

"I don't understand. Nothing Doramos said really contradicts Church teachings."

"Nothing known to the public, no. But when speaking to those in the know, he revealed beliefs that only our order has yet grappled with. Oh, not heresy. Nothing that dire. Heterodox, perhaps. Revolutionary and groundbreaking? Definitely."

"I doubt there are many beliefs which would surprise me anymore. Not after my travels."

"Hmph," he said, lifting himself up the rickety ladder to examine the fourth shelf from the bottom. "No, I suppose not. Imperial Cohort these days, is it? Questing Knights and dangerous missions are your lot, yes? Not my cup of tea. An Eskatonic's true place is here, in the library."

"I don't dispute its importance. Am I not here? But surely these books had to come from somewhere. Someone had to collect them. If we don't quest, what do we have to feed the mind?"

"Bah! Too true, I suppose. Not for me! I read your journals. Oh, yes, many in our order do. Many more don't. Jealousy or disapproval, I'm sure. I know about your time in barbarian space. Barely made it back. I'd hate for my divine spark to find its way to the Empyrean through such ethers as they have there — full of demons, I'm sure."

"I saw none. People there are as we are: struggling to survive with dignity and faith. A different faith, to be sure, but a yearning for light nonetheless."

"After all you've been through and you still see the good in men, eh? I can't see past their vile treacheries. Every man wields a dagger aimed at another's back. Most are simply too afraid to take the blow. Others take it and miss. Those who rule are those whose aim was true."

"I wonder how you call yourself a priest, sometimes. You're cynicism is as strong as most priests' charity. If I didn't know you personally, I'd think that it was stronger than your faith."

Jefers turned and smiled a conspiratorial grin. "Ah, but you do know me, Guisseppe. And you know better."

"I do. Which is why I have never condemned you for your beliefs. And why I came to you now. The Church may not think them useful, but I do."

Jefers cackled and snatched a book from the shelf, and then jumped down to the floor, kicking up a cloud of dust as he landed. "So do many others who come to see me from time to time, looking for books such as these." He placed the old, dusty, leather-bound tome on the table between us.

I read the title on the spine, its gold-gilt letters still quite legible. "The Annals of Buttercup Vale, by Friar Puddleton? You must be joking. That's one of the most wretched children's books to survive the Fall!"

Jefers cackled again, his sides shaking with uncontrollable glee. "I know! I know! The last place anyone would look!"

I grabbed the book and flung open its cover. The title page had a very different name: *On the Harmonics of the Geo-Astral Grid, or the Alignment of the Leys*, by Doramos of Tyre. I gasped.

"This is it! You actually have a copy!"

"Of course, of course," Jefers said, pulling up a chair and sitting down. "I've read it many times myself. It's practically scripture, you know. Should be amended into the Omega Gospels, if you ask me."

"I don't think the Bishopric Council will ask you, Jefers. Not anytime soon." I pulled up a chair and began reading furiously. Jefers watched me for a while, a look of pleasure and contentment on his face. Those who share his beliefs are rare. He knows I am not a convert to his cause, but my interest in Doramos's work made me somewhat of a fellow traveler in his mind.

I read for hours. During that time, Jefers puttered about with his own research, leaving now and then to replenish the teakettle he kept there. Most of the book was beyond my knowledge, written with terminology only a terraformer would know. I suspected that even most terraformers of Doramos's day and after wouldn't have understood much of it, either.

Doramos wrote much of his science in a special metaphorical language couched in religious references. Or so later terraformers tried to describe it. What they refused to see was that, to Doramos, it wasn't metaphor. In his metaphysics, subtle realms of unseen energy existed all around us and yet followed certain principles that could be harnessed to change the material world, to transform it as an alchemist turns lead into gold. Nobody fully understood his work, however, and most of his secrets died with him.

I realized as I came near to the end of the work — many pages of which I had to skip out of sheer incomprehensibility — that I would need to enlist Jefers's aid if I were to answer the questions required of my quest. I had hesitated to do so, for I did not want to get him into any trouble. More than that, I feared that the lore he would gain from it might later fire his will towards a task not necessarily healthy for his soul.

"Have you ever heard of the Jovian Beacon?" I asked, the first words I had spoken for some time.

Jefers looked up from where he scribbled into a large notebook with a feather-quill pen. All his access to technology and he still preferred to write by hand. "Oh, yes. Of course I have. Doramos' theoretical satellite. Designed to align interspatial leys with planetary system lays. Part of his program to stellarform entire solar systems."

"Yes, I believe that was his intent. But he also speaks of it as a tool to better understand the jump routes. He thought that the Anunnaki had used such interstellar ley lines to plot their routes. Using the Jovian Beacon, a technological array placed near a system's largest gas giant — such as Holy Terra's Jove — he would supposedly be able to plot such lines and devise his own jump routes."

"A noble idea. Too bad he never built it. If only we had his notes on such a device, we might build one today."

"We do."

Jefers stared at me as if I were mad — or a king promising to grant a knighthood. "What... what do you mean?"

"We found his notes. In a lost bunker under Megiddo. We had to evade Avestites to escape, but we did. They don't know it was us yet. But we got them. I didn't know what they were at first, but I've spent some time deciphering them, and there's no doubt that they pertain to the Jovian Beacon."

Jefers was speechless. He opened and closed his mouth a number of times, but no sound came out. I thought I may have even seen a tear well up in his eye.

"I came to find out how to build it," I said. "But the information isn't in this book, as I thought it would be."

"No," Jefers said. "Not that book — you want this one." He ran to the bookcase and skittered up the stairs like a daplu monkey in a tree heading for a zuglar fruit. He yanked a book from the top shelf and slid back down the stairs. He thrust the book open in front of me and I read the title: *On the Manufacture of Stellar Arrays According to Harmonic Principles,* by Doramos of Tyre.

"It's an early one," he said. "It contains none of his later work on the Jovian Beacon, but he used it as a basis for that theory. Would it help?"

I nodded. "I'll need assistance deciphering it, but yes, it should."

Jefers sat down across from me, staring into my eyes. "Do you intend to build such an array?"

I hesitated before answering. How far could I involve him? I certainly needed his expertise, but it came with a price — the risk of heresy charges for us all, my Lady too. But I saw no other way.

"Yes. We have... allies who intend to fund us."

"To what purpose? What do you seek?"

I was silent again for a while, but then spoke. "Yathrib."

He stared at me with wonder in his eyes. "Can it be done? Could the Beacon lead the way there?"

190

"I hope so," I said.

"I beg you, Guisseppe, let me help! It would be the culmination of my life's work!"

"If we succeed, Jefers, there will be much scrutiny. You may not survive it."

"If we succeed, Guisseppe Alustro, the Worldshapers will not have to hide their faith any longer. Delivering to the Church the jump route to the world where the Prophet saw the Holy Flame would be enough to redeem even an Antinomist."

I hoped he was right. For all our sakes.

"Then yes, we shall have you. And I thank you for it."

"No, Guissepe, I thank you, with all my heart and soul. Where shall we build this array?"

"Why, Holy Terra, of course," I said, smiling.

He smiled, too, but not without a hint of nervousness. Once off Pentateuch, he had no guarantee of safety from Inquisitors and others who looked down on the Worldshapers. Indeed, even I had reservations about turning so much knowledge over to one of them. Their past hubris in terraforming has harmed the very balance of nature on some worlds — or so the Church claims. And yet, I saw little choice. For my Lady Erian's quest to succeed, we must build the array in the Holy Terra system — from where all Doramos's equations were drawn— and if it worked, then place it in Aylon's system. There, we might have a hope of finding the way to Yathrib.

I silently prayed to the Pancreator to protect us from our own sin and deliver us unharmed from our own folly.

Lost Time

And so begins another day of my exile.

Today, as dawn rose above the Verona Mountains, I marked the twentieth day on my calendar. Twenty days since I was stranded here in this remote region of Rampart, abandoned by necessity. My Lady and our crew fled in the Resurgent, under heavy fire from an unmarked frigate, although I am sure it was one of the pirate fleet owned by her brother. I had disembarked to trade with the locals for food, and had no time to reach the ship before it launched. Julia maneuvered deftly to avoid the frigate's guns, taking the ship into the clouds and beyond my sight.

I have waited here since, at the foot of the mountains, anxious and soul-sore with dread that they have been shot down or captured. I have haunted the local taverns, plying travelers with drinks in the hopes that they have heard some rumor of the chase and its outcome.

But nothing.

In this place, far from the high-speed rails that connect the major cities, news travels slowly. This is why we chose this place to restock our supplies; it was remote. That very remoteness keeps me safe from our enemies, but leaves me ignorant of the fate of my friends. Each hour of the day, I dearly wish to hear the whine of the engines and to see the Resurgent set down again, her door opening to admit me to the company of my friends, to my home.

But nothing.

No noise here but the rustle of the wind in the evergreens. Silence.

A silence the locals fear.

The silence, they say, of the ghosts of Sallow Hill.

As I paid for the drinks of travelers and locals, I heard on more than one occasion tales about the "strange goings on" at a place called Sallow Hill. From what I could ascertain, the site is located half a day's ride from town, in the wilderness near the foot of the mountains. It is a haunted site, where chilling apparitions are seen and unholy energies are said to sometimes light the night. Animals avoid it, and it is hard to get horses near.

None of this was too unusual. I had heard many stories about strange places on nearly every world of the empire. I had even been to some of them, and found that they sometimes even deserved their reputation. As intrigued as I was, I nonetheless had no desire to visit this place. If I left town for the day, I might miss my friends' return, and there was no guarantee they could wait for me if trouble still dogged their trail.

But the mayor's tale changed my mind. Donatius Otalo is an ex-Reeve, retired from what he calls the "hectic dance of hypocrisy," by which he means the doings of the outside world. He prefers this remote rural existence, and claims its lackadaisical pace has cured his stomach ailment. He got wind of my sojourn at the local inn and my questioning of travelers, and he came to buy me a drink and ply me for answers. I assured him that I was but a priest on pilgrimage, and that I waited for the return of my ship, which was chased away by pirates. This is not untrue, if not the whole truth. He liked me, though, and sensed that, even if I were not telling the whole tale, I at least lacked the sort of guile he had come to this hamlet to escape. We spent many an hour talking of the local territory and marking its pleasures and drawbacks.

Eventually, the subject of Sallow Hill arose. Since Donatius had found in me someone learned, who, unlike the locals, had studied the lore of the past, he smiled conspiratorially and drew me away from the common room in which we had been relaxing and into a private room in the back, with a cozy fire crackling to warm it. There he regaled me with his theories about the place. Although the tales of ghosts and disappeared travelers varied, often with what are obvious elaborations added to increase the effect of horror on the listener, one thread seemed to run through all of the more genuine seeming accounts. The re-occurrence of the past.

It seems that the most trusted reports all involved the eye-witnessing of a crew of Republican scientists, identified by their unique uniforms and scientific equipment, the likes of which are unknown even today among the wealthiest of guildsmen on this world.

Donatius chuckled as he related this, and then revealed his theory: Sallow Hill hosts an ancient magic lantern device with images of a scientific expedition from long ago. For whatever reason, the device was buried deep enough to be undiscovered by travelers, but with its emitter field still shallow enough to project its recordings into the air above ground. It was this display that accounted for the sightings of ghosts.

I asked him how this explained the disappearances in the region, and he more seriously opined that a gang of bandits had obviously discovered the truth and used the ghost stories as an excuse to hide their murders. I nodded. It seemed like a good explanation.

What I did not tell Donatius was that his story made me even more interested in visiting the site. If there was a Second Republic cache of scientific gear buried there, my lady Erian would certainly want to know of it. I smiled to think of her surprise when she returned, to find my gift of priceless relics from the past.

But I first had to get out there. Earlier today, after asking around among some of my new friends among the locals (it's amazing how many doors a few drinks can open), I was directed to a local prospector, a man named Pino. He was no guildsman, but an independent operator, traveling into the mountains on his own in the hopes of finding valuable veins of metals. He had been lucky enough to discover one valuable vein, which he promptly reported to the Merchant League in return for decent recompense, and that allowed him to winter in the town between spring and summer explorations.

Upon meeting him, I doubted he'd have many more years of exploring. He was only in his forties, but was clearly afflicted with some form of wasting disease. He came right out and revealed it: "Rad poisoning. I got too deep into a cave up there," he said, motioning at the Verona Mountains, "and came out a few weeks later practically glowing. It don't matter none; it's the life I chose."

I broached the topic of hiring him as a guide, and he seemed most interested... until I mentioned Sallow Hill. He looked at me with such pity, like I was a madman but had not had the sense to realize it, that I lost my temper. I won't record my words here, but suffice it to say that my exile was wearing on me and had eroded my seminary discipline somewhat. I think it amused him, but he also clearly felt guilty, causing a priest to curse. He agreed to lead me there, saying "I'm already a dead man, or will be in a few years at best. I don't know why you want to rush the process yourself, but you clearly need to go. I might as well at least keep you from getting lost on the way."

My money was running out (I had already spent too much on drinks for my informants), but I nonetheless bought us enough provisions for a few days (in case we become waylaid and cannot return by evening).

We shall leave early tomorrow morning. This will be my last entry for a while, as I won't have time during the trek to add new reports. May the Pancreator bless our expedition.

* * *

So much to tell. My hand trembles as I write, but I shall endeavor to record events in the order in which they occurred.

We had no trouble getting to Sallow Hill, Pino and I. He knew his way around the woods unerringly. He admitted that he had only been to Sallow Hill once, and did not stay — "I didn't like the odor of the place." — but remembered perfectly how to get there. As we approached within what he claimed was "a smidgeon more than an hour away," I began to get nervous, although I knew not why. I eventually figured it out. The woods had gone silent again. Even the wind seemed still here, and no sound of bird or animal could be heard. I mentioned

195

this to Pino and he nodded. "They don't like the odor, either."

Soon, the horses began to snort and shy, resisting us as we attempted to move forward. Pino sighed and slipped from his horse, and tied it to a branch near a patch of grass. He motioned me to do the same. "We'll have to go on foot the rest of the way."

When we finally arrived, it was not what I had expected. The "hill" was really just a large mound, nestled within a small valley that was darkened by the high walls of the mountains on either side. A shallow brook ran down from the northernmost wall and trickled around the mound and then disappeared into a hole in the ground. Atop the hill was a circle of standing stones, looking almost natural, but this was a trick of their age: erosion had so worn them down as to make them appear to have fallen there during some distant glaciation. They were, in fact, man-made, having been carved and set here in formation.

I knew this because I had seen something similar once, on Tethys. Not as an object, but a sketch, a drawing in the notebooks of Victor Domokos Erling, the uncle of Saint Amalthea. The thrill in the pit of my stomach combated with my sense of dread. If my memory was correct, this was no mere magic lantern. It was a Second Republic-era recreation of an abandoned experiment in Pan-Physics. It would be at once priceless, but also potentially damnable. The chaos such technology invoked could serve either the Empyrean or Gehenne.

Pino must have discerned something in my expression, as his eyes narrowed and he cast his gaze about the place. "What is it?"

"I... I think I know what this is," I said, cautiously. "I'm not sure I'm paying you enough to go any farther."

"That either means it's dangerous," he said, scratching his scalp, "or it's valuable. Since you're a priest, supposed to look out for souls, I suppose you mean the former."

"Both," I said. I saw no reason to hide the truth from him. I was no greedy merchant seeking to hide the truth of a claim, and I didn't think he was the type to kill me over such knowledge. Besides, his sickness prevented him from being much of a physical threat, and I had a gun hidden in my robes just in case.

"Well, I'm going in anyway," he said. "You've got me curious, and like I said before, I don't got much time in my bones anyway. Might as well spend it marveling at something new."

We cautiously approached the stones, finding the slope of the hill very easy going. I looked carefully for any signs of the technology hidden there, while Pino began to climb one of the stones. There was a crackling sound and I heard a grunt from him, and then something large and heavy hit me with incredible force, knocking me to the ground. I lost consciousness.

When I again opened my eyes, it was dark. Although it had seemed that only moments had passed, by the position of the constellations, it appeared that hours had gone by. It was perhaps midnight by now, or sometime after. I got to my feet, feeling none the worse for the blow, and looked about. I saw no sign of an attacker or any object that might have hit me.

Pino lay on the ground, having been clearly thrown from the stone he was climbing. I rushed to him and found that he was unhurt, at least with no external injuries. I splashed some water from my canteen onto his face and his eyes fluttered open.

"What in the name of Cyrus?" he said, sitting up, staring in consternation at the night sky.

"Who is Cyrus?" I asked.

"Saint Cyrus of Vasilgrod. A local saint. Local for this world, that is. I'm sure you've heard of more saints than I can count, you being worldly and well-traveled, that is." He stood up and seemed to take an inventory of his bones and muscles, flexing his arms and twisting his torso.

"I haven't heard of that one," I said. "What is his patronage?"

"Astronomy. A dead art. Except among the Charioteers, of course. Cyrus had foretold the coming of Kung-1, the meteor that destroyed his beloved city. But that was after his death." He walked about the circle, peering at the stones in the dim light of the half moon. "What do you suppose hit us?"

"Ah, I've been thinking about that," I said. I pointed with my toe to a distinct line in the grass. Before it, the grass lay flat. Past it, the grass grew straight. "Whatever hit us also flattened this grass. If you look at the pattern, though, it clearly came from a central point — there." I gestured to a small rock roughly in the center of the circle. "I think I've seen something like this before, on Malignatius, although there it was a jury-rigged trap left behind by the Li Halan and meant for the Decados forces."

"So what is it?"

"A stunner. A Second Republic weapons technology. It emits an invisible field of force that radiates outwards in a wave. I think your climbing on that stone must have set it off."

He looked skeptical. "Are you sure? I don't see a weapon."

"I think it must be under that rock. It would have risen up as needed, then slid back into its casing once it had discharged. The one on Malignatius was only a one-shot device. I suspect this one will go off again if we're not careful."

"If you say so." Pino shrugged his shoulders. "What now then?"

"Well, maybe you could try to disable it."

"Me?"

"I notice you've got tools on your belt. That puts you a few steps ahead of me."

Pino grunted and seemed to sulk for a moment. He then shrugged again and began to cautiously move toward the rock, drawing a tool from his belt. I wished him luck.

He bent down by the rock, ready to roll to the side if he needed to, although by the stunner's pattern of effect on the grass, I judged it would hit both of us should it go off again, regardless of where we stood in the circle.

He lifted the rock with his left hand and peered down the hole that was revealed. He grunted again and reached down with his tool. A whining sound grew louder and a metal tube scalloped up from the hole. Pino rammed his tool into the opening and jumped back. The whining turned into a crackling bang, and then silence. He appeared to have shorted out the device.

Pino stood up and shrugged. "Well, we're still standing."

"We're not alone," I said, my voice almost catching in my throat.

Standing in the circle with us were three men dressed in strange uniforms of silver. They stared intently at unseen things, speaking to each other with words I could not understand. As I looked around, I noticed that a smooth metal floor had replaced the grass, and the stones were no longer aged and eroded; they were newly carved and worked with all manner of odd inscriptions and sigils.

Pino was frozen in fear, just as I was, although I was beginning to realize that these people weren't real. They were Mayor Donatius' magic lantern show. I chuckled, relieved to know they weren't ghosts.

At the sound of my outburst, one of them turned to look at me.

"Are you here to observe? I don't recognize your robes. Are you from the Phavian Institute?"

I froze. Magic lantern images rarely talked back. Those that did were usually run by an advanced pygmallium-based intelligence. But this man who spoke to me… he seemed more than real.

Another one of the men looked at me and spoke. "No, he's clearly one of the gospelers. Come to see if Amalthea's uncle was right? Well, we'll prove it to your people's satisfaction, I think."

"And who are you?" the first one said, looking at Pino.

"We don't have time for that," the third man said. "Oscillation is in 10 minus." They all turned back to peer at invisible objects, which I now realized were holovids projected into their eyes, like those I'd seen used by Baroness Sahid Azula on Criticorum.

"Wait!" the second one cried. "There's something wrong — the chamber is not on the right frequency."

"That can't be — I calibrated it myself earlier today."

"Something's thrown it off. I'm showing that the defense grid has been triggered, and there's a short in the system."

199

I shook my head. This was not possible. These men were living in the past, a point in time so distant from me as to be nearly unimaginable. And yet... they reacted to events that took place here and now. Pino's disabling of the stunner was clearly interfering with their experiment. But how could that be? Their experiment had taken place over a millennium ago.

The first man to speak looked at me gravely, with a strange look on his face. The look, it seemed to me, of a man who had just realized the universe was not what he thought it was. "I understand now. Erling's missing factor, the reason he didn't complete this experiment — it's time. Time is a circle."

"What are you talking about?" the second man said.

"We are experiencing two moments in time, ours and... theirs." He looked at me as he said this. He swallowed and his eyes pleaded with me. "Am I right? Did we unite time with P-Physics? My name... my name is John Lakos. Am I famous in your time?"

I could not answer. My mind had frozen in shock. The enormity of the event was too much for me to comprehend.

"Oh my god," the third man said. "The waves are polarizing. We're all going to—"

The hill exploded.

The very atoms of the place shivered and separated, scattering in chaos. I felt my own body separate in all directions.

I prayed.

And for a moment, I was back at the time before the catastrophe, with John Lakos still pleading with me. I felt a hand on my shoulder and turned my head to look at it. Female, smooth, brown, and shining with a light I will never be able to describe for as long as I shall live. Her voice spoke to me: "You called me here. From the eye of the soul, time is simultaneous. Do not worry. Loyalty shall be your salvation."

I opened my mouth to say something, but she removed her hand. Then something hit me, something large and painful and my body was thrown off the hill just before the explosion shook it.

I hit the ground hard and heard the snap of one of my left ribs. The weight lifted from me and I could see the hill. Where the stones had been was… nothing. A void, as if a hole into darkest outer space had opened.

Then it closed and the stones were back, as if they had never been gone.

The sharp pain in my side cleared the fog from my mind and a smell came to my nose — a smell I almost cried at. So real, so close. I was losing my mind. But then a grunt and four hands around me, patting out the fires on my clothing, and then lifting me, convincing me it was real.

"Ong? Is that you," I whispered.

"Yes, Alustro," Ongangarak said, his deep Voroxian voice rumbling. "I am here."

"Thank the Pancreator." I wept for a little while as he carried me to the edge of the woods and put me down. I smiled to see him. "Where are the others? My lady?"

"They are coming. We could not land here — something got in the way of the instruments. We saw you on the hill and called and called for you, but you didn't respond. I jumped from the ship while the others flew to land as close as they could."

"Pino? There was a man with me? Where is he?"

Ong sniffed the air. "I smell him." He bounded away, into the woods. I heard a yelp and the thumping of Ong's feet as he bounded back to me, bearing Pino in his arms. He set him down beside me.

Pino looked at me as if he saw a ghost, and at Ong with a sense of wonder. "Did you see her?" he said.

I nodded.

"She cured me," Pino said. "I am whole. See?" He lifted his shirt and revealed a healthy looking torso. "My rad poisoning! It's gone! No marks!" He laughed with glee and jumped up and down, dancing in a circle around Ong and I.

"Who is he talking about?" Ong said. "I saw only you and he."

"I… he means… the Lady Amalthea. She saved us. Her uncle's forbidden experiment… they were trying to perform it. I mean they did perform it. But I think they're trapped, caught in a pocket of time. Or they were. I think she freed them." I did not add that I believe it was my faith that had brought her there, somehow, to free those poor souls, trapped for so many years. Or was it that long? For them, maybe it was only a mere moment.

Pino stopped his capering and stared soberly at me. "Amalthea? But… she wore a silver suit, like them. She grabbed me before the explosion hit and pulled me out of the way. She then scanned me with some sort of ray. She called it a Zinn Reducer, said it reversed radiation damage to living cells. Then she faded away. I thought she was part of the AI's force projector — the magic lantern theory, like you said."

I didn't know what to make of this. I knew it was Amalthea, with a conviction that came not from reason but from some place deeper in my soul. Perhaps she had appeared in a different form to Pino, a form he could more readily accept. Of all the Prophet's disciples, she was the one most comfortable with Merciful Technals. So it made sense for her divine aura to take the form of such technology.

I looked at Ong and smiled. It was good to see my friend again. I heard someone calling from far off, and Ong roared an answer.

"They come," he said.

I said, "I knew they would."

FINIS

Thank you for reading this book. Please consider telling others about it by writing a review at your favorite bookseller.

May the Pancreator bless all your endeavors,

— Bill (your humble author)

Would you like to hear from me whenever I have a new book or story available? Sign up at bill-bridges.com to be notified by email of my new releases. You can read my blog there and find out about my appearances.

Want to know more about the Fading Suns universe? Visit fadingsuns.com.

Appendix: The Fading Suns Universe

Once the suns shone brightly, beacons in the vast night of space, calling humanity onward. The stars were symbols of humanity's vast potential, a purpose and destiny revealed in progress, inciting an exodus of unlimited growth to the distant stars. Once people looked to the heavens with hope and longing in their eyes.

Then the suns — and the hope — began to fade.

It is the year 5014 and history has come to an end. Humanity's greatest civilization has fallen, leaving ignorance and fear scattered among the ruins of many worlds. A new Dark Age is upon humanity and few believe in renewal and progress anymore. Now there is only waiting. Waiting for a slow death as the age-old stars fade to cinders and the souls of the sinful are called to Final Judgment.

But not all believe in this destiny. A leader has arisen, an Emperor sworn to unite the worlds of Human Space together again under one banner. To once more ignite hope in people's hearts.

It is a monumental task, for most people have already given up and fallen into the ways of the past, playing serfs to feudal lords. What is hope to them now but a falsehood that leads to pain? Better to leave the hard decisions to their masters and let the Church console their souls.

There are enemies everywhere, those who seek to selfishly profit from humanity's demise: vain nobles ruling far-flung worlds, power-hungry priests who seek dominion over the lives of men, the greedy merchant guilds growing rich from bartering humanity's needs and wants. They are not alone. Others are out there among the darkening stars, alien races angry with humankind for age-old slavery, and enigmatic alien empires with agendas too paradoxical to fathom.

History

The chronicle of humanity's history among the stars is a long one, stretching over two millennia. It is not a quiet story. From the greedy planet-grabbing of early colonists to the bloody battles of the Emperor Wars, humans have rarely slept peacefully in the void. They have prospered, suffered defeat, and dared to hope again. And they have not traveled down the paths of history alone; aliens walk among them, with long histories and destinies of their own to complete.

First Republic

Humanity first reached the stars under the auspices of the First Republic, a one-world government run by the "zaibatsu": greedy mercantile barons whose corporate states replaced the nations of the earth. The zaibatsu colonized the solar system in search of new sources of wealth and mineral resources. At the edge of the solar system they found the jumpgate.

This ancient artifact of alien manufacture baffled and awed humanity. It took many years of research to unlock even the most basic secrets of its technology, but its main function was clear: it opened portals to distant star systems. Diligent scientists constructed the first jump drive, an engine installed on a spaceship that could propel the ship through the gate, transporting it instantly into foreign space light years away.

The exodus began.

At first, the zaibatsu carefully controlled the manufacture and ownership of jump ships and reaped the resources of the new worlds and solar systems. Additionally, they outlawed and suppressed a religious movement which grew around the jump experience, based on a mystical experience common to many jump pilots: the Sathra Effect, so called because of the first words from the lips of the ecstatic pilots. The zaibatsu installed dampers on ships that ended the communion and halted the rebellious religion.

But repression was not long suffered. After anarchists leaked the secret of the technology to all, nobody could keep back the vast wave of people seeking to escape corporate tyranny and claim worlds of their own. The First Republic collapsed in a civil war over ever-expanding territory and diminishing loyalties.

Diaspora

The new universe of Human Space was made up of fractured, planetary nations, some democratic, some totalitarian. Many of the original rulers of these worlds created dynasties which would last for millennia: the first noble houses to rule the stars. But years of political and social experiments yielded only chaos and strife between worlds. Into this dangerous universe came the Prophet, a man with a vision of Creation he claimed was gifted to him by God, whom he called the Pancreator. The Prophet gathered disciples and followers about him and performed many miracles. A humanity desperate for unity and hope looked to the Prophet for their answers.

During this time, humanity met its first sentient race, the ungulate Shantor. At first, they were thought to be merely clever horselike beings. But it was soon realized how intelligent they were — and how dangerous. Another sentient race, the Ukar, was gifted with psychic powers — powers that they used to goad the Shantor into a bloody revolt. By the time the truth behind the Shantor's rage was discovered, it was too late to reform the beasts in humanity's eyes: the "dangerous and uncontrollable" Shantor were enslaved and moved to reservations across the Known Worlds, breaking up their families and culture.

The following Ukar War united humanity against another star-faring race, one inimicable to human interests. With the aid of the Ukar's cousin race, the Obun, humanity gained ground in their galactic war. Finally, Palamedes Alecto, follower of the Prophet, led the newly formed Universal Church of the Celestial Sun against the Ukari on their homeworld. Humanity was victorious, and the place of the Church in future politics and martial power was cemented.

Humanity marched across new worlds and subjugated the sentients living upon them, most of whom were incapable of star travel and thus considered inferior.

Until the Vau.

Humanity met more than its match when it subjugated a peaceful race of gardeners known as the G'nesh. When their overlords arrived from unknown worlds in vastly superior starships with devastating energy weapons, humans had no choice but to fall back and go no further. Luckily, the Vau were non-expansionistic, and pursued no vendetta against humanity. As long as they were left alone, they would cause no trouble — or so most humans believed. But enigmatic "gifts" and lore from the Vau over the centuries have been curiously effective at starting conflicts among humans.

Second Republic

Eventually, with the unity provided by the Church and economic interests heralded by mercantile leaders, the Second Republic was born, a democratic government that eventually spanned all the worlds of Human Space. Under its auspices, an unprecedented era of prosperity and high technology was initiated. It seemed that there were no limits to human development, no secrets that could not be unlocked by the power of the human mind, along with a little ingenuity and grit. Scientists even tapped into the very genetic code of humanity, creating mutated beings later known as the Changed.

But power eventually seems to coalesce into the hands of a few, especially when the people are no longer vigilant. The noble houses of the Diaspora, still rich but now relegated to meaningless roles, hungered for the vast power they once had and plotted against the Republic. They were aided by a new millennialism and apocalyptic fever, for scientists had discovered a new, dread phenomenon: the suns were fading. The stars grew dim and no one knew why.

The government could not calm the fears of all the worlds, and the untimely crash of the welfare computer system caused riots in every major city on every planet. Rebels rose up and with lightning speed, claimed the central government on Byzantium Secundus. The nobles joined together with the Church to free the capital. Victorious, they refused to return power to the senators and instead seized power for themselves. This ushered in a new age for humanity: a Dark Age of feudal lords, fanatic priests and scheming guilds.

New Dark Ages

The new lords of the Known Worlds quickly began to war upon one another, with only the largest, most cunning or richest houses rising to prominence, while many others were destroyed. In this chaos, the common people were left defenseless. In desperation, many signed generational contracts with the noble houses, swearing fealty to their local lords for themselves and their children to come. At first, the Church fought such indenture, but it eventually adopted such contracts itself when they proved the only reliable means to raise armies against rivals — and the Church was just as combative and martial as the nobles.

The corporations of the Second Republic were left with little of the spoils. With their holdings seized or signed over forcefully, they had little overt power. But a conglomeration of these corporations banded together to form the Merchant League, and rewrote their charters to form guilds rather than corporations. Guilds could more easily control membership and advancement within their ranks. In addition, the League maintained their secret technological patents, often paying for this privilege with the death of many agents charged with wiping such data from computers the universe over lest it fall into the hands of the noble lords.

Without the means to repair their starships and high-tech weaponry, the nobles and the Church could not long stand. After a vicious campaign against the guilds failed to free the League's secrets, the lords had little choice but to admit the merchant guilds into the halls of power. Even the Church was forced to concede their power, and issued a Patriarchal Bull allowing only them (along with the nobles and priests) to use certain proscribed high technologies. Once these scientific secrets were kept from the people, the Known Worlds' descent into a feudal society was complete: only the upper classes moved among the stars; the peasants lived and died on the planets where they were born.

But the Known Worlds were not the only words of Human Space. During the Fall of the Second Republic, many planets were lost, their jump coordinates stolen or the jumpgates sealed. After centuries of absence, some of these worlds reappeared, heralded by barbarian hordes who swept into the Known Worlds, wreaking havoc and looting noble lands.

Only a powerful coalition of nobles could defend against the scattered barbarian clans, and only a master tactician could form such a coalition. This man was Vladimir, whose campaign against the barbarians propelled him to power. After his victory against the raiders, he declared himself the first Emperor of the Known Worlds. A campaign of pacification convinced the noble houses to accept his rule. But upon his coronation day, when he placed the crown upon his head, he mysteriously died in a sudden conflagration. His coalition fell apart, and house fell upon house, each blaming the others for the death of Vladimir. Eventually, peace was secured again, sealed with Vladimir's reforms: all the houses, sects and guilds would vote equally to choose a noble to become Regent, to rule until a new Emperor could be decided upon.

It would be nearly half a millennium before an Emperor was again chosen, and only after nearly 40 years of violent war. The Emperor Wars lasted for two generations, and saw a greater rise in technology than any time since the Second Republic. But it was war tech: powerful killing machines, chemical weapons, fusion bombs and other means of destruction. Finally, one man was victorious: Alexius Hawkwood, the new Emperor of the Fading Suns.

In his newly forged reign peace has finally come. The jumproutes are open again, and pilgrims can travel safely to other worlds. Merchants can once more ply the starlanes, selling exotic goods to people who have not seen them within their grandfather's lifetimes. And adventure awaits, for Alexius has called for a great quest: to explore the stars, discover the lost worlds of the Second Republic, and solve the mystery of the fading suns.

The Noble Houses

Of the many noble houses throughout the Known Worlds, five have achieved prominence and effectively rule most of the Known Worlds — under their new Emperor, of course. The Emperor Wars took a toll on many of these houses: the losers now struggle to regain lost lands or power, while the victors fight to ensure that their rivals stay down.

The life of a noble is not the leisurely idyll one might expect: there are fiefs to manage, rivals to crush and wars to wage. While there is much power to be gained, there is always the risk of humiliation or loss of holdings and position. It is no wonder that they know how to party: their gala affairs are lavish and awe-inspiring — but also rife with intrigue, innuendo, back-stabbing and even sword dueling. To escape such pressures, noble sons and daughters often take to the stars with only a small entourage of friends and retainers, to better know the worlds they wish to one day rule.

The five major houses (called the Royal Houses) are:

House Hawkwood

Prideful yet honorable, the Hawkwoods have seen one of their own take the Emperor's throne. While Alexius Hawkwood has since distanced himself from his family to appear more impartial, the Hawkwoods take such political setbacks with stoicism — the same fierce perseverance with which they beat back the barbarian raiders to their worlds. A Hawkwood does not give up. House Hawkwood is more beloved by its vassals than any other house, for they treat them fairly and with justice.

House Decados

Slimy, cunning and extremely successful, the Decados have risen to power through treachery and an uncanny understanding of their rivals — helped in no small part, no doubt, by their vast, invisible intelligence network. While the other families accuse them of a number of crimes, the Decados are here to stay and thus must be dealt with on their own terms. Decados vassals despise their lords but are kept in line through fear or the promise of power for those who make good quislings.

The Hazat

Hot-blooded and intense, the martial Hazat know how to field an army but are also no strangers to intrigue. When they can calm the vicious infighting from family to family, they can present a formidable front against rivals from other houses. Left with less land after the wars than they began with, they now pursue a campaign against a barbarian world, seeking new lands outside of the Empire. Hazat vassals are loyal, for they know that sacrifices for their lords are often rewarded.

House Li Halan

This pious and disciplined family was once the worst behaved of all nobles. Their immoral exploits are legendary, as is the tale of their overnight conversion to the Church. They now pursue the scriptures as fanatically as they once chased pleasure. While other nobles may snicker at the faithful lords, they more often fear the Li Halan, for this family has proved implacable on both the battlefield and at court. Their vassals are fiercely loyal, for they know their place as vassals in the Pancreator's plan.

House al-Malik

The exotic and inscrutable al-Malik are often accused of being mere merchants, for their ties to the League are well known. But they have proven their noble legerdemain many times, through the acquisition of land and a unique understanding of human nature and politics. It is very hard to pull one over on an al-Malik, but it is likewise hard for them to resist the lure of a good adventure or challenge. Vassals of this family are treated well and return the respect with solid service.

The Church

Although the Universal Church of the Celestial Sun may present a unified front for the faithful of the Known Worlds, its cathedrals are rife with sectarianism. While the Patriarch has rule over all aspects of the Church, it is often difficult to manage the actions of priests the universe over. Many sects and orders have arisen, powerful enough to earn official status from a reluctant Orthodoxy. Even more heresies have arisen, forcing the Patriarch to spend his time hunting heretics rather than unifying the present sects.

A priest's life is often a trying one: If it's not local disasters or famines they must try to relieve, it's occult threats to the faith, from demon possessions, zombie plagues or malicious psychics. Church magical rites are effective, regardless of whether they are considered merely a form of psychic power by the more skeptical.

The five major sects/orders ordained by the Church are:

Urth Orthodox

The largest sect, it is the Orthodoxy that most people associate with the Church. Its priests can be found on all worlds, from the ostentatious bishops of the capital cities to the more humble parish priests in the most poverty-stricken fiefs. While the Orthodoxy has gained a reputation for their cunning political maneuvers, most priests know little of such things, being entirely too busy protecting the souls of the simple faithful. While many may spurn the Orthodoxy for its martial role in the Emperor Wars, when tragedy strikes, it is the Orthodoxy they return to for consolation.

Brother Battle

This order of monk knights is the most elite fighting unit in the Known Worlds, surpassing even the Emperor's Phoenix Guard in martial prowess. Originally initiated to protect pilgrims and pursue heretics, the order is now chartered by noble houses, Church sects and even guilds to perform elite military operations on many worlds, including the deadly Stigmata Front against the Symbiot alien invaders. Despite rumors of heresy and usury within their ranks, everyone wants a Brother Battle monk by their side in times of trouble.

Eskatonic Order

These hermetic sages are often thought of as wizards by the common folk, but the nobles and guildsmen know them for the kooks they often are. While there are many within the order who possess profound wisdom and learning, there are just as many who are obsessed with the end of the universe and who stand on street corners telling everyone about it. Once considered a heresy by the Orthodoxy, the Eskatonics were admitted into the fold when their theurgical rites proved effective against the Symbiots.

Temple Avesti

Dreaded inquisitors. The Avestites long ago seized most of the seats on the Inquisitorial Synod, and have since then made it their duty to search the Known Worlds for signs of heresy, demonism and any other threat to the faithful. Their illiteracy, fear of learning and dogmatic adherence to certain extreme scriptures makes them feared and hated throughout the empire. But they are obeyed nonetheless. Only the most fanatic and ascetic initiates are admitted to this sect.

Sanctuary Aeon

Healers and compassionate mystics. Everybody loves the priests and priestesses of Sanctuary Aeon, followers of Saint Amalthea. When an Amalthean comes to town, there is always someone willing to provide hospitality for her. Indeed, so beloved by the commoners are they that when one was once accused of witchcraft by an Avestite, the Avestite was seized by the populace and burned at the stake instead.

The Merchant League

The remnants of the Second Republic mega-corporations can be found among the many guilds of the Merchant League. It is the League which controls high technology: invention, manufacture and distribution. It is the guilds who pilot noble starships or repair Church think machines. If any one of these factions were to anger them, a League blockade would quickly end the argument.

The guilds gladly accept their role as second-class citizens at the royal soirees, for they know that there is little profit to be made arguing over the best or worst dressed. They instead charge high dollar for the privilege of hiring a guild specialist — and their enforcers ensure that only the guild specializes in certain skills and tech; black marketers and tech counterfeiters are thrown from airlocks.

While the guilds are numerous, only five have risen to intergalactic prominence and regularly travel the jumpweb in the employ of nobles, priests or other guildsmen:

Charioteers

Star pilots and merchants marine, this intrepid guild is what most people think of when they imagine the Merchant League, for it is the Charioteer merchants with their exotic, traveling medicine shows who are most often seen by the commoners. They own the star lanes — literally. Without their secret jumpcode technology, travel through jumpgates would be impossible. In addition, the best pilots come from this guild.

Engineers

High technology is rare in the Dark Ages, and most people fear it, for as the Church teaches, it is the symbol of human hubris that brought down the Republic. Few dare to delve into its secrets anymore, and those that do are considered mad — like the Engineers. These strange technicians often modify their bodies with cybertech, becoming more machine than human. While they creep out the commoners and disgust the priests, everyone knows just how valuable their lore is in maintaining intergalactic power and communication.

Scravers

If you can't find what you're looking for legally, chances are the Scravers can get it — for a price. Scravers specialize in all sorts of activities normally viewed as anti-social (but often fun): gambling, black market goods and even thievery. Of course, they deny it all, hiding behind the guise of a salvage and reclamation guild. Since they possess blackmail on just about every major official — even bishops — little is done against them.

The Muster

Professional soldiers, these mercenaries are essential to most military operations throughout the Known Worlds. Even the Brothers Battle rely on their orbital artillery support, and most noble houses have hired them to either assault their rivals or quell rebellions. But soldiery is not the only labor this guild contracts; they specialize in all sorts of trained help: cooks, technicians, animal trainers, butlers, etc. In fact, it's very dangerous to hire trained labor without contracting this guild — their enforcers ensure that they get the largest and juiciest contracts.

Reeves

Somebody's got to do the paperwork, and this job is left to the Reeves. They do it quite well. So well that they are the de facto bankers of the Known Worlds and probably one of the richest factions in the universe — although few realize just how rich they've become through their loans to noble houses. Just about everybody owes the Reeves, and when one comes calling on favors, few dare deny him.

Aliens

There are a number of sentient races within the Known Worlds: the simian Gannok, the ungulate Shantor, the avian Etyri, amphibian Oro'ym, insectoid Ascorbites and the reptilian Hironem. But three other races have achieved the most freedom of movement and self-determination:

Ur-Obun

This peaceful, philosophical race, like their Ur-Ukar cousins, claims deep Anunnaki involvement in their history. The Anunnaki (the ancient race who built the jumpgates) apparently engineered the two races' fates, separating them onto different worlds before they disappeared from history. The Obun are given positions of respect as councilors and advisors in Known Worlds society. However, while they are treated politely, their advice is often considered naive by the militant human culture. Nonetheless, an Ur-Obun became one of the Prophet's disciples, and is honored by an Obun sect of the Church.

Ur-Ukar

Due to their initial hostile dealings with humanity, the Ukari are now a broken race. Their homeworld is owned by the League, who reaps it for its mineral resources, selling the spoils off-world to noble houses. The have been removed from their ancestral, subterranean lands and herded into tight caves in poverty. Few humans care what happens to them. A resistance movement has responded with terrorist tactics, and has taken its war of hatred to other worlds. Nonetheless, the League values them for their shady, underworld skills.

Vorox

Huge carnivorous, multi-limbed beasts, the Vorox are new to civilization. That they achieved sentience at all on their toxic jungle world is a wonder. That they have come as far as they have since is a tribute to their adaptability and powerful attributes — valuable qualities in the Known Worlds. They are most often trained as elite shock troops by noble houses, but many have joined the League to see the stars firsthand.

Enemies

There are many dangers in the universe of the Fading Suns, not the least of which are humans themselves. The intrigues and conspiracies of the noble houses, Church and League are enough to keep most people occupied for a lifetime. The post-war years have seen an increase in such covert activity, for few dare to openly disturb the peace. The Emperor has his hands full trying to cement his rule against internal malcontents and external alien and barbarian empires.

Barbarians

Of the hundreds of worlds once part of the Second Republic, a handful remains in reach of the empire. Many more still exist in space, waiting for some intrepid adventurer to rediscover the jumpcodes. Some of these have new civilizations of their own, from the loose and fractious Vuldrok Star-Nation, whose raiders harry the Hawkwood worlds and to whom loyalty is only as good as the value of booty, to the regal Kurgan Caliphate, whose disciplined people follow the latest in a long succession of prophet-kings. Both of these cultures are labeled "barbarian" by the empire, and declared heretical by the Church. The spectre of a crusade looms over the Known Worlds....

Among the more dangerous, non-human threats out there are:

The Vau

This technologically superior alien empire has so far-proved little threat — as long as humans stay on their side of the border. The few times Vau ambassadors have parleyed with humans, trouble has resulted, although in forms hard to trace back to the Vau. For instance, the Vau "gifted" humanity with the jumpcoordinates to reach a previously lost world called Pandemonium. This world in turn revealed coordinates to another lost world called Iver. A cold war for the spoils of these new worlds began; the Vau's present has proven most troublesome.

If the Vau were to expand into Human Space, no one is sure if they could be halted, for their tech is impressive. Humans stole their own knowledge about energy shields and blasters from early Vau encounters. It is theorized that the Vau know far more about these fields than has been revealed.

Symbiots

A greater threat to Known Worlds hegemony, however, are the Symbiots, parasitic entities attempting to break through into Human Space and possess its inhabitants, turning them into hive mind slaves — or so the propaganda goes. In truth, nobody really knows what the Symbiots want or even just what they are. Everybody does know that they are dangerous and inimical to human goals. Rumor of a Symbiot infestation is enough to bring a squad of Church inquisitors with flameguns, ready to burn first and ask questions later.

Demons

The Church claims that demons exist and can possess people to perform their nefarious deeds in this world. The sad thing is that this seems to be true. Even the most rational scientists must admit to the reality of something out there, something often unseen but seemingly hostile. These entities, demons or aliens or whatever, can so far only be combated by Church theurgy and miracles of faith.

Glossary

Amalthea, Saint: Called the "Healer", Amalthea is the saint of compassion and was one of the Prophet's eight disciples.

Amen'ta: Omnivorous alien creatures native to Severus, resembling ratlike armadillos. Also called "hull rats"; a common pest on starships.

Antinomy: Magic that derives its power from malevolent entities.

Anunnaki: Also known as the Preadamites, or the Ur. An ancient spacefaring race (or races) which developed the jumpgates.

Ascorbite: Insectoid alien race, known as "blood-suckers from Severus" (a term also applied to members of House Decados). Their behavior is bewildering to humans, and they seem to possess some form of hive mind. Like many alien races encountered by humans before they attained star-travel on their own, Ascorbites are largely confined to reservations on their homeworld.

Changed, The: The Second Republic produced many experiments in genetic manipulation. Now reviled by the Church, the mutant products of such "sinful" science are hunted and burned by Inquisitors.

Dayside: A jump that moves closer to Byzantium Secundus.

Diaspora: The historical exodus of humanity to the stars.

Doppleganger: The dark side of a psychic's personality, which, if left unchecked, can develop a life of its own. Also called the "Dark Twin."

Etyri: An avian alien race from the planet Grail, often considered regal by Known Worlders.

Gannok: Simianlike aliens renowned for their clownish behavior. Their small size and mechanical aptitude makes them prized starship engineers.

Gargoyle: Ancient creations — sculptures, buildings — believed to have been left by the Ur. The superstitious believe them to be sentient beings of great power.

Horace, Saint: Called the "Learned Man," Horace is the patron saint of the Eskatonic Order and was one of the Prophet's eight disciples.

Jumpgate: A massive alien artifact which allows for interstellar travel. The inner workings and scientific principles of jumpgates have so far remained unfathomable to Known Worlders.

Keddah, House: A minor noble house, rulers of the planet Grail.

Known Worlds: The planets claimed by the Empire or which have Empire citizens living upon them.

Kurgan Caliphate: An empire of lost worlds ruled by a prophet-king. The caliphate wars with House Hazat over territory.

Leagueheim: Homeworld of the Merchant League, this planet host some of the highest tech wonders still in production, although it is considered a den of sin and villainy by the more extreme members of the Church.

Lost Worlds: Planets which were once part of the Second Republic but whose locations are now unknown.

Mantius, Saint: Called the "Soldier", Mantius is the patron saint of the Brother Battle order and was the Prophet's bodyguard.

Nightside: A jump that moves further away from Byzantium Secundus.

Omega Gospels: The teachings of the Prophet, and the basis for the Universal Church faith.

Philosopher's Stone: Objects of great power from past centuries.

Prophet, The: The man who united humanity with his vision of the Holy Flame. His miracles and the deeds of his saints are treasured by the faithful, who look upon his era with almost Biblical awe.

Psi: Psychic powers, possessed by psychics who — when recognized as such — are treated with distrust and outright fear by most Known Worlders.

Sathraism: The religion that grew up around jumpgate ecstasy, but was squashed by the First Republic. A later revival was crushed by the Universal Church, but adherents are rumored to still exist.

Second Republic: The golden age of human civilization and the peak of technological advancement. Relics from this period are highly valued.

Selchakah: A highly addictive drug known to be manufactured by certain devious Decados.

Shantor: An ungulate race from Shaprut that somewhat resemble earth horses. Treated the worst of all alien races during their first contact with humans, they are still largely confined to reservations and ostracized from Known Worlds society.

Symbiots: Insidious creatures originally born of a bizarre combination of a Xolotl and another plant or animal. Symbiots now breed among unwilling or human aliens. They threaten to invade the Known Worlds.

Theurgy: Church magic. Theurgy rituals are used by the faithful for a variety of spiritual tasks, from blessing a congregation to protecting people from enemies of the Faith.

Trusnikron, House: A minor noble house known for its amazing ability to tame and train creatures of all kinds.

Universal Church: The dominant faith in the Known Worlds, based on the teaching of the Prophet. While there are many recognized sects or orders (Brother Battle, Sanctuary Aeon, Eskatonic Order), most are offshoots of the Orthodox faith.

Ur-Obun: A powerfully psychic alien race known for its dedication to philosophy and learning; its homeworld of Velisamil (called simply "Obun" by most Known Worlders) is claimed by House Hawkwood.

Ur-Ukar: Another race of powerful psychics with highly developed senses, the Ur-Ukar are thought to be violent and savage compared to their Obun cousins. Their homeworld of Kordeth (called simply "Ukar" by most Known Worlders) is claimed by the Merchant League and House al-Malik.

Urth: Also known as Holy Terra or, in ancient texts, Earth. The birthplace of humanity.

Vau: Mysterious aliens who control the high-tech Vau Hegemony, but whose goals and customs remain mysterious to the people of the Known Worlds.

Vorox: Multi-limbed alien creatures; "feral" Vorox retain their highly-poisonous claws, while "civilized" Vorox have them removed.

Vuldrok Star-Nations: A loose confederation of star nations ruled by warlords who often raid Hawkwood worlds. Called "barbarians" by Known Worlders.

Zaibatsu: The First Republic merchants who controlled Urth prior to the discovery of the jumpgate.

Jumproads of the Known Worlds

The following pages provide a map of Alexius' Empire and its borders. Each world is connected to the others by jumproads — known routes which lead from a system's jumpgate to another system's jumpgate. Many, many other worlds once colonized by humankind exist in space, but their jumpcodes have been lost or their gates locked shut.

KEY

Imperial crest

House Hawkwood

House Decados

The Hazat

House Li Halan

House al-Malik

House Keddah

Church (Orthodoxy)

Brother Battle

Temple Avesti (Avestites)

Eskatonic Order

Sanctuary Aeon (Amaltheans)

Merchant League

Ur-Obun

Ur-Ukar

Vorox

Vau Hegemony

Symbiots

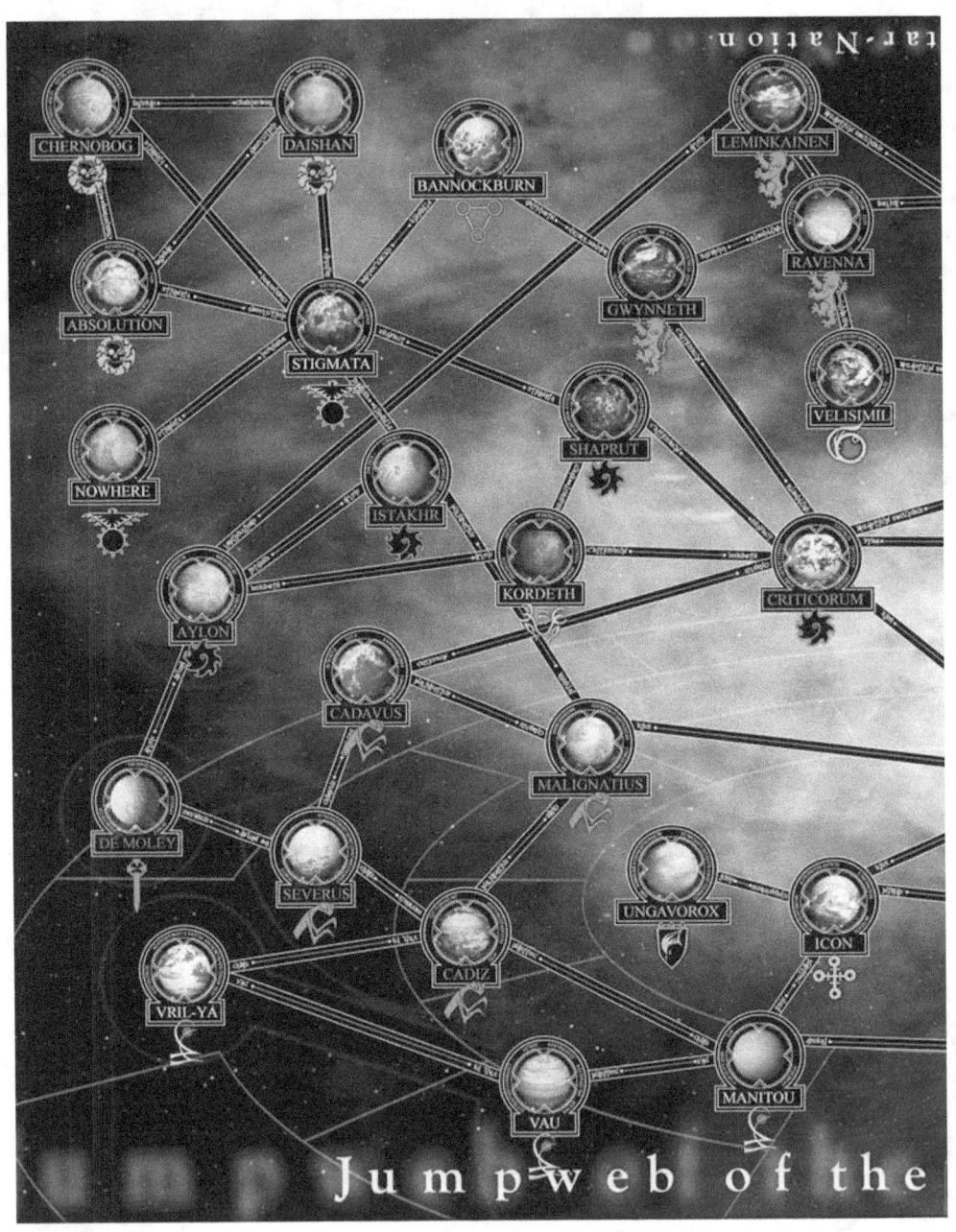

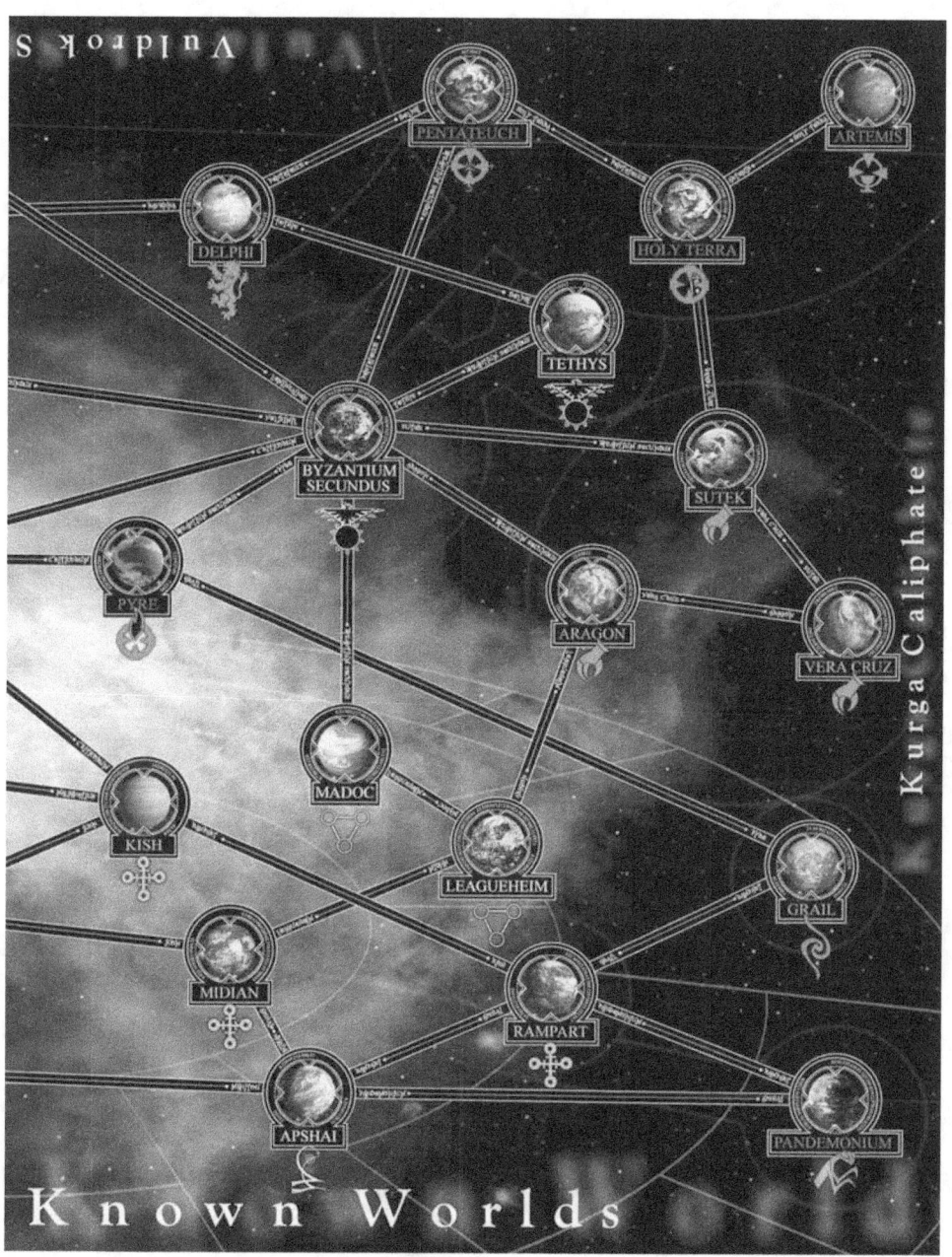

About the Author

Bill Bridges is an award-winning writer and narrative designer of numerous games. He was one of the original developers of White Wolf's *World of Darkness* and is the co-creator and developer of the *Fading Suns* science-fiction universe. He is a Fellow at Atlanta's Mythic Imagination Institute.

Formerly Senior Content Designer on CCP Games' *World of Darkness* MMO, he is now a full-time freelance writer. He was the lead designer of the award-winning Storytelling system rules for White Wolf's *World of Darkness* games, and designed and developed the award-winning games *Mage: The Awakening*, *Promethean: The Created*, and *Werewolf: the Apocalypse*.

His novels include *The Silver Crown* and *Last Battle* (both for *Werewolf*). Bill has written for Chaosium and helped develop Last Unicorn's *Star Trek: The Next Generation* and *Star Trek: Deep Space Nine* roleplaying games. He co-wrote the scripts for Viacom's interactive horror movie *Dracula Unleashed*, Interplay's *Starfleet Academy*, and contributed to world design for Segasoft's *Emperor of the Fading Suns*.

Visit bill-bridges.com for more info and links.

www.ingramcontent.com/pod-product-compliance
Lightning Source LLC
Chambersburg PA
CBHW071330250626
47159CB00004B/1543